Across the Distance

LINDSEY RENÉE BACKEN

Across the Distance

LINDSEY RENÉE BACKEN

Ever Ink Press

Ever Ink Press
P.O. Box 327
Palacios, Texas 77465

*To
Dad and Mom,
who have waited so long for this book.
Thanks for believing in
me.*

CLARA CASTLE
Summer, 1910

THE CLOCK SOUNDS ITS HUNDREDTH TICK. I OPEN MY EYES. NOTHING has changed. The yard is still empty, tinted gray by the screen on the front door. Our cow grazes alone in the field and beyond that, a boat drags a net back and forth through the sparkling bay.

I suppress a sigh and shift on the stair step. Two patches of wrinkles ruin my skirt where I have clutched the material. Father hates the habit, but I rarely realize I'm doing it until it's too late.

I close my eyes again, cocking my head toward the door to listen for the rumble of a motor car. There are a few Model Ts in town, but Grandfather has purchased a Lozier Touring automobile. I'm not sure if their engines sound similar to a Model T or not, but when he arrives, the entire town will know. I cannot even dwell on the excitement of seeing a new automobile because my thoughts return to Grandfather's other promise.

A boy.

I peek at the letter for the hundred and third time. That is what he wrote. After two years of travel, he is coming to visit, and he's bringing me a boy. A doll, perhaps? Or a marionette? I've never seen a marionette, but Grandfather has told me about them. Or perhaps it is a painting.

He can't mean a *real* boy.

I hear everything at once. The cries of the seagulls and the whirring wings of the doves sent into flight by the buzz of an engine. I stand, only to find that my hem has caught beneath my boot, causing me to nearly reel through the door. I catch my balance and press my palms and face against the screen, peering in each direction.

If I could only step onto the porch, perhaps I could see them, but I don't dare. I force myself to walk, instead of run, to pull aside the curtain in the parlor. I still cannot see the car, and now the engine has quieted, but when I step back, I collide into something warm, soft, and tall. Two hands seize my waist from behind.

I scream as Vincent howls with laughter, pulling me against him in a backward hug. He peeks over my shoulder, and I glimpse hints of Father's blue eyes and Mother's chestnut hair.

I laugh, spinning to face him. "You're with Grandfather! You're the boy!"

"No, no." Vincent adjusts the shoulders of his suit in mock offense. "For heaven's sake, I'm sixteen. Two years, and good riddance to school altogether. But I did my duty and earned back my final bit of summer. I've got two weeks to spend with you and convince Father to send you to school next fall."

I smile to cover the flinch. "Please, don't bring it up. I don't think Father will change his mind, and it only makes him cross."

"He should. Things are different for girls nowadays."

"But we haven't the money."

"Grandfather has."

"But Father hates to borrow from . . ."

Vincent cuts me off by placing a finger over my lips as Grandfather's voice carries from the back door, and Father rides into the front yard. It's hard to know whom to greet first, but Father is swinging down from his horse and Grandfather is already in the kitchen.

"Where is that granddaughter of mine?" he calls.

I have always thought if someone were blind and could not tell between an older and younger voice, they might mistake Grandfather for a college boy. His mustache looks whiter, though it's hard to tell because he's covered in a layer of dust. I hug him anyway, realizing he smells like Vincent, only with the added hint of cigars and new cloth.

"Clara!" He squeezes me so tightly I feel as though I could get lost in his jacket.

I hold him a bit longer than I should. No one has held me in a long time. He pulls back to survey me, keeping his hands on my shoulders. "Yes, yes. She's done well. Taller. Prettier."

I giggle as Father lets himself into the front door. Grandfather's eyebrows tuck as he continues his assessment without pause. "Thinner. Paler." He cocks his head toward Father who is removing his hat. "Gracious, Edmund, don't you feed this child? You could put her on a string and fly her like a kite."

Vincent barks a laugh. I almost do too, imagining being swept away by the wind, as Father clutches a string. But I glimpse Father's frown, and I realize it's not very funny.

"Of course I feed her," Father answers.

Grandfather glances back at me, though something dark lies beneath his smile. "And how is my favorite granddaughter?"

I laugh louder than I should, hoping to drive away the tension. "Your only granddaughter is quite well, thank you."

"Good!" He reaches into his coat and produces creamy white sheets with notes scattered across like a lovely poem. "Because I brought you music."

"Thank you." I study the pages, feeling trepidation mix with pleasure. "It will take some time to learn this song. I'm not very advanced."

"Of course you're not." Grandfather wags a finger in front of my face. "You can't become decent at reading music without a teacher. But you deserve some music, so I brought someone to play for you."

I glance up. "What?"

"Your boy," Grandfather says. "I promised to bring you a boy, remember?"

My heart pounds until even my ears pulsate as I glance from Father's cocked head to Vincent's grin. Wondering what the joke is, I stutter, "I thought Vincent was the boy."

"Andrew!" Grandfather calls into the kitchen. "Come in here!" His mustache twitches. "He's terribly shy at first."

I watch the doorway as though Grandfather has just called a dragon to his side. I can't breathe. We never have strangers in our home. Certainly not boys.

The doorway remains empty until I catch sight of Vincent's grin. Just as I turn to implore him not to tease, a boy with a violin steps into the frame.

Good god, it's a boy.

A real boy.

A living, breathing, trembling boy, who walks gingerly as though he expects the floor might collapse beneath him. His clothing is newer than mine, his coat tailored as crisply as Grandfather's, yet hanging a bit flat like it's strung on a washline instead of a person. His eyes are blue, his hair the color of copper, and he's not much taller than I am.

"This is Andrew Callaghan," Grandfather says. "Andrew, this is my granddaughter, Clara."

I realize my blush isn't covering the horror on my face, but it's not because of the boy. It's because I haven't an inkling about the correct response to meeting a young man that my grandfather has sprung upon me.

Andrew's eyes meet mine, looking as unsure as I feel. We search each other for clues and come up woefully empty. Then he nods toward me and I stumble out a curtsy, wondering if I shouldn't have offered a hand instead.

"Hello, Miss —" Andrew hesitates, glancing toward Grandfather like he's suddenly realized we don't share our last name. Receiving no help, he continues, "Clara."

I haven't the faintest idea where the boy is from, but his voice is mellow and the "r" gives a short flip that I've never heard. He makes my name sound beautiful. I hope he'll say something else, but his eyes return to the floor like Grandfather brought him to be our gardener instead of our guest.

Grandfather beams, then jolts like he's forgotten Father, though I'm sure he hasn't. "Andrew, this is Mr. Edmund Castle."

I see the war in Father's eyes, like he's seen right through the new jacket and can't be fooled. I hold my breath, but he replies to Andrew's greeting with, "Hello, Mr. Callaghan." Then, with duties aside, he calls through the door. "Hannah, we'll eat early. There's no use letting things grow cold."

He does not specify who "we" is, so I breathe a sigh of relief and follow Vincent to the table. Father presides at the head, and Grandfather takes the right where Vincent usually sits. I do a funny little dance, trying to decide on my own place, now that our table has four people instead of two. Andrew eyes the foot of the table, but Grandfather pats the seat beside him, which puts our guest directly across from me.

It is most inconvenient because every time I lift my head the tiniest bit, I see him. We take turns trying not to catch each other's eyes. I'm so curious that I can hardly help but watch as Andrew copies Vincent's manners. I wonder what he is like when he is at home with his own family.

Vincent doesn't notice our guest's discomfort—or perhaps he does—for he jokes and teases me throughout the meal. Grandfather relates his adventures in Rome and Pompeii. As Grandfather finishes describing the murals found as they excavated the Villa Item, I glance at our own dining room and try to imagine it buried under thirty feet of ash.

But Father lacks the sort of imagination that I have and turns his attention toward Andrew, speaking before Grandfather can launch into another story. I wish Father would soften his voice and face. He looks like he's cross-examining a suspicious business partner as he asks, "How long have you lived in America?"

Andrew swallows, lowering his fork. "Seven years, sir."

"What does your father do?"

Andrew hesitates before he replies, "He's a farmer by trade. Currently, he's a foreman at the wharf."

"Fulfilling his American dream, I'm sure," Father mutters, reaching for his glass. "How many siblings do you have?"

Andrew's eyes dart down before they rise to meet Father's scrutiny. Something flashes, then disappears like a match blown out. I think he says, "None," but Father chokes on his water and I realize that he actually said, "Nine."

"Older or younger?" I ask, because it's the first thing that comes to mind.

Andrew's shoulders soften as he looks toward me. "All younger. A younger brother and eight sisters. Two sets of twins."

Ten children sound like such fun. I try to imagine our house with ten children, all younger than myself. "Where in the world do you put them?" I ask. "How large is your house?"

Andrew swallows, making me wish I hadn't asked, before he replies, "It is one room."

"Oh," I say, because I can't think of anything else.

Feeling as though I've committed a transgression, I clutch my napkin to spare my skirt. I cannot imagine a house with only one room. How do twelve people eat, cook, work, play, and sleep in the same quarters? I desperately want to know, but I close my mouth as Grandfather tries to salvage the conversation.

"Andrew is a musician," he says. "We attended a concert together, and he could reproduce entire pieces by memory. It's quite extraordinary. I couldn't leave such talent behind, so I've arranged for him to attend school with Vincent."

"That's quite a leap," Father says.

Grandfather turns toward Andrew. "Why don't you play for us? Clara loves music and God knows she hears little of it."

"We have a phonograph," I say.

Father doesn't often let me play it, but Grandfather's implications embarrass me. Andrew only nods, pushes back his chair and retrieves his violin, handling it like an old delicate friend. He plucks a string and listens, then tightens the peg with a shake of his head.

I watch, intrigued by the instrument. I've never seen a violin. Andrew's face softens as he secures its base beneath his chin. When he draws the bow across the strings, the sound reaches through the room, snaking along the walls, both wrapping around me and going right through me.

It's not like the piano, which I play with limited skill. It's not even like the violins I've heard on the scratchy records with their crackles and pops and the voices that sound too high in pitch. This music is like lace, each delicate tone responding to the slightest movement of his fingers.

I feel Vincent nudge me and dimly see his eyebrows wag, but I hardly realize it. The song isolates me, offering to carry me to wherever has filled its maker's eyes with such wistful oblivion.

Andrew looks toward us, but his thoughts are somewhere far away. His eyes snag on me, holding steady as he smiles like the music told a secret and I'm the only one who understood it.

But eyes are a powerful thing, and I pull in a breath as my face heats. I study my reflection in the silver candlestick, unsure of what just happened and a little frightened. Andrew lingers over the last note before the spell is broken by a knock on the front door.

Vincent grins. "Someone wants to see the car."

Hannah's already moving toward the door, but Vincent shoves back his chair and dashes for the porch like a little boy bellowing, "Hallo!"

Grandfather chuckles. "Best put the violin away, Andrew, unless you wish to perform all night. The entire town will be here soon."

I laugh, but I don't recognize the voice that carries from the porch. Father touches my elbow as I pass. His chin hardly moves, but he snaps his eyes up toward my room.

Disappointment and desperation sear my heart. I could not speak loudly if I tried, but my protest is so soft that I can scarcely hear it myself. "But Father..."

He raises his eyebrows, ending the conversation. There is nothing to do, except excuse myself to my room to hide while all the excitement goes on without me. He's keeping me safe from something, but I'm never quite sure what it is.

I hurry up the stairs, slipping past the banister before anyone on the porch can see me. I stay in my room, swallowing the urge to cry, hoping Vincent doesn't look for me, and straining to hear snatches of conversation. Hannah says it's not polite to eavesdrop, but spying on the outside world is the only way I can learn anything. I listen for Andrew's voice, but he only offers a few more polite greetings. I peek from the window as Grandfather starts the car, circling the block with a few passengers aboard.

When darkness descends and politeness — or perhaps Father — sends the neighbors home, I creep into the hallway. There is a small square of slats in the floor above the pantry to encourage the airflow through the house. It carries voices as well, and I kneel next to it, straining to hear Father on the back porch.

"It's ridiculous," he says.

"It's my money, Edmund. I see potential and am quite willing to risk it."

"You know nothing about this boy or his background. He may be skilled with an instrument, perhaps, but he has little education or —"

"He is bright," Grandfather says. "A tutor could work wonders with him. And his talent is astounding. He's from a good Christian family."

"A good Christian family with ten starving children. That boy looks as though he hasn't eaten in his life." Father cuts Grandfather off without regard for Andrew's talent. "You have found an Irish immigrant from a family with too many mouths. Of course they'll allow you to do as you please. You could make him a slave, and I dare say they would not protest."

"Edmund."

"You have always wanted to find the next Houdini and now you have landed this boy."

"I have always wanted a son."

There is silence. I flinch for Father, since I am sure he will not.

"When Rose married you, I thought I would gain one. I could have made you into someone great, too, had you not been so bullheaded."

I grip my nightdress so tightly that it hurts. Father would never let anyone except Grandfather talk to him in such a fashion, because Grandfather is the only one with money. With Mother gone, he has little reason to come see us, since he and Father spend a good deal of the visit arguing. Grandfather's visits to countries halfway around the world, where he has spent enough money to buy our house over again, are always a stab at Father's pride.

Since Grandfather has no living children and Father hopes that Vincent and I will come into that money, he will let Grandfather scold, rant, and rave. I wish he wouldn't. It always puts Father into a terrible mood and after Grandfather leaves, poor Father becomes so...But never mind. I will not take sides between the two. Father does the best he can with what he has.

Grandfather's voice is harder than I have ever heard it. "Don't tell me whom I may or may not take into my care. He is Irish and Catholic, which is unfortunate but not insurmountable. You can't see the potential in your own children, Edmund. Clara looks paler than even the last time I was here."

"Clara is fine," Father replies.

"Girls need more than a pretty face and social graces. Times are changing."

"Times are changing for the worse."

"Edmund." Grandfather's voice softens in pain. "Clara is not her mother."

I close my eyes, trying to banish the haunted look I know Father wears when someone speaks of Mother. I know when he is wounded, though he is careful not to show it. I also know what those wounds do to him, festering inside until they all burst forth at once.

I stand, hoping Andrew cannot hear them through the plank floors. Slipping back into my dark room, I smooth the blanket before I climb between the sheets and listen to the crickets.

I wish someone saw enough potential in me to send me to school. I wonder what my future will be like. Most of the time, I prefer not to think of it. I cannot imagine anything other than living with Father in this big, lonely house. I try to think of being married, living somewhere else, and doing exciting things. Perhaps it is because it is night and the clouds cover the stars, but all I can see is black. All I can imagine is black.

2

SCARLET BELDON

Summer, 2012

THERE IS NOTHING QUITE LIKE THE SILENT TREATMENT ON A ROAD trip. I'm not sure exactly where we're going or when we'll get there, but if Dad doesn't tell me soon, I'm going to write *Help. I'm kidnapped!* on a sign and hold it against the passenger window. I'm still fuming at Dad, but it's been three days since we left New York, and so far the landscape is becoming less and less populated.

I fish my phone from its current hiding place between the seats and tap a message to Kate.

He's still driving. How are you doing?

Dad glances toward me as the phone buzzes.

Testing my theory that the world can be saved by chocolate. So far it's not working. Moods are not brightening anywhere. :(

"No kidding," I mutter. I stretch as best I can in the seat before rolling my head toward Dad. "So, where are we going?"

"A small bayside town in Texas," he answers, like the salt grass interspersed among fields of cows and random patches of marsh grass isn't speaking for itself.

Dad's been toying with me like a cat with a grasshopper, just waiting to see when I'm going to blow. Which might be very soon if he keeps this up. I take a deep breath before asking, "Called?"

"Not telling." He grins at me like Peter Pan, but I am no Wendy, and I am not in the mood to cater to his childish capers. He dragged my adolescent self from Texas to New York to bring a step-mother into my life, and just as suddenly he's decided to leave her and drag me back across the country? He hoodwinked me once, but it's not happening again.

"Why are we going there?" I ask.

"I own a house. Your grandparents willed it to me. I was going to sell it, but I'd like to take a vacation first. Get away. Go back to simple things."

"Oh." I shift. When I packed my bag, I thought we were changing apartments, not lifestyles. "Is it big?"

He shrugs. "It's two stories. I barely remember it. I was seven last time I was there."

Dad at seven is just a weird thing to imagine, but it occupies my thoughts for the next several minutes. I try not to think of Kate or Sherri, or how I won't see them because my father is going on a phony vacation to "get away." Literally.

I close my eyes and continue formulating my own plan of escape. Since the first semester of high school, I've been plotting my most effective route to college, saving money so I'm not dependent on Dad's stamp of approval for anything. I need to decide what I want to study soon and inquire about going early. This year would be good, if I can find somewhere that accepts runaway seventeen-year-olds.

Dad bounces like a toddler. "We're going to have so much fun. Sailboats, water skiing…"

"Mosquitoes," I reply. "Humidity. Heat."

He sighs, reaching to turn down the radio and I wish I hadn't started a conversation. "You need to learn to look at the bright side of life, Scarlet," he says.

I squint at a rain cloud that sprinkles us, even while the sun bounces off a sign, giving me the first clue of how incredibly far I am from home.

Palacios. The City by the Sea. Population: 4,718.

I crack a laugh. Some city.

I thought the bay would be blue, nearly matching the sky. It's not. It's a brownish-green color. The buildings in the old part of town look like someone waved a wand over a western movie set and made them all brick and concrete. Most of the doors are closed, but I note the location of the library and a coffee shop doubling as a bookstore. This may have been a main street at one time, but it's not anymore. And it's not the highway we've been traveling on.

"Dad?" I ask. "We're not staying here, right?"

Dad just wags his eyebrows, refusing to give any more information until he parks in front of a big white house with a gray roof. A rickety balcony with rotted wood shades a porch, hidden by three large trees and something that looks like a potted plant that's taken over the center of the yard. With the overgrown grass, it's like a jungle smack in the middle of Texas.

I blink.

"Isn't it great?" Dad beams.

"If you're looking for a set for a Hitchcock movie," I answer.

"Oh, come on," Dad says, sliding from the black leather seat. "You haven't even seen inside of it yet."

He slams the door and I stare before speaking to the window. "I really don't have to."

Watching for snakes or other unwelcoming creatures, I follow his trail to the door, then bounce impatiently as he jiggles the key in a modern lock installed above an old-fashioned keyhole. The door makes a sucking protest when Dad pushes it open. The breeze comes in with us, sending dust bunnies racing along the hallway that runs alongside the stairs. Dad goes straight, but I see my escape and head upstairs, turning into the first bedroom to dump my laptop and suitcase on a white wicker chest at the foot of a wrought-iron bed.

It stifling hot and the windows screech as I open each one, finding two more bedrooms at the end of the hallway. My favorite is a light blue room with windows that look toward the bay. A wooden four poster bed sports a flowery bedspread. A blue lamp hovers over the head of any who dare sleep there—which will not be me.

When my phone rings in my pocket with Kate's ringtone, I snap it open but the signal drops before I lift it to my ear. I search for signal bars in every room upstairs before I end up in the hall, holding my breath as I finally hear a ring.

"Hi." Kate's voice sounds surprisingly steady. "Where are you?"

"Palacios," I say.

"Where?" she asks.

"I have no idea," I sigh. "How's Mom?"

"Better than expected. She's moved away from the chocolate, and she's filling out job applications."

"Yeah? That's good." I pace back into the hallway before realizing I don't want Dad hearing this conversation.

"I am a woman, hear me roar," Kate says, but the catch in her voice reminds us both that Sherri is happiest as a homemaker.

"Roar," I say, and she laughs.

There's a moment when only the seagulls talk. I lower myself onto an old leather chest, glaring through the porch door.

"How's Dad?" Kate asks.

"Making all kinds of stupid jokes. This is the most bizarre life crisis he's had so far," I say, though Dad is really in such a good mood that it scares me. "He's decided to vacation in this house that looks like nobody's lived here since the Victorians left."

Kate laughs. "You're going to go nuts."

My heart aches. It took almost six months to warm up to Kate, but I haven't really thought of her as my step-sister for almost four years until Dad said 'Just kidding' to the blended family idea. Sherri whisked her one direction and he took me another.

Tears prick, but I palm them back. "I wish you were here. You'd love this place as much as I'm going to hate it."

"I'm actually really jealous," Kate says. "You should snoop. Maybe you'll find jewelry or something."

I wince at the mottled books in a shelf. "Anything valuable went the way of the rats years ago."

I sigh as Dad's exaggerated southern accent disturbs the entire house. "Where did Miss Scarlet go?"

"Ugh. I have to go. Dad's trying to sound like Prissy, and she's annoying enough on the movie."

Kate laughs, then mimics the tone. "Bye, Miss Scarlet."

I roll my eyes. "Bye." I punch the end button and call down the stairs. "What?"

"I'm going to find a store and get some stuff to clean. Do you want to come?"

"No. I just got out of the car!"

"Fine." He actually sounds a little disappointed, like he really thought I'd consider climbing back into the car with him.

I close my eyes, listening to his footsteps creak their way across the bottom story of the house. What am I going to do here for the whole freaking summer?

I lower my phone, glaring as the movement erases the signal bars. "What the..." The anger that's been welling inside for the entire weekend surges to the surface. I throw my phone against the chest like it's responsible for redirecting cellular waves. "Stupid piece of crap!"

"Hey, Scarlet?" Dad calls again. My eyes snap dully to the wall as he warns, "Someone's coming to mow the lawn in a bit. Don't kill him, kay?"

I grind my teeth as the door shuts, the screen bangs, and Dad's car roars to life.

The floor is littered with dead bugs, making me wonder where I'm going to keep my stuff. I eye the chest, then unlatch the lid, peeking inside on the off-chance that it's bug-proof or full of Kate's jewels. A pink quilt drapes across the bottom. I pull it away, and a glass music box glimmers with the promise of one clean spot in this house. As soon as I lift the translucent lid, the gears turn, tinkling out a song like someone left it wound and ready to go. I don't recognize the tune, but it's just eerie inside the abandoned house.

I'm still considering tucking my suitcase inside for extra protection until the other rooms feel sanitary, but this isn't just a storage spot. It's a careful arrangement of folded newspapers, a hand mirror, a stack of letters tied with a ribbon, and a shriveled bouquet of lavender nestled between moth-balls. A sheet of music with handwritten notes is rolled and tied with an old shoelace. It's like some sort of freaking shrine, and I cringe, replacing the box. I should leave it alone, but the letters make me curious enough to lift the top flap for a peek.

March 29, 1912.

I shut the lid, taking the letters downstairs to read where it's not creepy. The ribbon is knotted so tightly it doesn't look like whoever secured it was planning on ever reading them again. Lucky for me, it's so rotted that I easily snap the ribbon. The letters are backwards with the oldest dates at the bottom of the pile. I sort through them, watching the handwriting change from a me-ticulous script to uneven loops, though the date only creeps back two years.

September 15, 1910
Galveston, Texas

Dear Clara,

Thank you for writing me. Vincent said it would help me learn if I practiced corresponding with you. I send letters home as well, but no one in my family ever had a chance to attend school. The priest can read them the note, but no one can write back unless they beg it of a friend. Mr. Mordaunt has hired a tutor to help me learn what I have missed, so I may catch up with the other boys in the school. He re kopid this leter for me and korrekted the speling.

I huff a laugh. Awkward, but apparently necessary if his spelling is that bad. The hum of an engine grows louder until it's followed by the screech of a mower blade dropping. I glance out the screen, spying a guy about my age on a lawn mower that moves closer to the speed of a go-cart. He weaves between the trees like he's in a video game. I suck in a long breath as he peers at the house, sees me behind the screen, and waves with a grin. I move away, before his peeping causes a collision with the potted plant.

I want to read the rest of the letter, but the sun's already sinking, so I leave it and spend the afternoon running the sheets through the washer. I'm not sure how much soap to use — Sherri's always done the laundry — but there are instructions on the back of the bottle. By the time it's dark and the lawn is finished, I've created an oasis of fresh bedding, safe enough to curl up and check my computer for my own letters. There's one from Blake, another boy who has serious issues with spelling.

Hey Babe. Wut's up? Ur sis said u had 2 leave with the old man. U ok? I still want a date when u get back, k?

I wish he'd use proper sentences. But at least someone noticed I was gone. I hit the reply button.

I'm fine. We're taking a vacation for the summer. Kate stayed because she's in a play and can't get away. We're in a family home down by the beach, enjoying sun and seagulls. When I get back, I'll let you know.

I press the send button and lie back. Blake's dreaming if he thinks he'll get a date. He's the guy every girl wants, and he's cute, but there's not much to him. When I bring up college or news or anything that really matters, he laughs and tells me to lighten up. But I can't. With Dad as fickle and irresponsible as he is, I'm going to be on my own after I turn eighteen. Unlike Sherri, I don't want my world to revolve around depending on a man or anyone besides myself.

I crawl across the bed and reach to pull the string that turns out the light. It's hot, even with the windows open and the fan whirling at its highest speed. I sweat and fidget, listening to the bed squeak and watching the moon rise and disappear past my window.

A tinkling song carries from the blue bedroom. I bolt upright before I'm frozen by a dim light in the hallway. It creates dancing shadows that shrink as the light grows brighter.

A girl in a nightdress tiptoes past my room, lighting her path with a candle. I clamp my hands over my mouth, hunching forward against a rising scream. She's blocking the freaking stairs, and I seriously consider bailing out the second story window.

Don't see me. Don't see me.

She pauses at the door across from mine. The flame illuminates the red highlights in brown hair that fluffs past her waist. She squirms, glancing down the stairwell again before she knocks softly on the door across from mine.

I hear the knock, coming way too strong to be a ghost, but her voice sounds nearly as terrified as I feel when she whispers, "Vincent?"

"Dad!" My voice frees itself from my throat, making up for its captivity in volume.

The girl gasps, whirling to face my room. Her eyes are wide, but she inches to the threshold to look around.

"Father?" she whispers.

Dad's feet shake the entire house when they hit the floor downstairs. The girl backs up, blows out her candle, and hurries down the hall.

Dad swings around the top of the stairs, glowing white because he's only wearing boxers and socks. "What? You okay?"

"There's a girl," I squeak, pointing down the hallway because I can't get any other explanation out.

And then I can't help it. I freak out. Face it. You'd freak out too, if you'd seen some girl sneaking down your hallway.

Dad should believe me because I'm not the panicking type, but he doesn't. I demand that he check every room, closet, balcony, and behind and under each bed.

He says I was dreaming, but I wasn't. There is a girl who roams the halls at night. I don't believe in ghosts. But I don't know how to explain this one, and I stay up all night trying to figure it out. Maybe reading those letters wasn't a good idea. I don't think about them until the music box plays again, this time so muffled inside the chest that I can barely hear it.

Okay. I'm officially creeped out.

3

CLARA CASTLE
Summer, 1910

IT'S MORNING, AND I'M ALREADY IN TEARS. I'VE TRIED THREE TIMES TO PUT MY hair up and all I can manage is a lumpy, loose bun that falls out before I can finish pinning it. I brush out my curls and pull back half, securing them with a ribbon. I'm fifteen, not twelve, but I'd rather approach Father with a neat and young style than be sent upstairs to fix a messy updo.

I retie my sash three times, trying to make a perfect blue bow in the back. My day dress is white with half-sleeves and embroidered holes that create raindrop designs at the hem and neckline. Hannah has scrubbed and starched it, so I know that it will meet Father's approval, but I wonder what Grandfather will think.

I slip past Vincent's room where Grandfather is likely still asleep. The boys started out on the balcony, but the mosquitoes must have driven them back inside. All is quiet from behind Vincent's door, but I hear Hannah in the kitchen. Holding onto the stair rail, I tiptoe downstairs, smelling eggs and biscuits.

"Good morning, Hannah," I whisper, stepping into the kitchen.

Hannah is tending three pans at once over the stove. Her hands continue their work as she glances toward me. "Good morning, Clara. Is Mr. Mordaunt awake yet?"

"I don't think so," I reply.

She shakes her head with a sigh. Sleeping past 7:00 is a sin in this house. "Well, we'll try to keep things warm, I suppose. Be a darling and put out the sign for the ice truck."

I slip past her to the pantry to retrieve the sign. "Shall I ask him for one or two blocks?"

"Two today. If the cow is willing, we'll make ice cream."

Elated, I snatch up the sign with a 2 printed on it and dance to the parlor window to indicate the joyful tidings to the ice truck. I peek to the field to see if Simon has finished milking the cow yet, but only Father's horse is grazing. Father must be in his study, probably budgeting ice cream into our monthly grocery allowance.

I hear the back door open and Simon's uneven steps as he hauls the milk inside. I want to see how much cream is available, but Hannah's pots grow quiet and I stand still, listening for their kiss. It won't last long. Hannah puts romance on the back burner when there are things to be done. When Father is around, you'd never guess they are married at all.

I hear their voices and words like "shop" and "dinner," so I slip back into the kitchen, shouting to greet Simon who has become nearly deaf to the high pitch of my voice. He peers at me, then smiles, rubbing down tufts of hair. "Good morning, Miss Clara."

I love watching them together, but today I worry about their whitening hair and thinning skin. Hannah was my mother's nanny, then mine and Vincent's. Now, Father keeps her on as a cook and housekeeper. I can't imagine life without them.

"Where's Father?" I ask.

"He's gone off to the mill," Hannah answers. "Some of the lumber toppled from a wagon, and a worker was injured. He said not to wait for him for breakfast, so we'll be serving it as soon as your grandfather and those boys come down."

I wonder about the worker, but Hannah returns her attention to the pans. Several times, she takes a breath like she's going to say something, then closes her mouth. Before I can think which question will break the dam and spill her thoughts, I hear soft footsteps on the stairs.

I can always tell a person's footsteps by their descent. Father's is flat-footed and careful. Vincent lopes down as though someone unleashed a golden retriever in the house. Hannah's are always slow, and she says, "oh, dear me!" over and over. And Grandfather usually takes four steps, then returns for something he forgot. These must belong to Andrew, for they hesitate at the top and bottom like he's unsure if he should be downstairs or not.

Hannah abandons the pots, bustling through the dining room to wave him in from the hallway. Her eyes sparkle and I stare, realizing with sudden amusement that she's taken with him.

"Come in, Mr. Callaghan," she says. "Good morning. Sit down. How do you like your eggs?"

Simon stoops and hurries out the back door, unwilling to be seen by any guest of Grandfather's, no matter how questionable his origins.

During Hannah's flurry, I realize I'm the only one available to entertain, so I take a breath and step back into the dining room, managing to say, "Good morning, Andrew."

He's wearing a different suit than yesterday, but it looks just as hot and heavy. His face shows no misery though he shifts, casting an uncomfortable glance toward Hannah. But he replies, "Good morning, Miss Castle."

"Oh, I wish you'd call me Clara," I say quickly, realizing I probably should have called him Mr. Callaghan. "We're not terribly formal around here. I was just conspiring with the servants about making iced cream." I wave toward Hannah, before wondering why in the world I'm calling her a servant.

She laughs softly, probably realizing I'm flustered. "I'll have breakfast ready in two shakes of a stick," she says. "You two amuse yourselves. You're both musicians. Why don't you show him the piano?"

She almost grins at me as she ducks back into the kitchen, leaving me standing with a slamming heart. There is really only one musician in the room, and it's not me. I walk toward the piano, an extravagant thing someone gifted to Father when the storms demolished half their house and sent them back north. Hannah showed me how to read notes, but for the most part, I've been left to bumble through my own training.

"Do you play then?" Andrew asks after we stand through an awkward moment.

"Not—not well," I sputter. "I've never had a teacher. Do you?"

Perhaps if I can coax him to play, I won't have to show my lack of performance skill. But he shakes his head. "Only the violin. Your grandfather says they will teach me to read music and play the piano at school."

I blink. "Can't you read music?"

"Not a bit," he replied.

"How do you play?"

He cocks his head a bit, like he doesn't understand the question, then shrugs one shoulder. "I hear the music."

"That song you played yesterday, you just heard?" I ask.

He nods. "Most Irish don't read music. We pass it on by ear. That song I played, I heard in New York. I have a friend named Patrick, who is a bellboy at a hotel. We always sneaked into the back alley to listen to the musicians."

We wince at the same time, realizing his nerves are playing as much havoc on his mind as mine are. I wonder again where in the world he met my grandfather, but perhaps Grandfather stumbled on him coming out of a hotel. I'm about to ask before I remember that I'm not supposed to know anything more than he's a talented musician with lots of siblings who live in one room. I suppose that is quite enough to deduct that he shouldn't even cross paths with my grandfather, but I'm glad he did.

"I'm not very good at playing," I warn, before he has a chance to hope for anything decent. "But I'll show you what I can."

The parlor is the nicest room in our home. It has a golden loveseat and the only rug in the entire house. The stool is a round seat, only big enough for one person, so I stand, pressing the keys.

"The lines and spaces tell you which note to hit." I point to the first line of the treble staff. "That one is E and they go straight up on the keys."

Andrew listens, watching my finger on the paper, but he becomes distracted with the keys themselves, picking out a song I've never heard on the high notes. Something flashes in the mirror and I lift my eyes, realizing the wallpaper has disappeared, replaced by a blue wall. I glance backward, then toward the mirror where the reflection has returned to perfectly normal.

"Did you see that?" I ask.

Andrew tears his eyes from the keys. "See what?"

Before I can think of how to answer, Vincent stomps drunkenly down the stairs.

"Good morning!" I call, glad for the interruption. I suppose it was a trick of the light. And anyway, one can't go about trying to convince their guests that the walls changed colors.

Vincent steps into the doorway, slouching against the frame. His hair is combed, but his face still bears marks of a rumpled pillow. "We've been over this, Clara. There is nothing good about mornings."

I giggle. Vincent always takes a while to fully wake, but his humor bleeds through even when he's grumpy.

Vincent stumbles to the table, flopping into his seat. "Hannah?" he calls, rubbing his face. "Do you have coffee with that breakfast?"

"I'm not desecrating my cooking with coffee!" Hannah calls. "I'll make you a good, stout cup of tea."

Vincent lays his head into his arm and moans.

I glance toward Andrew asking, "Do you drink coffee?"

He grins. "Occasionally. Da and I drink it on the way to work."

"Do you work at the wharf, too?" I ask.

He reddens, then shakes his head, glancing back at the keys. "No. I — I worked in a factory in a boiler room."

I shut the piano as I hear Grandfather on the top of the stairs. True to habit, he takes four steps, then returns for something. Father arrives just in time for breakfast and the meal stays quiet. Grandfather leaves directly after to call upon acquaintance, and Father eyes Andrew before ordering me to stay inside and Vincent to chop up a fallen tree.

Vincent's shoulders fall in irritation, but I take up my journal to write by the screen window where we can call back and forth to each other. Andrew seems nearly as eager to work as Vincent does to avoid it, but it gives them both an excuse to shed their coats.

I think they forget I'm here, because Vincent begins throwing tree bark at Andrew, and it's the first time I've seen Andrew laugh as he dodges around the fallen trunk of the tree. Andrew stops the capering before Vincent does, but he's still laughing. He cracks an imaginary whip over Vincent's head, then carries the wood to the pile himself.

I'm trying to decide who is better at chopping. Vincent is stronger, so he more often cleaves the wood with one stroke, but Andrew has better aim, nailing the log right in the middle.

It's really quite fun to contrast the two. Vincent exudes confidence. He says what he thinks and doesn't care how anyone sees him. Andrew has a sort of confidence too, but it's quiet. It's almost as though he has learned to expect rejection and disapproval, so he just keeps on doing whatever he was planning in the first place.

I stand to check the progress on the ice cream just as Andrew drops his entire stack of wood, jumping back and flapping his hands.

"Did you get into the ants?" Vincent calls with a heartless laugh.

"Ants?" Andrew looks as though Vincent just asked him to saddle a cow.

"Don't you have ants in New York?" I ask.

Andrew's head snaps toward me with a bewildered look. "They don't sting!"

I grimace for him. Stepping into a fire ant bed is a childhood rite of passage here. Adding to their grievances, you don't always see them creeping on you, and they have some sort of signal because they all bite at the same time. I never thought to warn Andrew because I didn't realize there was anywhere in the world where they don't bite.

Andrew shakes his head as he kneels to regather the wood. "Biting ants and bloodsucking insects. Anything else I should know about while I'm here?"

"Spiders?" I suggest.

Vincent takes up the list. "Snakes, alligators..."

Andrew's head jerks up. "What's an alligator?"

Vincent starts explaining, and Andrew looks more disturbed by the moment. I slip to the kitchen door so he won't see me laugh, but Hannah is still washing the dishes from breakfast.

When I return, Vincent stands just on the other side of the screen. "How's the ice cream?" he asks.

"She hasn't started yet," I moan.

He peers at my journal. "What are you writing?"

I set my chin in my hand. "I was writing about you."

"All good, I hope?"

"But of course," I answer.

Vincent strikes a pose with his chest puffed out, then teases, "What are you writing about Andrew?"

"That he has good aim with an ax," I answer quickly.

Vincent laughs, and Andrew flushes. "I thought perhaps you were working on a story," he says. I wish that he would say it again, just so I can hear his accent.

"My life's not that interesting," I reply, though I've really never thought of writing a story before. "It would make a terrible story."

"Then write it like you'd like it to be," Andrew suggested.

Vincent snags the idea, pointing toward me. "You can change one thing about life. What is it? Go!"

"Mother's alive." Again, I speak without thinking.

Vincent's face changes, jolting as though I've just fired a gun at him. His throat pumps twice. "That would make life interesting."

Then he turns to gather another armful, and I close my eyes. Why did I say that? Of course, that is what I would change, but mother heads the list of unmentionable subjects.

But now that Andrew has kindly followed Vincent and left me to myself, I step through the doorway I've opened and imagine Mother into this scene. I pretend she's playing a cheerful song on the piano, even though Hannah said she hated to practice. What has that simple act changed?

Well, for one thing, I didn't just run off my brother. The truth is stranger than fiction, for if I were entirely creating this scene I would never think to make Vincent chopping wood. So I imagine him in front of the house, leaning against the tree trunk as he reads Sherlock. He looks quite fetching there, and if we had any young ladies living next door, I would think that they'd be taking turns peeking out the windows. I've made Father drive up in a new automobile and climb out with a smile.

"How's the reading going, Watson?"

He's talking to Vincent, and I really feel quite startled, for I had forgotten that he ever called him that. Vincent has always loved Sherlock, and Father used to tease him that he could only be Watson.

Vincent closes the book, saying something about hounds. I suppose I haven't put myself in this story yet, but for now, I don't. Instead, I follow them inside, where Vincent explores Hannah's offerings for dinner, while Father lingers in the doorway, listening as Mother finishes the song. She lets the last note linger before smiling mischievously at him. "You're home early."

Father's not playing along well with this, even in my imagination, for I really can't come up with a response for him. Hannah says Mother brought out the best in Father. So I try to smooth the lines in his forehead, along with his stiff movements. He slips a necklace from his pocket and drapes it around her neck, whispering something into her ear.

Oh dear. This wasn't a good idea at all.

I stare at the empty piano and wonder why I can't imagine myself in the picture, and I think it's because I haven't any idea what I would be like if I'd grown up with a mother and a father who was not terrified to let me try new things.

I don't like myself at all, and it must show in my face because Andrew steps to the window.

"Are you well, Miss Castle?" he asks. "I didn't mean for you to think about things that make you sad."

"You didn't," I say, though he doesn't look like he believes me. I suppose it isn't quite true, but he had no idea his suggestion would bring up Mother. "We don't talk about Mother, and I wish we did."

He puts his hands to the windowsill, and I notice his poor skin is still red from multiple bites. Ants really are evil creatures.

"Do you remember her?" he asks.

"Not well," I answer. "Only fragments of memories. Hannah says I look like her."

"You do."

I cock my head at the quick reply.

He explains. "Your grandfather showed me a portrait of her while we were on the train on our way here. She was very pretty."

I'm so startled that he has seen her that I nearly interrupt him. "Grandfather has a portrait?"

Andrew nodded. "In his watch. Don't you have one?"

"Not out. Most of Mother's things that survived the storm are in Father's desk upstairs, and he keeps it locked."

"Can you ask him to open it?"

"No." I shake my head. "I don't think he could bear it."

"Oh," Andrew says, and now it seems he's the one blundering into awkward conversations. He winces and offers an apologetic smile. It's only after he turns that I remember the rest of what he said.

Mother was pretty. And I look like her.

My face pricks. Does that mean he thinks I look pretty?

4

SCARLET BELDON
Summer, 2012

ALL ARGUMENTS ASIDE, I SPEND THE MORNING FOLLOWING DAD around the house, parroting the same phrases. "Dad. I'm telling you. There was a girl in the hall."

He sighs. "I looked. There was no girl. I don't know what you saw, but it's only me and you now. Kay?"

"That music box was playing in the chest," I insist. "You had to have heard that, even if you didn't see ghost-girl. It was right above your bedroom!"

Dad rolls his eyes. "It was not."

"It was. I recognized the song."

"How do you know what song it played?"

"Because, I listened to it earlier yesterday when I wound it."

"Well, it probably just wasn't all the way unwound and started again. They do that, you know."

"I'm telling you —"

Dad's phone buzzes, and he slides it from his pocket like it's a lifeline away from me. Then he goes to the porch for a better connection. This house eats signals for breakfast. I swear the walls are made of concrete.

But it doesn't matter. I already know if I am going to stay in control of my life, I have to take it by the horns. Relying on Dad is not an option. If I can figure out Clara's last name, I can find out who she is — was. If she matches her picture. If she's a ghost or was murdered or something.

I saw a girl. She didn't see me. I have no idea what explanation I'm going to tack onto the event, but I have a pretty good idea of who it might be and the only way I'm going to get answers is if I find them myself. I seriously question my sanity at the moment, but I don't have any better ideas, so I decide to finish reading the letters. But they're not on the table. I look under it, around it, and under things around it.

Dad must have moved them. I growl and roam the house. Maybe he put them back in the chest, since I told him that was where I found them. I inch near the chest, telling myself not to be stupid. After all, I'm only approaching a piece of furniture that contains a self-winding music box, to get information about people who shouldn't be wandering the halls because they wrote letters back in 1910.

I blow out a yoga breath as I kneel by the chest and lift the lid. I snatch the stack of letters, let the lid slam, and make a run for it. Settling on the porch swing, I ignore the seagulls' calls as I rifle through the letters. The guy with the pretty handwriting doesn't sign his letters with his last name, but I find it written on the back of one piece of paper folded like an envelope. Andrew Callaghan. From New York City.

I wish I was in New York City.

It's addressed to a Clara Castle in Palacios, Texas.

"Clara Castle," I mutter. "At least I know what to call you when you come back."

I glance toward the old house, wondering what the odds are that she'll go through Dad's room tonight and they'll spook each other. That would serve him right, though she doesn't deserve that sort of shock. Even if she is a ghost, she doesn't seem really scary, but a shiver goes down my spine as I flip open another letter.

Oct. 20, 1910
Palacios, Texas

Dear Andrew,

I hope things are going well for you at school. We are all fine here. My life continues as normal. There is nothing much to write about it, honestly. I am reading "A Connecticut Yankee in King Arthur's Court." Vincent said that he is reading it with you. Can you imagine hitting your head and waking up in another century? I can't decide if I would be excited or terrified.

Sometimes I sit up too late reading and my eyes hurt in the morning, but I cannot tell Father why. Is it wicked of me, Andrew, to deceive him in such a manner? I suppose I should not read without his permission, but Father would never let me read anything at all, and I do so love learning new things. He nearly found our correspondence. I keep your letters in a wooden box in my chest, but some made it all the way down to the dining room. I found them sitting on the table, and I cannot think how they got there.

Andrew, something dreadful has happened since I last wrote. Father's lumber mill burned. Vincent says it was a malfunction, sparks from the blade that ignited the sawdust or something like that. Everyone got out, but I could see the blaze from my window upstairs. We haven't a fire station here, and there wasn't anything to be done, except toss buckets of sea water around the perimeters and watch it burn. I ran all the way down the street, worried that Father was inside, and no one paid me any heed at all, so I stood there and watched it go down with the rest of the town.

Father looked so defeated, and I can't get the memory out of my mind. Of course, everyone assumes that we have enough savings to get back onto our feet, but I don't think we do. Sometimes I wonder if it doesn't make you as sick as it makes me that the whole world seems to be struggling just to make ends meet, and my grandfather dances around, paying exorbitant amounts to eat fish eggs. Then again, I suppose it is his money to spend as he likes.

Now that I look over this, I see all that I should not have written. I shall start again and not send this letter. If the truth be told, I write you lots of letters that I don't send. I cannot talk to Vincent, for he would be sure to start a fight with Father. I just want a confidant. You are that, even though you shall never know it. Now I am off to write another, lighter, happier, and probably duller letter. I do wonder that you put up with them.

Clara

I fold the letter again, wondering what Andrew would have made of that if he ever read it. Did Clara ever tell him he has a stack of unread mail? I flip through the envelopes until I find Andrew's handwriting again, though it takes a few minutes to realize that a year's worth of practice has greatly improved it and that beautiful scroll belongs to him. He'd be bullied in school nowadays coming with handwriting that pretty.

August 2, 1911
NYC, New York

Dear Clara,

Here I am again, trying to write before the coal is used up and the fire burns too low to see. I feel like a fool tonight. Your grandfather has been kind to me, and I am grateful. I have never seen my father so proud that one of his children is attending school. But honestly, Clara, I'm not sure how your grandfather persuaded them to allow me into school in the first place. Even with a tutor, I barely passed the year. I honestly don't know if I can make it through another. There is so much from the earlier classes that I never learned. I feel hopelessly lost. Even when I memorize the correct answers, I'm not always sure what they mean.

But your grandfather still believes I could become someone important if I'll let him teach me how. My youngest siblings don't remember me at all, and the children all think I'm going to become rich and take them away from New York. But my older siblings, Fiona, Lauren and Tommey, think I'm getting above myself, even though I'm doing everything I can to help out. Tommey's lungs are so bad now that he can hardly work. I told him perhaps if I returned with your grandfather, I could find a way to make him better. He turned on me, telling me he had worked so I could go to school. And he must listen to Da brag about Andrew, who is going to school. Andrew, who is going to make something of himself.

And never Tommey, I suppose. I did not realize that he was jealous. I never imagined the money I sent from playing at the hotel this past summer would make him feel unneeded. We do need him, Clara. I hate to see him so unhappy.

Before I left for home, your grandfather implied that the best way I could help my family was to completely remake myself. He's promised to help them, but only if I exchange my life as a Callaghan and let him adopt me. I don't know how such consent would affect you and Vincent, though your grandfather says that no one shall do anything except benefit from the arrangement. But how can I do that, Clara? Can I look my father in the face and tell him for all his honesty and work, even though he taught me to play the violin, he's not good enough? I can't, Clara.

But Da fell asleep two hours ago from sheer exhaustion. The baby rarely stops crying. Everyone is hungry. Tommey is coughing up blood. Would you despise me, Clara, if I said yes? I'm not trying to infiltrate, and I would never ruin your family. I'm only desperate to save my own. There goes the last of the embers. Good night, Clara.

Andrew

I close the letter, feeling like I've stumbled on something I should have never seen. If someone came along and offered to send me to college and set me up for success, I'd walk away from Dad in a heartbeat. But this letter is dripping with agony, and I'm starting to wonder if there isn't a guy ghost walking around here too, who's going to be ticked off that some modern intruder is reading his girlfriend's mail. I mean. I don't know that she is his girlfriend, but he's pretty worried about whether she's going to think he's a big, fat fraud after her family's money.

His mention of the violin makes me remember the roll of sheet music in the trunk, and I abandon the correspondence until I'm brave enough to snoop again. The song is handwritten with Andrew's name printed neatly at the top.

I had six months of piano lessons in second grade, just enough to make me curious to hear what kind of song was written by this boy. I approach the piano, hoping to coax enough noise from it to at least hear the rest of the melody line. Most of the keys are dead, giving a plunk or a feeble note so loose that you can hear the string vibrate. The higher notes sound better, so I move the entire song up an octave, and the song sounds sort of like a music box. In fact, the song sounds a lot like *the* music box.

When I first see the movement in the mirror's reflection, I think that it's Dad. It isn't. Clara's back. She comes in a flash, sitting on the piano stool as solid as I am. She jumps, sucking in a sharp breath as her head turns toward me.

"Clara!" I sputter.

Clara screams, leaping from her seat. She takes two steps back and fades. I can't move. I can't even breathe. She saw me? Should I feel safer knowing that she is terrified of me, too? At least I don't think she's going to come strangle me in the middle of the night.

Over the next few days, I see her again — a lot — though she no longer seems to see me. I glimpse her at the vanity in the morning. Then outlined in the window at night, humming to herself as she watches the water. I call her name again, but she doesn't respond to it. Even playing the song at the piano again does nothing. But that music box goes off as faithfully as an alarm clock — only at night instead of in the morning.

My email becomes replaced by snail mail. I write Kate, then leave it alone. No social media. No surfing. Just letters between two people who would probably die if they knew I found them. If I'm reading between the lines correctly, there are some feelings blossoming between these two. Which is cute, because I can't figure out if the other one knows it or not. It's like two little kids on the playground.

Andrew gets lots of letters over the course of a year that he doesn't know exist. Clara writes with abandon, asking questions and coming up with imaginative answers. She seems apologetic — like everything that goes wrong is her fault. Outside of the mail, I can find little about her. Her name is in the family Bible. She was born in 1895, which would make her close to my age when the letters end, soon after Andrew asks his big question.

Clara must have received it and sent the first letter that she wrote because there is nothing after that date. Which sucks. I'm dying to know if she and Andrew ever married, and especially if they married each other and the sudden silence doesn't look promising. Most of his letters are from the year before, relaying pranks at school and glossing over lessons, painting a very different image than a boy who is desperately trying to keep up in high school when he's never been to kindergarten.

I scour the chest, looking for any letters that I've missed, but there's none. I have only one left. One that fell out of the stack, and I wasn't sure where to put it back in. I've been saving it, not wanting the story to end.

It is another from Clara that was never sent to Andrew. I grin and lie back on the bed, glad that the guilt of reading their mail is almost over. If I've read the letters once already, there's no reason why I shouldn't go ahead and read them all over again, right?

Feb. 11, 1911

   Dear Andrew,
    I have the strangest thoughts today. I cannot stop the pen from shaking. I cannot stop myself from shaking. I have seen the strangest thing. I cannot tell anyone. They would not believe me. I am not certain that even you would believe me, though I know that you would try. There is a girl in the house.

"Whaaaa?"

I bolt upright, hunching over the letter, feeling the blood pound through my entire body.

    There is a girl in the house, only she is a strange girl. I was playing your song at the piano and she just appeared, right next to me. I swear I saw her and she saw me, too. She knew my name. How did she know my name? And then, she vanished. What is it, Andrew? Who is it?

My brain shuts off. I stare at the words, letting my mouth hang at an unattractive angle. She apparently never finished. Maybe she was as freaked out as I'm feeling. Has this letter been here the whole time, or did it separate from the stack because it came after? What if… what if…

I press my lips together, hunting for a piece of paper. Old houses don't have paper sitting around, but I find the back of a pizza flyer and sit down, clicking one of my pens on the table.

July 12, 2012

Dear Clara,

I stare. I'm officially crazy. I'm writing to a dead girl. I bite my lip and start again.

> *I know this is weird and I'm creeped out too, but I'm the girl that you see. The one that was playing the piano. My name is Scarlet. I don't know how this works, but I have seen you too. I am living in your house, but not at the same time as you. For me, you lived here almost 100 years before. Kind of like when the Yankee went back to Camelot in King Arthur's Court. Except that was fiction, and this is real.*
>
> *I have seen you a few times around the house since we moved here a few weeks back. I was really scared of you at first, but now I like to spot you. I startled you that one time when I was at the piano, but you don't have to be scared of me because I am a friend.*
>
> *I'm going to leave this with your letters inside your chest and see if maybe you get it. I think if you left me a letter, I would probably find it there. I really hope you get this, because I've been feeling like I'm crazy too, but now we can figure it out together. I promise I will never hurt you or tell anyone that I saw you here. You don't have to be afraid.*
>
> *Scarlet*

> *P.S. I hear your music box every night. It kind of creeped me out at first, but now I'm used to it. Where did you get it?*

I take the letter before I can think twice and deposit it beneath the music box. I rock on my heels in a classic pose of someone who has completely lost their mind. I don't know what I'm expecting it to do. Poof and disappear or something.

It doesn't.

It's still there the next day.

And the next.

So I decide that it won't travel back to her time, and I can only try and talk to her when I see her again. The next night when I hear the music tinkling, I run to the chest anyway. She's not there, but a neat envelope lays beside the music box.

"Holy crap," I whisper and reach for the white paper. It's crisp, unfolding stiffly, though it's already yellowed.

Feb 13, 1911

Dear Scarlet,

My name is Clara, but you know that, of course. I found your letter here. I cannot believe that it is here, but I cannot explain how else it would have come. So I have no choice but to believe you. Your stationary is very bright.

I have seen you twice here, but I cannot think of how you have so much information about me. Please do not think me rude. I do not have any friends, except the servants that live in the house. Father does not like me to go into society often, saying my health is too delicate. That is why I was so startled to find you.

I could not write for a day after I found your letter. I think perhaps you are the reason things keep moving around the house. I find my belongings downstairs on the table sometimes, and I have no idea how they got there. Please don't think me unkind if I ask that you keep my things upstairs. My father becomes very upset when they are out of place, especially where he can see them. I do not mind you looking at them. I hope you receive this letter, and that we may be friends. It is the most exciting thing that has ever happened to me, and there is no one that I can tell, except you.

Yours fondly,
Clara Castle

P.S. What music box?

What music box?? I jolt, then glance at the top of the letter. Spring of 1911. This is before the last of the letters. Clara is sixteen. Andrew's going to school, pretending he's not struggling. Clara's father already lost the mill, but Andrew hasn't stayed there for the summer to play at whatever hotel their later correspondence refers to.

I bring my hands to my face, realizing that I know parts of Clara's story that she hasn't experienced. I just discovered some sort of time portal, at least for paper.

I want to write another letter right away without waiting for good paper, but I really can't find anything, so I force myself to pull on sandals and jog to the bookstore. I wonder if my letters crumble like Clara's after they've traveled back in time. I'm so busy with the debate, that I hardly notice that I've arrived until the door swings shut and hits me from behind.

"Careful!" Someone calls as about five people turn to look at me. "The wind is strong today."

The lady behind the counter smiles and says, "Can I help you?"

"I'm looking for stationary," I say, like that's a completely logical thing for a teenager to be searching for.

"Okay..." She glances toward the back of the store where old and new books mingle on the shelves. "We have some cards."

I follow her past two men who are talking from different tables.

"I'm telling you," one says. "They need to knock that building down and replace it with something that's going to attract tourists. Otherwise, this place is going to die."

"Right here," the shopkeeper says. "Did you just need one? The museum dropped off a set with historical pictures on them. I think there are ten in the box."

Usually, I wouldn't care a bit about black and white photographs, but these look like they're from Clara's time, and I snatch them, resisting a squeal. "That looks perfect."

"Hey, boy! Where you been?" A man with a white mustache calls out as the wind whistles another person through the door.

I recognize the teen Dad hired to work on our lawn, but he doesn't see me. He smiles at a couple at the table. "Oh, just looking for a job."

The lobbyist for the tourist building snorts. "Good luck."

"Well, get some coffee and have a break." The only woman at the tables pats the spot across from her.

The guy moves to the coffee urn, helping himself to an insulated cup before he spies me over the short wall. "Hey!" The smile is back. "Girl in the house on the corner."

"Yeah," I say. "Mower man."

"Mower man." He quirks an eyebrow, then grins. "That sounds like a really lame superhero."

I flinch. "It does, doesn't it?"

He laughs, then sticks his hand over the wall between us. "Keith Castle."

I snap and point at him. "You're related to Clara!"

He rocks back on his heels like my finger is a gun. "Who?"

"Clara Castle," I say. "From like...way back."

Wow, I just made an idiot of myself.

Keith cocks his head as I blunder on, unsure how to explain that I'm buying notecards to write one of his ancestors. "She lived in our house," I say. "I found a record of her name from 1911."

I don't want to tell him about the letters. Those are mine. Well, mine and Andrew's and Clara's.

"Uh." Keith glances toward the others at the table. "Yeah. Dad did say that house used to be in the family."

"Do you know anything about them?" I ask, trying to figure out how to sound cool about researching someone totally unrelated to me.

Keith laughs awkwardly, like he's unsure if he wants to talk to me or not. Or maybe he's just trying to figure out how to be cool about all this, too. Then he looks back up. "I'll buy you coffee?"

I glance down at my cards. Writing Clara right away or having coffee with her great-great-something-relative? "Sure," I answer, wondering if this counts as a date.

"Splendid," he says, and pulls another cup from the stack, pumping the coffee into it before I can change my mind. "Here. You get your own cream and sugar. What's your name, by the way?"

"Scarlet. Scarlet Beldon."

He motions me to my cup. I snag the sugar packets, tearing open two. Then we move to the stools at the counter as I try to figure out how to interview him without looking completely weird. "Your family's been here a long time, I guess?"

"Sort of," he says. He stirs his coffee, watching it turn a shade lighter. "My parents are dead, and I bounced around foster care for a while. I'm living with my aunt now, but I've only been back for a little over a year."

"Well, that sucks," I say. "My dad divorced—twice. I'm kind of used to bouncing around, too. I have no idea where my real mom is anymore."

"How long are you going to be here?" he asks.

"I have no idea," I answer. "Dad's not sure what he's going to do with the house. He's thinking about selling it, but he wanted to vacation here first."

Keith's head snaps up. "Oh, he should keep it!"

"The house?" I ask.

"Yeah." He shrugs, then sips his coffee. "I mean. It's a cool house."

He senses me staring and his shoulders collapse. "I mean..." He leans toward me, trying to look cool and conspiring, but he nearly knocks his cup over with his elbow. "I heard it has a secret passage, or room, or something."

"What?" I say it a little louder than I mean to, but the coffee shop has cleared out.

Keith nods, and the reflection from the fan makes his eyes sparkle. "When I was little, I lived in Galveston with my grandma until she got too senile to keep me. She always told me that I looked like her grandfather, Vincent. But, as she got worse, she started thinking I was Vincent."

"Your grandmother thought you were her grandfather?" I ask.

"Yeah. It was weird. She kept asking if I'd unblocked the secret door in the house." He catches me staring and then shrugs. "It was probably just crazy-talk, but I did always kind of wonder, you know? I love old buildings, and if there's a secret passage—"

"If there is a secret passage, we are so finding it." I slap my hands on the table surface and stand, though I can't think of any place where even a small passage could be tucked into the structure of the house. I already know that house has at least one secret, but I can't share that with him yet.

He pays for my coffee, and I pay for my cards, and we run down the street like a pair of hoodlums. Clara's letter is burning a hole in my pocket, but I promised her I wouldn't tell anyone. Besides, I have no idea if I can trust this guy, and if anybody discovers a way to pen-pal people from the past, it's going to be me. The wind is picking up, and the clouds threaten rain by the time we barge through the front door. I slow to catch my breath, wincing as Dad's voice carries from the kitchen.

"I said 'no' and that's final!"

I don't know who he's talking to, but he sounds mad enough that I slow and scrunch my nose. He must have heard us coming, because he's snapping his phone closed as he strides into the hallway.

"This is Keith," I say quickly, like Keith isn't standing behind me peering at the ceiling and walls like he's casing the place. "We're just going to hang out."

"Okay," Dad says, and I know he's upset because he doesn't even say hi to Keith. "I've got some errands to run. You guys have fun."

I should be glad that he's not detaining us, but I watch him move to the porch, thinking it probably wouldn't matter what kind of stranger I brought into the house. As though he's just remembered some secret pact of fatherhood, Dad sticks his head back into the door. "Hi, Keith." He points at me. "Don't smoke."

And then he's gone, shutting the door and completely missing my hands flying out. Whatever.

Keith's already exploring a closet under the stairs. We pry open the door with our fingertips, but it's just storage with old jars stuffed on shelves. Keith keeps peeking around door frames, then muttering, "Not wide enough."

I find a square jutting from the kitchen wall, just wide enough to be a door, but the room would only be about the size of a wardrobe. "What about this?" I ask.

Keith knocks on the wall with solid thumps, and I take advantage of his distraction by scrawling onto the first note card.

Dear Clara,
Longer letter later. Is there a secret room in your house?
Scarlet

I stuff the card into my pocket, already plotting how to get it into the chest as Keith steps back, pushing his lips to one side. He shakes his head. "It's probably a chimney."

"Well, that's boring," I say. "Why would you block off a chimney?"

He shrugs. "It's the kitchen. They probably stopped using it when they got an electric stove."

We go around knocking on walls, even knowing they're too thin to conceal a secret room. The excitement evaporates into disappointment and then impatience. I don't think we're going to find anything, and I have a letter to write. When Keith's not looking, I slip the note into the chest, hoping it will travel back to Clara's time much faster than the first one did.

Keith plants his hands on his hips. "The stair rail looks original," he says with disappointment. "The walls have been redone. If there was anything, the workers would have found it."

I sigh. "Well. Maybe you could try to find out more about Vincent? Maybe he wrote something about it that your grandma was referring to."

"Yeah." Keith still peers around. "Okay. Okay, I'll do that. Um." He points to me. "Phone number?"

"Uh, sure." I pull out my cell, and we exchange numbers. Then, to my relief, he takes off on his own. I slide into a chair like a baseball player to home base, using the second card and a pink pen. I'm about to tell Clara that I just met her great-something nephew, but then I decide that's a lot to drop onto anyone. Writing by hand is so much slower than typing, but I scrawl as quickly as I can.

> *Dear Clara,*
> *It worked! We can write each other! Are my letters crumbled when you get them? Yours are. I have to be careful to open them. I'll never bring any of your things downstairs again. I don't want you getting in trouble. Is your father really strict? Sometimes I watch movies (those are like books, but different) and anyway, they're about people who live back when you do and the dad is super strict. Do you have to dress up for dinner?*
> *My dad's a jerk, but he's not strict. He lets me do whatever I want. I can't imagine him getting mad because I left something laying around. Tell me about yourself.*
> *There is so much I could tell you. I can even tell you when your father died, but I can't find anything about you, really. Maybe I shouldn't have written that. He's really old when he*

dies. I think. I don't remember. Anyway, we all do, right? You know what? I'm gonna start this letter over.

I complete a second letter that is not so giddy or saying stupid stuff like, 'Is your father a jerk? Don't worry if he is. He dies.' Then I put it in the chest with its friend and check every ten minutes, but it's still there white and clean and laying on top like a straitjacket.

It's cool, but I wish I hadn't told her I wouldn't tell anyone. Kate would find this awesome. She might actually believe me. Actresses are weird.

I check the next morning and it's gone, but there is no letter in its place, so she must be writing it. I practically prance until Dad asks what in the world I'm up to and gets a long explanation about nothing.

I don't know what to do with myself.

I wish Clara had email.

Or chat. Chat would be better. After lunch, a letter returns. I nearly tear the stationary trying to get the envelope open. Clara's handwriting is so much nicer than mine.

February 20, 1911

Dear Scarlet,

I am very glad that it works. It is such fun. We are like secret friends. Father is not terribly strict, but he is very protective. I do not know quite how to tell people about myself. My days are nearly alike. I rise in the morning before it is light. Hannah has breakfast going, so I can smell it. Don't you love the smell of breakfast in the morning? I dress myself and do my own hair, though often I leave it down. Father does not mind that I look younger. I usually read until I go down at half past seven for breakfast. Father talks to me sometimes, and other mornings he simply reads the paper or his correspondence. He always tells me what he expects of me for the day. Most of the time it is the same, but occasionally he has something in particular he wishes me to work on.

After he leaves, Hannah clears the table. I usually help her, though it is not proper. I have even scrubbed the floors on occasion. I tell you this, only because you cannot tell anyone else, for you are not in my time and have given your word as well. I hope you are still my friend after I send this. Perhaps I shall not.

After the table is cleared, I make out dinner plans or any household managing that Father has placed in my care. I am also to know what supplies we need. Then I practice music and correspondence. Father says it is important to learn to communicate well, though he would not be pleased with the informality of this letter if he saw it. A year ago, I only wrote to him, Grandfather, and Vincent.

Now I write to Andrew as well. Andrew is my grandfather's ward who attends school with my brother. Vincent doesn't like to write, but Andrew will. He knows I like learning things, so he'll often write about his lessons. And now I have you as well, which is by far the most peculiar. The letter I write to Father, he reads when he comes home in the evenings.

After the letters, I work on my skills such as embroidery or help Hannah mend the clothing. Father has me learn arithmetic as well, but he won't let me keep the financial records. I spend much of my day making sure that the house remains clean. When he returns in the evening, I must be changed again for dinner and waiting fresh and cheerful for him. He says he likes to see that sort of daughter when he arrives. Even if I am not at all cheerful and feeling terrible, I still pretend that I am.

Hannah has supper waiting, and Father and I sit down for the meal. Sometimes he will tell me a story of something that happened to him. Sometimes he is silent. He is a good father. He cares very much about me, and I am grateful to have him.

But I do not go out often, so I am sure that my life must be quite boring to you. I cannot think of anything more to write, and I still must write Father and Vincent. I did not intend to spend so much time on your letter. I hope that I may finish theirs in time.

Clara

P.S. What is your day like?

I grin, imagining what I might say.

> Dear Clara,
> My days are like this: I get up when I want. Eat what and when I want. Talk to my dad anytime I want. Argue a lot and spend my spare time snooping through your love letters.

Of course, I will not say that to her.
But her dad sounds like a jerk, no matter what she may think about him.

> Dear Clara,
> I think your dad must be a bigger jerk than mine.

I don't say that either.

But I do wonder what would happen if Clara did not finish her letter to her father or learn a piece of music. What would her father do?

I have no time to figure it out, before my own dad is bellowing up the stairs that he's going for hamburgers and if I want one, I'd better get my tail into the car. I wonder, as I stand, if Clara is right next to me, peering into the trunk and waiting for a reply.

CLARA CASTLE
Fall, 1910

A MONTH HAS PASSED SINCE HER LETTER CAME. I'VE READ HER WORDS UNTIL I have them memorized, simply to convince myself that I did not imagine them. I only allow myself to check once every morning now, for the empty chest is too disappointing to dwell on.

I glance inside today, so quickly that I almost overlook the envelope with my name scrawled on it. My heart pounds, but Father calls from the dining room with an edge of disapproval in his tone.

There is not enough time to read it before I must go to breakfast. I slip the letter into my pocket and hurry downstairs, keeping hold of the banister. Father worries if I do not descend with one hand on the railing.

He is sitting at the table already, and my heart thumps. I glance at the clock, finding it just three minutes past 7:00. Four now.

"Sit down, Clara." Father folds the paper and sets it aside. "You are dawdling today."

"I am sorry, Father."

He nods toward my chair, then searches my face.

"Are you feeling ill?" he asks.

I wave him off as he sits up. "Nothing is the matter. I didn't sleep well last night."

"What were you doing?" he asks, as though he can't imagine why anyone wouldn't be able to sleep as soon as the lamp is blown out.

"Nothing," I answer. This time, it's true. After Christmas break, Vincent whispered that he 'may have forgotten' something, and I found three novels hidden in his room. I started one, but it became so frightening that I set it down again. I'd rather think about Scarlet. Receiving a letter from someone who hasn't been born yet is far more exciting than the most scandalous novel.

Father glances up. "What time did you go to bed?"

"Half past nine," I answer.

"Did you not fall asleep?"

"No, sir."

His eyes rove over me and I try not to squirm, hoping this does not trigger the most extreme form of his anxiety. He has forced some of the most horrible concoctions down my throat when he thinks that I am ill, and once, when Hannah missed a bad egg, he threw out the entire lot.

"I was only thinking, sir," I say.

Father leans back in his chair, then reaches for his napkin. "You think too much. Night is for sleeping. You must learn to set your thoughts to the side. They will be waiting when you awake."

"Yes, sir."

My face pricks as Hannah pours Father's coffee, eyeing me like she suspects I'm hiding secrets. I glance back down at my hands, waiting for Father to finish filling his plate and then mine.

Today he hesitates, scanning the dishes with puckered eyebrows as though one is poisoned and he must guess which. He looks so distressed over the decision that I can nearly imagine two men standing behind him, holding him at gunpoint. His spoonfuls are tiny, as though the bread is the only thing he knows is safe and he hopes that if he did choose wrong on the fruit, the amount will not kill me.

"If you are not feeling well, you should eat little," he says. "Simple food."

"Yes, sir," I answer.

I shall have to content myself with toast. I don't dare ask for butter. Father does not forget things. He leaves them out. I accept the plate with a smile as though it was filled with a king's feast. "Thank you."

He smiles back and the haunted look evaporates like steam rising from cast iron. My heart warms, despite its longing for butter.

Is your father strict?

I glance back at him, trying to see him through Scarlet's eyes.

No. My heart answers. But I'm not sure he's sane.

The thought swoops in like a bat startled out of a dark corner, and I banish it just as quickly. My father gave me toast without butter. That's not insanity. That's protection, even if it is unnecessary. Who knows? Perhaps butter causes insomnia.

Father says little for several minutes. I concentrate on swallowing dry toast, wondering what Scarlet's letter says and what I will tell her.

"Eat, Clara. I won't have you wasting away."

I force my thoughts from Scarlet. The sooner I finish, the sooner he'll leave for the mill, allowing me to read the letter.

"Yes, sir."

"You must try harder to sleep at night. I will not have you tired during the day."

"Yes, sir."

"I have many things for you to do today," he continues. "But you must be careful if you are feeling ill. We are having guests for dinner tonight, and I'm leaving every preparation to your care. Hannah will do as you say, but you mustn't spend more than five dollars if you can help it.

"However, they are important people, so it is imperative that we make the best impression. The house must be cleaned and dinner prepared. Tonight you may be called upon to play the piano. I believe the lady is fond of music."

Every sentence that comes from his mouth creates more panic inside my chest. Last time people came to the porch, he sent me upstairs. Now he wishes me to host a dinner party for complete strangers? I've never even been to a dinner party.

My stomach churns, but I smile, though I'm sure my face reflects the expression he wore only moments ago. "Yes, Father."

"Clara." Father's eyes meet mine, and my stomach tightens with a fresh wave of panic. "I want you to wear whatever you have that is nicest."

"Of course. I will take care of everything," I reply.

The guests will arrive, no matter what I think of it. Hannah will know how to prepare for them and, good heavens, if I'm to wear my best dress, Father's planning on letting me stay downstairs.

I smile a little as excitement replaces a bit of the fear.

Father stands and kisses my forehead. "Be a good girl. I'll see you tonight."

The breeze comes through the door when he opens it, leaving me sitting in front of my crust. I push it away, no longer hungry.

Hannah hurries in, wiping her hands on her apron. "No need to repeat. I heard it." She surveys me. "And I must have your help because I can't do it all myself, but I won't have you doing the hard things. We can't get those pretty little hands of yours all rough, where your father might see."

She has a point, but I hesitate. "You cannot do all the hard work yourself," I say. "I am younger than you."

She laughs and reaches for Father's plate. "Younger, but not stronger. I've been working all my life, and if you lived like everyone thinks you should, you'd be a chronic invalid."

"But I'm not ill." Frustration leaks through my voice as I squeeze the napkin in my lap.

"I know you're not," she says. "But no matter. You're small. You'd wear right down under the strain." She motions to the table. "Finish. No use letting it go to waste."

Tears prick as I try not to panic. "No, don't ask me to."

"You don't eat enough to keep a bird alive, Clara."

"I'm not hungry."

"I don't believe that."

"It's true."

She sighs, and I persist. "Please, do not ask me. I cannot deceive him."

That settles it. I shall go without. She can't afford to lose her place, and I can never hide anything from Father. I feel guilty enough over concealing my letters to Andrew though they've never been forbidden.

It is enough food, really. I don't eat very much, even when Father fills my plate with everything on the table. I stand and gather a serving dish, asking, "Do we have food for a good meal tonight?"

"We have food enough to pretend we have a full larder," Hannah replies, "though it will not be as extravagant as they wish."

"No. I suppose it won't," I reply.

Hannah gathers her favorite hat with the blue feather, which is as extravagant as she ever allows herself to become. "Don't you worry, Little Missy. We put up a good amount of fruit last year. I'll go and won't spend a penny over your allowance."

As soon as the screen slams, I pull the letter from my pocket. It's difficult to decipher. Her letters are wide and round.

> *Dear Clara,*
> *It worked! We can write each other. This is so cool! Are my letters yellowed when you get them? Yours are. There is so much I could tell you that I'm not sure where to start.*

I jump as the door shakes beneath a knock. My eyes freeze on Scarlet's words that suddenly don't make any sense at all. Simon isn't in the house. Hannah won't answer.

I am alone.

I swallow as the knock comes again. Do I answer? Is it safe? I glance at the clock, realizing it's the only movement in the room, then push to my feet. Perhaps Father sent something for the dinner tonight.

A young man stands on the step with a parcel tucked beneath his arm. He gives a little start, then cocks his head. "Oh. Hello. I have a package for Clara Castle."

For me? My eyes shift down to the package before I remember I haven't answered him. "I'm Clara."

"You..." He cuts his words short, regaining his stunned smile. "Very well, then."

He hands over a small, wooden box and tips his hat to me. After taking a step back, he turns back. "Forgive me. Are — do you — live here?"

No. I live in a tree in the backyard.

I fold my hands, balancing the package in front and press my lips together, catching the thought before it slips out. Father is right. I think too much. The poor man cannot help that he's never seen me before.

"Yes," I reply. "I'm Edmund Castle's daughter."

"Well, I'll be..." The man brushes the front of his coat, though it looks like he's trying to keep himself busy. "Forgive me. I didn't know he had a daughter."

Father's never mentioned me? I wonder how often they see each other. It's true that Father rarely allows me out of the house, but we go to church on Christmas and Easter every year. I have no idea how to respond, so I only offer a smile. "Thank you for the package," I say as I shut the door.

Only after I carry it to the dining room do I wonder if I should have offered a tip. I hurry back to the porch, but the poor man has already gone.

Spying Grandfather's handwriting on the package, I instinctively glance toward the yard, ready to stow it from sight if Father should return. Grandfather always gives such elaborate gifts that sometimes I wonder if they're not specifically chosen to somehow humiliate Father.

When I manage to pry the boards off the box, I find it filled to the brim with rice. I know of several farmers who would be elated for the chance to grow a new strain of rice, but I can't imagine what Grandfather fancies I'll do with it. An envelope peeks out and I pull it free, brushing off bits of grain.

> *To Clara,*
> *In a corner of New York lives the world's most clever man who makes oddities that most people have never seen. He is too shy and silly to be well known, but here you have the final work of Mr. Simon Mondeau. He says it's his perfect piece and shall be his last. Happy birthday, darling.*
>
> > *Grandfather*

> *P.S. The box is from me. The song inside is Andrew's creation. Take care of it, darling. That boy is going places.*

I feel my entire face warm and I'm only glad that no one is here to watch me blush. When Andrew spent Christmas with us, he told me all about his family and his hopes to return home this summer for a visit. Though Grandfather lavished us all with expensive gifts, my favorite was from Andrew; an original song written on white paper.

I run to the kitchen for the milk pail drying by the back porch and return to scoop away the top layer of rice. The box is wrapped in several layers of brown paper, but when I unroll it, I find it entirely made of clear glass. Inside, I see the gears of a music box like tiny fingers brushing the bumps on the roll.

A music box.

I gasp, abandoning the box of rice to run to the chest. I have the music box that Scarlet hears every night. My fingers tremble so hard that I can scarcely wind it. The melody tinkles through the still house, alternating between a cheerful and haunting tune. I watch the levers plink into place, creating the tune and then start again, playing the same wistful call.

The music box dips in my hand like a light tug-of-war, and I cling to it so it doesn't fall. My fingers brush flesh as hands materialize on the opposite side of the box. I scream, nearly dropping the entire thing. Scarlet answers my scream with one of her own, scrambling to her feet and backing against the wall. Then we both stare and laugh.

"Oh my gosh, you're here!" she cries. "You — you're here."

She's wearing heavy blue pants and a black short-sleeved shirt with a portrait painted on the front. Scarlet spins, gripping hair that seems unusually flat and straight. "Wait, no! I think I'm back in your time."

I glance around the hallway with its gleaming floors and floral wallpaper. "Everything is normal," I say, though nothing is normal at all. "I just received your letter. What took you so long to write?"

Scarlet tears her eyes away from our surroundings and back onto me. "I wrote it yesterday right after I got yours. Well, a few hours after."

"But it's been a month," I say.

"That's weird." She huffs a breath, looking around. "But so is this. My gosh. It's 1912?"

I laugh. "It's 1911."

I'm not sure she's even heard me. She's already stepping into my room, still gripping her hair. "This is trippy."

I'm not sure what she means, but none of my thoughts are making any sense either. How did she come here, and what will I tell Father if he should see her? I think I must know what it feels like to be intoxicated and unsure one is seeing correctly.

Her lips are stained unusually bright and it looks like she's outlined her eyelids with coal. I suddenly wonder if she's what Father means when he calls a woman "loose."

She spins around and steps toward me, studying me with high eyebrows and a close-lipped smile. "You're small," she says, in the same tone that Hannah talks to baby kittens and chicks.

"You're tall," I answer.

She laughs. "Yeah, I know. Don't remind me. But you are *really* small."

"I'm not very small," I say. "Vincent says most of the girls are my size, just a bit taller."

But again, she seems too preoccupied to pay attention more than a second. She peers into Vincent's rooms, then moves down the hall. "This is so cool!"

She stalls in front of Father's room at the top of the stairs, opening the door before I can warn her to keep away. "Wait. Whose room is this?" she asks.

"Father's," I answer quickly. "Best not go in there. I'm not even allowed in there."

"That's the room I'm sleeping in." She shuts the door with a shudder. "Okay, yeah. I'm switching rooms. I'm not going to wake up in bed with your dad."

I jolt at the very idea. "Well, I should hope not!"

But I do wonder, suddenly, if she's indirectly responsible for Father's prowling around like he's looking for a danger none of us can see. "You mustn't let Hannah see you when she returns. I'm not allowed to have guests."

"I won't." She glances at me. "My gosh, and I was just waiting for a letter."

"I would not be writing any replies today, anyway," I answer quickly, remembering what I have to do. "We are having guests for dinner, and Father says I must prepare. Hannah and I must tidy the house and make the meal and everything. There is silver to be polished, and I must be sure my dress is ironed. Oh, out of all the days you could have come!"

Her eyebrows rise, and I stop, covering my mouth with my fingers. "I am sorry," I say. "I am speaking too fast."

"No. Not that. I lived in New York last year. Your voice is fine. It's just, that's a lot of stuff for like, what, two people? Can't your father order in food or something?"

I have no idea what she is talking about, but he cannot do whatever it is. "No."

She plants her hands on her hips. "I guess it's good I'm here then. I'll help until I have to hide."

I hesitate. "Perhaps we can finish the table before she returns."

"I'm good at sneaking." Undaunted, she pushes past me. "I've already cleaned like tons of dust from downstairs anyway, so I know my way around."

"Dust?" Horror leaks into my voice.

"Yeah." She spins at the top of the stairs. "In my time. Not yours."

6

SCARLET BELDON
Fall, 1910

THE FIRST THING I NOTICE DOWNSTAIRS IS THE GORGEOUS CHANDELIER IN the hallway. In my time, there's this dumpy little light in its place. I gawk, but Clara doesn't notice. Her heels thud over the varnished floor into the dining hall where a breakfast still sits on the table.

"Yeah. I'd definitely like the smell of breakfast in the morning if I lived here," I say.

Clara laughs and sweeps one arm across the spread. "You may eat anything you'd like."

I reach over to snag a sausage. "I thought you guys weren't rich."

She flushes. Apparently it's different now that I'm not some random stranger living a hundred years away. "It's okay." I shrug. "I mean, this is nice."

She smiles softly. "I suppose."

"So what do we do first, besides the obvious clearing of this table?"

She begins listing off chores in the quaintest voice I've ever heard, with the soft tones of a southern girl who's been heavily influenced by pronunciations from people born in England.

I grin as I clear a plate with a crust of bread, stacking the plates and silverware and serving dishes until I see that she carries them one by one into the kitchen.

"What do you do with your leftovers?" I yell.

Clara reappears in the doorway with her head cocked like a spaniel.

I point. "The extra food. Where does it go?"

"Oh. We leave it in the kitchen for the servants."

"Wow. Kay. Is that what they eat for meals?"

"Yes."

She pauses, studying me like I'm the most fascinating creature she's ever seen. "What do you eat for breakfast?"

"Cereal, mostly," I answer. "You know, like Corn Flakes?"

Her eyes light. "Like Post Toasties?"

"What?" I laugh.

"Wafers of toasted corn," she explains. "Served with milk and sugar?"

"Yes!" I stare. "You guys have those?"

"Well, I've never had them," Clara says, "but I've seen an advertisement. It's called the Hurry-Up breakfast, but Hannah says she'll hurry it out of the house if they ever sell it nearby."

I laugh. "Next time I come, I'm going to bring the most sugary cereal I can find."

We carry the food to the kitchen, which is much nicer than it is in modern time. The walls are white. There is the chimney Keith and I discovered, though its main use is escorting the smoke from the wood-burning stove. Pans hang from the ceiling, polished and gleaming. Best of all, it's clean.

"Hannah likes to keep her kitchen perfect," Clara explains.

I gape all over again, remembering where I am and who I'm talking to. I hope Dad doesn't worry about me. No way am I going back any time soon.

We alternate between bursts of chatter and points when it's too hard to concentrate on work while comparing worlds. Clara and I work like dogs. All this time I thought that she did nothing but trot around the house and drink tea and write letters. Everything must be dusted and swept, which is no easy feat with the breeze blowing the dust around. There's no air conditioner either, and I wish I hadn't worn my skinny jeans today.

Clara moves around in that dress pretty well, though she keeps looking at my pants. Maybe she's wishing for a pair. I don't know. She asks who's on my shirt, launching me into describing a rock concert, which makes her face alternate between amusement and disbelief.

"We're making pretty good timing," I say.

She glances at the grandfather clock. "Good. The silver will take a long time to finish."

"Oh. You have a lot of it?"

She nods. "For these dinners, yes. Though I'm not sure where all of it is. Some of the things disappeared from the china cabinet."

We settle into the dining room chairs with cloths and begin to rub the silver.

"No. Lighter than that," Clara says, as I try to scrub the thing.

"Oh." I search for a way to ask the things I really want to know without giving away my snooping habits.

"So, do you have a boyfriend?"

It's a lousy start.

I search for a sign of blushing, but she shakes her head. "No."

But she's been writing Andrew. I try again. "What about that boy you said you wrote?"

Clara shrugs. "He is my brother's friend."

Uh-huh. I've seen your letters, sweetie. Even if that's true now, it won't be for long.

"Oh yeah?" I ask. "What's his name again?"

"Andrew."

Bingo.

"Yeah?" I ask. "What's he like?"

"Actually." She blushes for the first time. "I just received the music box this morning that you were speaking of. Andrew wrote the song it plays."

"Really?" That's why I hadn't heard the song. "How'd he get it made into a music box?"

"Oh, Grandfather did that," she says quickly. "He knows the maker and asked a favor. Grandfather likes doing things out of the ordinary."

Like plucking random Irish boys from their homes and plopping them into foreign circumstances as part of some weird social experiment.

"It's nice of you to write him," I say. "He's probably really homesick." Even if he won't admit to Clara that he's struggling to keep up in school, it doesn't mean I can't hint and move things along.

She nods. "I think they must miss him as well. All of his siblings are girls, except for one brother who is often ill. Andrew and his father were the main breadwinners. He says that four of his sisters are working in the factories now, because the twins started after he left."

This I hadn't read about, but I'm sure Andrew has glossed over factory life the same way he has put a rosier slant on school struggles.

"It takes two of them to replace his paycheck?" I ask.

She nods. "His mother and other sisters make lace from their home, but Heather and Esther found they could earn more in the textile factories. They still don't earn as much as he did."

"That's not fair," I say, even though I probably won't be paid as much when I start moving up the corporate ladder, even living in the age of equality.

"Life is never fair," Clara says. She plunks down a candlestick with a bit more force than before.

"So tell me about your brother," I say, realizing I can glean all sorts of information for Keith. "What is he like?"

She smiles into the silver. "Vincent is an imp."

I laugh. I was not expecting anything like that to cross her mouth.

"An imp?"

She grins and almost looks like a normal girl. "He plays the most horrid pranks on people."

"Like what?"

"Well, he doesn't do it as often as he did when he was young. Now only on me and Andrew, and friends who don't mind. But once when Mother was alive, he took a scrap from the ragbag and ripped it right as a woman stood."

I snort. When I see those stuffy old pictures of people, who look as though they'd rather be doing anything else than standing in front of the camera, I think that they were prim and proper. Maybe they're not as boring as I thought.

"What happened?"

"She left in a fluster, but Vincent giggled from the hallway and gave himself away. Mother only scolded him, but Father made him hold the back of a chair and thrashed him until he cried. But Vincent still says it was worth it."

Whoa. That's just weird.

"Did he do it again?" I ask.

"Not the cloth but when he was ten, he replaced the sugar with salt."

I laugh and pick up another piece of flat round silver. "Is this a plate?"

"It is a charger," she explains.

"What's that?"

"It goes beneath the plate."

"How annoying," I say.

"What is your father like?" Clara asks.

It's a fair question. I've snooped into her life so much that it's only natural that she turn the tables, but I wince anyway.

"Like a toddler," I say. "My grandfather was really rich, but he developed cancer when Dad was little. He made this trust fund that releases money to Dad every January. So for the first quarter of the year, Dad lives like a party animal but every freaking year he ends up going broke and then has to get a job to keep the electricity on for the winter. And then in January it starts all over again."

Clara frowns, and I wait for her to say something about the ridiculousness of spending large sums on caviar, but she only asks, "What part of the year is it now?"

"Well," I say. "It's summer which is usually when he gives the last of the grand bashes, but he's living here so there's no telling. I just hope I can get out before the trust money runs out again."

Clara nods, then replies slowly, "It's funny how things lose or gain value. One year, you contemplate whether or not you want to top your iced cream with peaches, but the next you keep the jars on the shelf as long as you can just to assure yourself that there is still food in the house."

"Supply and demand," I answer. "I guess that's why I . . ."

I trail off, but Clara presses anyway. "Why what?"

"Why it's so hard to decide if I ever want a man or not," I say. "I've seen so many women on Dad's arm that it's kind of amazing he married any of them. He goes through dates like candy, and I don't want to be candy."

Clara frowns. "But surely not all men are like that. Father's never had anyone except Mother. She's been gone for eleven years now, and he won't even consider remarrying."

I try to imagine finding a man who sees something so unique in me that he doesn't think he can find it in anybody else. Maybe men have changed. Or maybe Edmund Castle knows he was lucky to rope a woman the first time around. Then again, strict or not, he can't be worse than my dad, can he?

"I guess," I say.

She picks up a charger to shine for a second time and I stop rambling about men. "What? You did that one already."

She inspects it and shakes her head. "Not well enough."

Well, good point. The rest gleam, but I'm not sure it's necessary for something that is going to be hidden under a plate.

The porch door slams, and I dive beneath the table as a woman bustles through the house. Clara leans against the table, trying to shield me with her skirt, though it's not wide enough.

The woman, who I assume is Hannah, enters with an armful of parcels. "I got them, darling, and not a penny over."

"Oh, good!" Clara smiles, but her face is pink.

Hannah stops to eye her. Then the woman looks right at me. Well, actually, right through me.

I hold my breath, waiting for her to cock her head and say, "Lord have mercy! Who's under that table?"

But she doesn't. Her eyes glide past me as she says, "I'll get these hopping, and you can work on that silver."

"Of course," Clara answers.

I thought this woman was her servant, not her grandmother. Clara glances down at me and breathes again. "I don't think that she can see you," she mouths. And, proving it, Hannah looks into the room three more times before I'm convinced that she really doesn't see me.

"Clara, you should go change. Your father will be coming home soon."

Clara gasps, glancing at the clock before she rushes upstairs.

"Do you need help?" I yell after her.

Hannah keeps working in the kitchen without even looking up.

"If you can!" Clara calls back.

Hannah glances up with a frown. "If I can what?"

"Never mind!" Clara answers.

I race upstairs and find her lacing the front of a corset over undergarments that cover more than I'm wearing.

"You have to wear that?" I ask, sitting on the bed. "Does it hurt?"

"What?" Clara asks.

I point at the contraption. "That."

"This?"

"Yeah."

"It is stiff, but it doesn't hurt."

I'm about to explain how it has to hurt and is probably deforming her ribs, when I notice that she doesn't tighten it too much and that her figure really is matched to it.

Dang.

Maybe we should use those.

"I don't wear corsets," I say.

"I know," Clara answers, winding the loose ends around her waist before she tucks in the strings.

"How?"

"You slouch."

I sit up. "I do not."

"Yes, you do." She glances up. "I do, too. I never wear a corset, except when we have company."

She slides on a green dress and asks me to help her clasp it. There are a billion little hooks and eyes. I suddenly realize why they need servants. She looks pretty in a classic way that matches her clothing. I watch her pin her hair up, because I don't know how to do it.

"Do you have to wear it up?" I ask.

"Yes."

"Yuck."

She glances sideways and speaks through the hairpins in her mouth. "What do you wear when you have guests?"

I sweep my hands down to indicate my clothing.

She takes the pins out and pokes them into the braid. "You eat dinner in your day clothes?"

"I practically sleep in my day clothes," I say.

We hear hooves clamoring against shells. Clara jumps up, pulling the curtain aside to look at the road.

"Father's home." She smiles, but her voice drops. I follow her down the hall, stopping halfway down the stairs because her dad is coming into the house.

He has dark hair, broad shoulders, and those watery blue eyes that kind of seem like they'll slice through whatever he looks at. He's striking — that's for sure — but he doesn't look a thing like her.

"Father!" Clara calls.

I half smile, trying to imagine myself hurrying down to greet my dad with a "Father!" and a hug. He'd probably ask what I've been smoking.

Edmund drops a kiss onto her head, which freaks me out, but she doesn't seem to think much about it.

"Hello, darling. Did you get everything finished?"

"Yes, Father."

He surveys her, half kindly, half critically, and I slip down the stairs as they walk together into the dining room to scrutinize our work. Edmund circles the table, glancing at the napkins before he switches a fork. "Why are these backward?"

Clara and I both flush.

"I — I suppose I looked wrong," she stutters.

But she didn't. I did. I swallow, hoping she won't get into trouble. Edmund frowns, eyeing every place setting. Then he fidgets with his coat, and I realize he's just as nervous as Clara.

"They will be coming soon," he says. "Hannah has dinner ready?"

"Yes, sir. We bought some things, but did not go over your allowance."

My eyebrows rise. We definitely aren't in my world anymore.

"Good. Well, then." Edmund's eyes sweep the room, moving through me and landing on the piano. "All shall be well. We have nothing to be ashamed of."

"Of course not," Clara answers, but she sounds confused.

She glances at me, and I suddenly wish I could join their little dinner party just for moral support.

"It was easier with your mother," Edmund says.

Clara flinches. "Well, I suppose we'll manage."

He turns to study her like he's comparing her to this elusive woman he can never consider replacing. For a split second, he looks like a lost puppy and I almost feel sorry for him. But then he sits at the table and reaches out to Clara.

I can't tell what he's thinking, and I don't think she can either. She takes his hand with a smile, but it looks more like Sherri used to do when she tried to keep Dad from doing something reckless.

"Let me hear your song," Edmund says.

Clara's mouth drops and she looks even paler, glancing toward the piano before she recovers with an unconvincing smile. "Of course."

She walks to the piano, though it looks as though she's forcing her feet not to drag. She fumbles through the sheet music, taking a few breaths.

She plays a few chords. The song is decent — better than what her letters made me believe — but I still wait, feeling her terror and wondering where it's coming from. The song is pretty, but it trembles, too, like the singer who gets stage fright. Like me, when I sing. She bites the very edge of her bottom lip when she makes a mistake.

Edmund watches, frowning outright now that her back is turned. He turns his head toward the window, clenching his jaw as she wavers through another measure. Halfway through, he slams his hand against the table, making the china rattle.

"Stop!"

When Clara turns, her eyes are just as wide as mine. Edmund's fingers clench and release, and I see his head shake like he can't believe his daughter is capable of hitting a wrong key.

"I told you to have a piece prepared," he said.

"I'm sorry," Clara whispers.

Edmund stares at her. "Well, did you practice?"

"No. Not today."

Before I can even move, Edmund stands, brushing against me, but he doesn't notice. His eyes are glued on his daughter who shrinks back as he strides toward her. "Clara, you deceived me! You told me that you had finished everything."

"I was not intending to deceive you," Clara sputters. "I forgot."

He stops just short of her bench before his shoulders collapse. His breath goes out through his nose, and I hold mine. This is the moment where, if I was in my world with normal people, I'd be the best friend saying, 'I'll see you later.' Clara would smile like there was nothing wrong, then yell at her dad for scolding her in front of me. Except he doesn't know I exist, and I think she's forgotten about me. Even if I wanted to leave, I can't convince my feet to move.

Edmund's words come in little more than a breath, but I strain to catch them as he says, "We can't afford to make mistakes, darling."

There is a knock at the door, and he looks toward the hall before whispering, "Don't play tonight if you can't manage a decent tune. Don't speak unless you can be charming. I know you can, Clara. I know you can."

Mr. Castle strides from the room. I watch Clara mouth a confused, silent response as he greets someone at the door. She stands, clutching her skirt, and shuts her eyes suddenly looking like she's going to panic.

"Hey," I say. When she looks toward me, I give her two thumbs up. "You're going to be fine."

She opens her mouth like she'll speak, but glances toward the door to the hall where voices are ringing out with greetings. Clara nods, then turns to walk to the door. She pauses, then whispers, "Good heavens. It's another boy."

"Just act like everything he says is the most fascinating thing you've ever heard in your life," I say, patting her shoulder. "You can do this." And then I realize what she means. The table is only set for four.

I run to the kitchen for a plate, snatching the silverware and sneaking the entire thing past the cook, wondering if it's going to look like it's floating through the air. I don't have a chance to find out because they step into the parlor.

I arrange the place setting, then peek around the French doors. Edmund smiles, shaking hands and speaking in a rich voice that makes me almost like him.

The entire family has shocking red-orange hair, though the woman's curls look in need of a deep conditioning. But she's dressed like a benevolent queen. She smiles as Clara is introduced.

"At last, we meet," Mrs. Meyers says. "It's truly lovely. I've heard so much about you."

"Really?" Clara's head cocks again as surprise overrides whatever should be her proper response.

Edmund winces, then continues the introductions, "Mr. Phillip Meyers, and his son, Billy."

Clara dips with surprising gracefulness. Her dress looks plain next to Mrs. Meyers's, but the English flavored accent I'm assuming she picked up from Hannah gives her an edge against the nasal tones of the family. Billy's is the heaviest, sounding like it gets caught in his nose before it comes out of his mouth. Alone it wouldn't be bad, but mixed with the fast words and pumping Adam's apple, it's a bit much.

Clara's face melts into relief as her father motions them all to the dining room. She spies the new plate, then glances around for me.

Billy gawks openly at Clara and laughs at the end of each sentence. He has freckles and cheekbones that are too big for his face. I have no idea what Andrew looks like, but I'm willing to bet he's got the upper hand in that department.

Clara waits for everyone's plates to be filled, then looks to her father, receiving a subtle nod. She reaches for a spoon, then glances back at him. He nods again, so slightly that no one catches it. She puts a spoonful on, then moves her hand to the next dish, but this time he shakes his head. She skips it. She's asking what she can eat. I stare. What? Her father decides that, too?

The men talk about the lumber yard. Mrs. Meyers fusses over Billy until he whispers, "Mother, please."

Clara ducks her head and pretends not to hear. She squirms, eyes roving again and again toward me until Billy asks what she's looking at. Then she doesn't look anymore, but her eyes keep twitching like she wants to.

I hold my fingers against my temples. Maybe I don't want to get married, but Clara doesn't really have a choice. She's going to need help. I'm already making a mental list of techniques for the fine art of man-catching, when the table begins to fade. I blink hard, but suddenly I'm sitting back on the floor by the chest, holding the music box.

I rush downstairs, but instead of a dinner party, I find Dad eating a taco. I stare lightly as he motions toward a paper sack, saying through a full mouth, "Dere's wun fo' 'ou."

"Thanks."

I take it, wondering if Hannah would chase this out of her house too.

I stare until Dad asks, "What?"

"Nothing," I say.

Except he's sitting in Clara's chair.

7

CLARA CASTLE
Summer, 1911

Dear Clara,

Sorry about disappearing on you at the dinner party. Your boyfriend's little music box put me right back at the chest where we started. I tried to wind it again, but no go. I hope we can figure out how to see each other again, but in case it's another week or month before you get this, I'm covering every base.

So, how was the dinner party? Did you ever figure out why your father went all ~~Martha Stew~~ perfect host?

Hey, does Vincent have a girlfriend? I met this guy at the coffee shop who has your last name and a great-grandfather named Vincent. Related, perhaps?

Dad's already banished ideas of remodeling. Yesterday, he went out looking for a boat, but came home with some lady on his arm. Sometimes he truly disgusts me. I keep thinking of running away back to New York, but I'm broke and Sherri can barely afford to pay for herself and Kate. Besides, then I wouldn't get to see you again. Guess I'm back to plan A, which is applying for scholarships. Speaking of which, how is Andrew doing? Heard any news about the boys at school? Write as soon as you can. I'm bored out of my tree.

Scarlet

April 27, 1911

Dear Scarlet,

Alas, it has been nearly two months since your letter even
showed up, though I see you wrote the day after the dinner party.
I wonder why that is. I've wound the music box several times, but
I suppose we haven't discovered the trick to using it yet. I wonder
though, if we must wind it at the same time. I'd say let's wind it
at noon, but your days pass differently than mine, so it's likely your
time does as well. It's terribly vexing.

Father has finally consented to letting Hannah teach me how
to cook. She says I am better at it than Mother, for Mother never
had the patience to keep at anything that didn't catch her interest.
He hasn't invited anyone back to the house, so the only person I've
seen all this time is James, the doctor's apprentice, when he came
to care for Simon after he got a touch of sunstroke.

I asked Vincent if he had a girl anywhere, and he wrote back
and asked what put such a funny idea in my head and where was
he supposed to meet a girl when he was cooped up at an all-boys
school. Which I suspect really means that he actually does have a
girl somewhere and just doesn't want to say. I can't imagine him
as a grandfather—and barely a father—but I suppose 100 years
means we all have grandchildren running around. Good heavens,
I mustn't let that thought linger or it'll turn my head.

Father wants Vincent to learn the ropes at the lumber yard,
which he's taken out a loan to rebuild. If it doesn't do well this
year, he won't be able to pay it back, so he says we must be
economical. Andrew is hoping to see his family this summer.
Poor boy. He thought he was going home at Christmas, but
Grandfather changed plans and brought him here instead. I'm
sad for Andrew, but selfishly glad that he was here. We did have
a good time, and he told me all about Christmas Eve Mass.
Vincent says it's all nonsense, but I like the idea that there is a god
somewhere who listens to your prayers. Andrew prays to the saints
and Hannah says she prays directly to God. I've been praying
directly to God quite often lately because we're having such terrible
storms.

Father always gets antsy when it rains, but yesterday the wind
was strong enough to take down some of the branches. He prowled
the house the entire night and I suspect if the rain becomes much
heavier, he'll be coming home from the mill. I do wish it would
stop. But I shall stop writing and put this in the chest, so that you

may find it as quickly as possible. Do continue winding the music
box and let's see if we can't find each other again.

Clara

I sigh as I blot the ink, then glance outside at the sheet of white rain that
is trapping Father. A flash of lightning crackles down the sky, blinding me
and I brace, correctly anticipating the following boom that shakes the house.

It's only a storm. A typical storm that comes to those who live on the
coast. It's been raining for days, filling the yard with water. It wasn't like
this during the Great Storm in Galveston. The day that storm began, the
weather was beautiful.

I close up the letter and go to the chest, winding the music box and
setting it back on top of the letter. As it plays, I wonder if Scarlet can
hear it. I keep my fingers on it, but jump as another boom rattles the
windowpanes. This time, the door downstairs is responsible for most of
the vibration in the hallway as Father slams it shut, calling in a terrified
tone. "Clara?"

Relief slides through my body, even though Father sounds more frightened than I feel. "I'm upstairs."

His feet pound the steps, and he swings around the banister, dripping in
his best coat. His hair hangs in wet clumps that poke his eyes as he kneels
next to me, pulling me against his chest.

"It's all right," he says. "The shutters are closed, and the rod will direct
any lightning to the ground, away from the house."

I nod, wincing at the glaze in his eyes. It's only a few blocks from the
lumber yard, but he breathes so heavily that I realize he must have run all
the way home. With the lightning, who can blame him? Still, perhaps he
should have stayed there.

"I'm fine, Father," I say.

His mouth opens like he's about to remind me that the wind could collapse the house, trapping us upstairs, or the water could rise, flooding us in
the lower rooms. The safest room in the house seems to shift, depending on
the storm and Father's mood, but today he truly seems at a loss for where
to go.

Another gust of wind rattles the shutters. Father turns to put his back
against the chest, tugging me into his side. His breath continues heavy and
harsh, and I wonder how much is from the run and how much is his own
fear leaking out. He closes his eyes and lets his head fall back. We're going
to be sitting here for a while until the storm lessens.

"Oh, dear me." Hannah's voice at the bottom of the stairs brings relief
as she takes unsteady steps up the stairs. I glance backwards, seeing her

carrying a tea tray. She sets it on the trunk, and I smell peppermint in the steam. Whether she is being economical with the herbs from the garden or realizes that a comforting beverage is the best thing for the moment, I am grateful for her braving the stairs.

"Clara and I wanted to have a picnic outside today, but I suppose we'll have to make do here," she says, like huddling in the hallway is the nicest place in the house and it's perfectly logical to take tea here.

I push to my feet to retrieve the rocking chair for her from my bedroom. She sinks into it with a grateful sigh. "Thank you, darling. Sir, you really ought to go change into dry clothing. You'll catch your death in a wet suit."

"Wet clothes never killed anyone," Father says, keeping his eyes closed. "It's everything else."

I nibble my lip as I pour the tea into three cups. Simon must be in their cottage, enjoying his reprieve from yard work. Mother would know how to lighten up this moment, but then again, Mother is the reason Father's so traumatized by storms in the first place. I suppose I would be too if I watched Andrew stranded on the rooftop across from me, helpless to do anything as the building collapsed and washed away.

Father's never talked about the storm, but I know what happened. I was so young that all I really remember are the sounds; the cracking of wood and roaring wind that covered most of the screams. Hannah says if I don't remember it, I shouldn't try, but Vincent argues that I probably jumbled it in my mind because I was too little to grasp everything.

Personally, I think I don't remember it because I don't want to. If Father hadn't found us and snatched me up, I'd have died with Mother. I think that's why his first reaction is to snatch me again the first time lightning flashes across the sky.

But Hannah always pretends things are less worrisome than they should be. She had a "spell" when James says what she really had was a stroke. And this is just a spring rainstorm that canceled an imaginary picnic. Between the two of them, it's hard to tell how much danger we're actually in. I try to think of what Vincent would say if he were here, for he is usually more truthful.

But I really can't, so I repeat to myself that we will be fine and wind the music box, half for something calming to do, and half in the vague hope that I can contact Scarlet, even if I couldn't talk to her with Father and Hannah in the room. Andrew's song plays again, the wistful, hopeful little tune, and I wonder what he was thinking about when he wrote it.

Father lifts his head from his knees, watching it dully, before he blinks and his eyes turn curious. "Where did you get that?"

Oh dear. I'd forgotten about that.

"Grandfather found it in a shop in New York," I say, as though it's nothing more than a souvenir. I hold it out to him but before he touches it, it lurches again and I pull it back.

"You!" Scarlet says.

I draw in a sharp breath. Father and Hannah have disappeared. The wall has brown wallpaper covered with baskets of flowers and the door posts are covered with chipped paint.

Seagulls call and sunbeams filter through the screen. I can't see the bay, because there are trees in the way. Scarlet takes over the music box as I stare at the changes. And then I realize I'm in the future.

"You're here!" Scarlet says again, and this time she's right. "Oh my gosh, you're here! You did it!"

I look from the towering tree that Simon and I planted, to the cluttered rooms that smell like old paper, to the girl whose arms and legs are completely exposed.

"Am I?" I ask.

"I heard it playing," she says, "so I wound it, too. That must be the trick. We have to play it at the same time, but if I wind it first, I go back and if you wind it first, you come forward."

Scarlet speaks so quickly that I can hardly understand her words. Before she finishes her sentence, the toilet flushes in the bathroom and a man opens the door. His beard is brown with bits of gray and his stomach looks swollen.

"Scar, I'm gonna go down and get . . ." He sees me and trails off. "Oh. Hi. I didn't know you had company."

Scarlet and I exchange panicked glances. "Um. Yeah. This is Clara."

"Hi, Clara." He waves with a grin.

"Hello, sir," I stutter, but I remember not to curtsy. I don't suppose they do that sort of thing anymore.

"Good to meet you." The man turns back to Scarlet. "I called for pizza but no one delivers, so I have to go pick it up. Want to come?"

"Um." Scarlet's eyes grow as they dart toward me. "I think we'll pass."

"Okay. I'll bring it back."

"Thanks, Dad."

"No problemo." He waves at me and nearly jogs down the stairs. Scarlet and I stay still until the screen door bangs into place.

"How did he see me?" I whisper.

"I dunno," Scarlet answers. She sets the music box carefully into the chest. "I don't think he even noticed your clothes. What a dingbat."

I fidget with my dress, spying a cobweb in the corner of my room. "I need to go back. Father will miss me."

Scarlet shakes her head. "No, you don't. Remember? When I was at your house, no time passed. When I got back, I was just where I left off. They won't even know you're gone."

I am not sure if that is comforting or not.

"I should—"

"You can't." Scarlet shrugs lightly. "You can't get back until it takes you, so you may as well hang out with me."

This is what I've been wanting, but now that I'm here, I don't want to see how things have changed. I point a shaky finger toward the arching branches outside.

"I planted that tree with Simon."

"Really? That's awesome." She pulls on my hand. "Come on. See the rest of the house and tell me what else has changed."

But almost everything has changed. The air is musty. The chandelier is gone. The carpets are faded. The curtains are missing. Some of the furniture is replaced, and the pieces I recognize have been moved around.

"Come on!" Scarlet nearly dances, oblivious that I feel like crying. "Back upstairs. My dad's going to wonder when he comes home if you're still in those clothes. You can borrow some of mine."

"But..."

I have worn my mother's clothing, but I am quite sure it is not proper to wear something that belongs to someone else.

"We'll get you a dress. I've got one. Don't worry." She pulls me up the stairs to my room, pulling clothing from a suitcase until it looks like an erupted volcano. "Here. This one should do." Scarlet rummages through the piles until she finds a pink skirt with a very slanted hemline made of clear material over a darker pink. She hands them to me, along with a white shirt. "Come on, try them," she says. "I'll leave if you want."

I stare at them, but before I can say anything, she is gone. I slip on the clothes, finding they cover less than my chemise. Is this all there is? My hair is only a foot shorter than my hemline.

"You look great!" Scarlet says as she peeks into the room.

"My legs are showing." I peer into the mirror. "I look like a bird."

"Well, that's the longest skirt I have. It's that or pants."

I swallow. "Pants are for men."

She snorts. "Not my pants. They're tight and sparkly, and nobody is going to mistake them for guys' jeans." When I frown, she steps closer. "You look fine. Really. Most people wear even less than that. Trust me, nobody's going to look twice. Except for your boots. We'll have to get you some flip-flops. My shoes will be too big."

I take a breath.

She laughs. "Don't look so scared. It'll be fine. I promise. You want to go to the beach?"

"I don't have permission."

"Well, your father's not here to ask, and he'll never know."

"Pizza!" A voice bellows from below.

"Eat first," Scarlet says. "Then we'll figure it out."

I take a breath. I can't walk around one hundred years in the future and not raise questions about my clothing. I must pretend I belong here and wear this sort of thing every day, even if it does feel like going to dinner in my nightclothes. Scarlet grins and bounces down the stairs one step ahead of me.

"Hey, Dad," she calls, reaching for the box the man holds. "We're going to the beach after this."

He steps back, holding the box above his head. "Hey, I didn't bring this for you! This is my pizza. Go get your own."

"Yeah, right!" Scarlet jumps, grabbing a corner.

The box tips and they both lurch for it.

"Don't drop it! Don't drop it!" Mr. Beldon calls. He catches the box, steadying it as he carries it to the bare table. "Sheesh, woman."

"Sheesh, nothing!" Scarlet opens the box, letting out a puff of steam. "Who's responsible for bringing me into this world?"

"I brought you in, and I can take you out," Mr. Beldon says.

"Only if you want to go to jail." Scarlet pulls a wedge from the box and transfers it to a square of indented paper.

I brace and laugh at the same time. I expect him to scold her, but he just sighs heavily and shakes his head. Father would be appalled at this display.

"Come on, Clara. Just ignore the man. That's what I do," Scarlet answers lightly.

There are no place settings. No utensils. The plates Scarlet retrieves are white and flimsy. No one says grace. They simply pick up the food and eat with their hands.

"Here." Scarlet tosses a wedge onto my plate. "You'll like it."

"She's never had pizza?" Mr. Beldon asks.

"No. Her family is vegan."

"Oh." He glances toward me. "Tree hugger?"

I laugh. "Why would I hug a tree?"

"Do we need to get you something special to eat?" he asks.

"No, sir. Thank you." My hands hover over the food, before I pick up the piece to eat it like they do. It is like a greasy pastry. I taste tomato and cheese and something I've never had before.

Scarlet laughs and hands me a napkin. "Here. It's messy."

"Thank you." I place the napkin into my lap wondering if it's paper or cloth. It doesn't feel like either.

"So, Clara," Mr. Beldon addresses me. "Do you live around here?"

Here. But I cannot say that.

"Yes. Nearby," I answer.

"Do you like it?"

"Yes, very much."

"We're thinking of maybe moving down here."

"We are?" Scarlet asks.

"I see." I exchange looks with Scarlet. Of course I want her to stay in the house, but it somehow feels like a betrayal to Father to encourage this man to become the new master. "I am sure that you would enjoy life in the town."

I wonder briefly if he will ever travel back to my time and meet my father. The idea might be amusing, if it was not so terrifyingly possible.

"Yeah?" Mr. Beldon asks. "What does your dad do around here?"

"He owns the lumber mill," I answer, because I have no idea what to say. Then I realize he could ask at the mill and find the lie, so I add, "on the outside of town."

"What's his name?"

"Castle. Mr. Edmund Castle."

"He's away on a business trip," Scarlet speaks up, smoothly adding to my fabrication.

"Busy man?"

I smile. "Yes, sir."

"We're all busy. Everyone. Sometimes I want to just shout out, 'stop the world! I wanna get off!'" The man shouts, flinging his arms out.

I stiffen so I don't jolt, but I think he might knock over his glass if he's not careful. Scarlet's eyes roll toward the ceiling.

"What do you do for a living?" I ask. Then, remembering what Scarlet said, I try to change the subject. "It's just the two of you here?"

"Yep. Just me and Scarlet." He grins at her as though it's always been just the pair. "You have siblings?"

"A brother."

"How old is he?"

"Vincent is almost eighteen."

I am having a hard time finishing the slice, and I wonder how they are eating so quickly. Then I notice what large bites they take and how little they chew it. Vincent ate that way once, when he had come in from traveling and had missed the noon meal. Hannah scolded him terribly.

A knock sounds, and Mr. Beldon shoves back his chair to amble to the door. It's almost overwhelming, all these people coming and going from the house.

The voice is another young man. "Hi, is Scarlet there?"

Scarlet sucks in a sharp breath, then whispers, "It's your nephew!"

"What?" I whisper back.

But Scarlet is already pushing back her chair, scraping its legs across the wooden floor. "Keith! You're just in time! We've got pizza. Want to eat?"

"I never turn down food," Keith responds.

He steps into the room with a slanted grin like Vincent. His features are sharper, but his eyes are set at an identical slant and his hair is the same shade.

"Have a seat." Scarlet glances toward her father, then smiles at Keith. "Keith, this is Clara. Clara, Keith."

She conveniently leaves out our last name. I sit, because I'm shaking too hard to remain standing. This is far more uncomfortable than even our dinner party, but it seems to drive Mr. Beldon away, because he only stays long enough to eat one more piece of pizza.

As soon as he's gone, Scarlet leans forward. "So, how's operation secret room going?"

"No answers for secret rooms." Keith jumps into the conversation. "But more mystery. I looked through my grandmother's records. She never wrote his name. The lines end abruptly after my great-grandfather Michael. The only reason I know Vincent's name is because Grandma told me."

"What?" Scarlet and I ask together.

"Yeah." Keith nods eagerly. "It's almost like he didn't want to be found. But in a letter, he said he left something in the attic, so I think that's where Grandma got the idea that he'd come back for it."

"Do you have the letter?" Scarlet asks.

"Yeah." Keith digs a folded envelope from his pocket.

I'm not sure what they mean about a secret room and I certainly don't understand why they're discussing Vincent, but I reach for it, jolting to see the faded familiar handwriting in a place that feels so foreign.

Hannah's name is on the front of the envelope, but there's a second envelope inside addressed to me. I don't want to open it. I don't want to know. But I must. If Vincent is separated from our family, I need to know how and why.

> *Dear Clara,*
> *Forgive me for leaving so abruptly. I am at Grandfather's home, so don't fret on my account. Truly, I swear, I am all right. I am making every arrangement that I can to help Father and bring*

you somewhere safe. Please, believe me that this is as difficult for me as it is for you.

I know there is much friction between Father and Grandfather, especially now, but I feel we really must contact him for help if we are to save Father's life. This will kill him, Clara, if it's not checked. It will endanger you as well, so for goodness' sake, be careful.

I'm sending you money for a train ticket. Leave, the very moment that you feel you cannot stay. Don't tell anyone. Just leave and go to Galveston. James will escort you if you ask. If I am not there, I'm tracking down Grandfather. I suspect he's in England. Do not let mercy cloud your judgment. I know I've always said you have a good head on your shoulders, and you do, but please for this once, trust me that I know more than you can understand. We cannot pretend anymore.

V.

P. S. I may or may not have forgotten some things in the attic.

"What's it say?" Scarlet asks.

I can't answer. I cannot move. She pries the letter from my hand, frowning further as her eyes rove back and forth across the page.

"My gosh," she sputters.

"What's the date on that?" I ask.

"April 9, 1912," she says.

Less than a year. I'm going to receive this letter in eleven months, and I haven't the slightest idea what it means, but everything about it is terrifying.

Keith leans forward, oblivious to the shock he just foisted onto me. "It's probably not still up there, but — can we look?"

The attic. The letter is not going to explain itself, but something in the attic might.

I stand. "It's upstairs."

Keith grins. "Attics normally are."

I run up the stairs faster than I have in my life. I've never been in the attic, and I can't imagine why Vincent would leave something for me there of all places. Aware that I am in a skirt, I open the closet and step away to let Keith crawl up first. He scrambles up the ladder and disappears halfway through the square hole in the top. A moment later a light flickers to life.

Scarlet follows, and then I go.

"Careful standing up," Scarlet calls. "There are nails sticking down from the ceiling beams."

"It's too dark to see the edges," Keith says.

"Hey, Dad!" Scarlet yells. "Can you pass up a flashlight? Dad?" When there is no answer, she growls. "I'll get one."

She disappears down the ladder as I inch along the rafters, thinking how upset Father would be if he knew what I was doing.

"This is amazing," Keith says. "Look at this."

Various pieces of furniture are scattered on loose plywood boards. There is the rocking chair that Hannah used to rock me to sleep. In the corner sits Father's bedside table. But there is nothing of great value.

Keith kneels next to a picture frame, wiping away a layer of dust. I see Father's eyes and turn away.

"I wonder who they are," Keith says.

I wonder who put them up here. It could have been Vincent, or any other homeowner in the last hundred years who didn't want to throw out the portrait of a stranger. I pull hair from my eyes and squint into the corners like Vincent is here to explain what is going on.

"Here guys." A light plays all around us as Scarlet reappears. "I got it." She shrieks as the beam lights up the eyes of my glass doll. I pick her up, dusting the grimy dress. What is she doing in the attic?

"Gah, I hate those things!" Keith says. "They have to be the creepiest toys in the world."

"Why?" I ask. "It's a doll."

"Those eyes. They look like they follow you."

I had noticed that about Emily. I liked it. It made her seem real, and I had no real playmates.

"Did you find anything?" Scarlet asks.

Keith points. "What's that in the corner?"

It is Vincent's writing chest. How strange to find it stuffed up here.

I step over beams and wires to the corner of the attic, where it's tucked beneath the slanted roof. Blowing off the dust, I open the lid. My brother's handwriting greets me like a familiar friend, sprawling across another envelope. There is no letter inside, only a few dollars bound together by humidity and age, and something else that weighs down the envelope. I shake it and a silver ring with a pearl falls into my palm.

Scarlet takes over, flipping through sheets of blank paper, looking for anything else. I spy Father's pocket watch and snatch it, like keeping it safe will somehow keep him safe. But it's broken. The glass is gone. The hands are still. The inscription from my mother inside is scarcely visible.

My throat closes as the words blur. The air is too hot, the roof too low, and the watch far too cold and heavy in my hand. I clutch it against the ring, turning to flee the attic in a reckless descent.

Scarlet follows, grabbing my arm once we reach the hall. "Clara!"

"I…" I turn, trying to say something, only managing a strangled whimper.

"We shouldn't have brought you up there," she says.

"Scarlet," I whisper. "What does that mean?"

"I don't know," she replies. Her eye gleams with determination. "But we have a year to figure it out. You can stop it. Somehow."

"How?" I clutch Father's watch.

The ladder rattles against the wall as Keith hurries down.

"Just chill," Scarlet whispers. "We'll figure it out."

Then Keith is standing in the hallway, staring at us. I force a breath into my lungs. Then out. Composing myself. I will find out what happened. I will do something. Anything.

If I can even get home.

8

SCARLET BELDON

Summer, 2012

"EVERYTHING OKAY?" KEITH ASKS. HE STOPS IN THE DOORWAY, EYEING us both like he's afraid to get any closer.

"She's claustrophobic," I say.

Clara turns her head away, but I see her tears retract before she faces Keith. "Why are you looking for a secret room?"

"His grandmother used to talk about one being here," I answer. "She sometimes thought he was Vincent."

Clara rubs her temple. "There aren't any secret rooms."

Keith's shoulders fall. "How do you . . ."

I cut him off before he tricks Clara into giving anything away. "Clara's my friend," I say. "She lived here when she was younger."

Keith frowns at her, then asks, "You don't look so good. Do you need to go outside?"

"No, I can't!" Clara blurts.

I wince, but she covers her face and I hope that Keith is buying this closed space act. I almost wish that he had not come. I wanted to have a good time with Clara, and now it's kind of like having a slumber party in an emergency room.

"Should I come back later?" Keith asks.

"No," Clara answers. She releases her breath slowly and repeats in a stronger voice. "No. I want to know what happened to this Vincent."

"Um . . ." Keith pulls yet another envelope from behind his back. "Well, I found another letter up there."

I take the envelope, but hand it to Clara. It's her brother, and as long as we're reading someone else's mail, it may as well be her. Her hands tremble as she opens it.

April 20, 1912
Galveston, TX

Dearest Vincent,
You may be penniless, but you are not alone. Destroy the papers
if you think you must, but do not tarry after the funeral. There
is nothing left for you in that house. Come to me. I'll wait at the
station every day until you arrive.

Anne

Distant cries come from the gulls as Clara refolds the letter, looking as clueless as us.

"What is she talking about?" I ask.

"I don't know," Clara answers.

"That's what I want to find out," Keith said. "If the papers he destroyed were personal records, then it makes sense that we can find so little of him."

"Why would he destroy his records?" Clara asks. "He wouldn't do that. Vincent isn't like that."

"Clara." I intervene. It really isn't nice, I suppose, to keep dragging her into discovering her own life. Not when it's so depressing.

"I want to go home," Clara says.

She doesn't wait for an answer. She's going to cry, and I'm not sure whether to follow her to the chest or keep Keith away.

Keith catches her hand. "Clara, stop. I didn't mean to upset you."

Clara turns with blazing eyes directed at both of us. "Well, you did. You haven't any right to go poking around in our family's business!"

"But Clara, if you know . . ." I cut off my own protest with a feeble shrug. "Don't you think it would be a good idea to find out what happened?"

"No!" Clara's hands fly out. "If my father is going to die within a year, and my brother will be alone and penniless, I'm going to stop searching before I find out what happens to me!"

Keith's eyes go from concern to confusion as he glances between the two of us. "Wait. What are we talking about?"

I can see the effort that goes through Clara as she sucks in a breath and faces him. "I am Clara Castle. Edmund's my father and Vincent is my brother. And I want to go home now."

Keith's eyes rove from her face to me. As eccentric as he may be, obviously time travel is a little far out. Yet, he doesn't call us freaks and flee. He watches slack-jawed as Clara opens the chest and reaches for the music box.

"Wait, wait! You can't go back until we know what's going on!" I rush over, but she's already wound it. We wait while it tinkles out the odd little melody.

I kneel beside her to touch her shoulder, but the moment I do, they begin to shake. Her cry is pitiful, high like a scared little child. I feel nauseous, but before I can say anything I'm left with my hand hovering in midair.

I bring it to my mouth as Keith lets out a slow grunt and sinks onto the floor. "Wha..."

He stares at the chest, and I stare at him. Nobody makes any noise, even when the clock chimes below. Finally, Keith sputters, "She wasn't lying."

"Nope," I answer.

A spark shows through the glaze in his eyes. "How?"

"I have no clue." I begin putting the things back into the chest before Clara's father stumbles over them in his time. "I think it has something to do with the music box. Usually, when we travel, we're both near it or touching it. I've been back once to her world. They can't see me there, I guess because I'm not born yet."

"Wait, wait, wait!" He snaps out of shock, and I see excitement already building. "Let's try it. Maybe you and I can travel back. We could look for clues there. I mean, we've got to do something!"

He's right. We have to do a lot of things, but I'm scared to death for Clara. "I don't think we can get back," I say. "Not without Clara."

He eyes the music box like it belongs to Pandora. "Can we try?"

I lift my chin. "Okay. If we can get back, we'll calm her down. And figure out what in the world is going on with this family."

"My family." Keith reminds me soberly.

"Yeah," I whisper.

Keith swallows and kneels down. "What do we do?"

"I'm not sure. Hold onto the box, or you won't go."

He grabs it, and I open the lid and let it play. We wait until it winds down, two teenagers holding a music box in an old house — and we stay two teenagers, holding a music box in an old house.

I bite my lip. "Try again. You hold it this time, and I'll wind it." It plays again, whispering, "Come on, Clara. Come on."

We try everything: playing it while he is holding the box, playing it while I'm holding the box, just me, just him.

"I think Clara has to be holding it too," I finally admit. "I guess she's not."

What if she doesn't? What if she tries to save her family on her own and never makes contact with us again?

I growl. Partly because we can't get back to help her. Partly because my hand just brushed Keith's and something warm, tingly, and wholly uninvited shot through my arm.

"We'll have to try again later." The sentence comes more abruptly than I mean it to, but I set the music box inside the chest. "It might be better if we search for answers on our own to begin with anyway. Clara can't handle much yet."

"And yet, she is our best asset," Keith replies, like he's been time-traveling, clearing up mysteries for his entire life.

"She'll be back," I say. "Let's just focus on finding as much as we can here, so we know what we need to convince her to look for in her time."

"Death certificates," Keith says. "We can find out how he died."

I stare a moment, then grab his hand. "Come on. To the computer." I settle the keyboard on my lap, twisting until I pick up a faint signal.

Keith perches on the end of the bed. "Wait, so...you've been back to when?"

"1911," I say.

"I want to go." Keith huffs a breath. "Do I look like Vincent?"

"I don't know. I've only seen Clara and her dad and her grandma-servant lady."

"They have a servant?" Keith grins.

"Yeah."

"That's awesome."

It's weird to see Edmund Castle's name on the Web, but link after link requires a subscription to actually open it. Which requires a credit card.

On the sixth link taunting me, I growl. "Gah, why am I not eighteen yet?"

"Could you use your dad's?" Keith asks.

"Dad is not going to let me use his credit card for a genealogy site," I say. "What about your uncle?"

Keith winces. "Failed business. Credit's shot."

"Well, would he know anything?"

Keith shakes his head. "He's in by marriage. Besides, we're looking at four generations ago. Nobody's going to remember much."

I scowl and type in Vincent's name, but for whatever reason he decided to go around destroying records, he did a fantastic job.

"Let me try," Keith says.

I hand over the computer and flop onto my back, blowing out a slow breath. "So something happens that Vincent knows puts Clara in danger and could possibly kill his father if it's not stopped. How would he know that ahead of time?"

"I don't know," Keith mumbles distractedly. The screen lights his eyes, and I watch them rove back and forth.

He pulls back slightly, then clicks. "April 16, 1912," he reads, then looks up at me. "Crushed skull."

"What?" I yank the computer out of his hand, peering at the medical jargon on the document. "Are you sure that's what it means?"

"Yep," he said. "That's how my dad went."

I'm full of questions, but the statement sends them all back. I glance up, realizing in a way Keith is going to be as fragile about this as Clara. "I am so sorry."

"But that doesn't tell us much," he says, ignoring his own tragedy. "I mean, that could be anything. He could have been thrown from a horse, or had some sort of fall, or something falling on him."

I wince for Mr. Castle though I don't even like the guy. Whatever happened to cause his death, it is sudden, violent, and soon in Clara's life. Keith and I study each other over the glow. Suddenly, I don't feel like a best friend trying to help out. I feel like a detective on a murder case.

"We have a year to stop it," Keith says. "We just have to get Clara to cooperate."

My phone buzzes in my pocket with Kate's ringtone.

"Hang on," I say, then punch the button to my ear. "Hi, Kate. What's up?"

I hear her take a breath and wonder if she's crying, but she says, "Just calling to see how you are."

"I'm okay." I wave at Keith when he picks up the music box, giving it another go. If he travels without me, I'm going to be mad.

"Yeah? What are you doing?" Kate asks.

Distraction, I decide. She's trying to distract herself from something. She used to get so nervous before auditions that she would call me and just say, "Talk."

"Um. Just hanging out." I eye Keith. "I met this guy in town and..."

"Oh yeah?" She perks, and I hope her voice isn't carrying through the speaker. Keith continues to study the gears of the music box, but he has to be listening.

"Yeah. He came over today. We've been eating pizza and exploring the attic."

"The attic?" Kate laughs. "Why?"

"Just bored. There's nothing else to do here." I turn the tables before she can ask more questions. "What about you?"

"Well," she says slowly. I practically hear her mind sifting which information she wants to disclose. "I got a job manning the booth at a skating rink."

"Good for you."

"Yeah. Um. Mom is still looking. She's been sending out stuff every day, and there's a restaurant I think will take her but I don't know if we can make enough unless she finds something better. Everything I can find is minimum wage."

She takes another breath. "Actually, I wanted to know if I could borrow about fifty dollars from you. I'll pay it back."

"Um . . ." I stall. I used my cash supply on the way down here, and my savings are neatly tucked into a college account that will not allow me to make withdrawals. "When do you need it?"

"End of next week," she answers. "I may be able to pick up another job, but I calculated my paycheck and I'm still going to be about fifty dollars short for what I told Mom I could help with the apartment rental. And I don't want to give her any more stress. She's trying really hard to stay here, so I can keep studying theater."

I grip the phone. Dad and I have a rule that I can use the emergency card, but I have to let him know when I did and why. Keeping a roof over my step-sister's head qualifies an emergency, but Dad has informed me that discussions on Sherri and Kate are off-limits.

"Yeah," I say. "I'll mail some to you. It might be a day or two, but I promise it will be there."

There is silence at the end of the phone, but I know her well enough to know that her face is probably scrunched up and she's holding her breath because she hates crying. It's so bizarre that she has one parent, I have one parent, and Clara has one parent, but all of us are facing completely different consequences for it. And unfair that Clara is trying to save her father's life, Kate, her mother's home, and I'm just worried about how to put myself through college without breaking into Dad's bank. Which I'm about to do. Again.

"Thanks," Kate says, and her voice is steady.

"Every millionaire has been broke at least once," I say. I'm not sure that's quite true, but I read that most of them have had to start over at least once in their life. "Things will get better, I promise."

"I hope so," she says. It sucks. Kate has that mix of boundless optimism and discipline that makes me think she actually has a shot of making it as an actress. If she's faltering, it means things are bad.

"Anyway, Mom is coming, so I have to go," she says. "I'll call you later."

"Okay," I answer, and she hangs up.

I wish I could wind a music box and transport myself over there to check on her. It also makes me wonder what else going on in Clara's life that she's not telling me about. I blow out a breath, slipping the phone back into place. If I give up my phone for a month, I could save the money that she needs.

Keith cocks his head, setting down the box which hasn't done anything besides play the same melody over and over. "You okay?"

I don't normally talk about money with my friends, but this is the dude who mowed my lawn without a shred of shame. He's not exactly rolling in dough himself. I plop onto Clara's trunk, ignoring everything about the 1911 mystery I've been distracting myself with.

"When I little, Dad went on a cruise with Mom," I say. "When they got off, she hailed a taxi and rode out of my life. I don't know if he told her to leave or she finally got sick of being on the back burner. He dated a bunch of women — the hot rich kind — but they were too smart to stick around. Not that Sherri is dumb, but Sherri can live with Dad when he flushes the money down the drain as well as when he's out buying fancy new rims for a car he's probably going to have to sell when things get tight again.

"Sherri made it work. She bent over backwards for him. She doesn't have much of a spine, but she kept me and Kate on time and she was just there, you know? Dad picking me up? He might be late. He might forget. He might get caught up with something shiny and tell me to call a cab. But Sherri would be there, five minutes early. If you needed something, she made it happen. Not even my mom was like that."

Keith pulls his knees toward his chest, sitting on the floor. He looks a little lost, but he's paying attention and that's more than Blake ever does. Which is good because words are pouring out of my mouth that I can't stop, even if I wanted to.

"And then, on their freaking anniversary, they go on a date. They come home. Sherri's crying. Dad says it's over. Sherri and Kate pack their bags, call a cab, and I don't even know where they went. And now Sherri's out trying to get a job, but she only has a GED because she had to support her parents in high school. And Kate still needs $50 dollars just to cover the freaking rent, and if they can't make things work there, she's going to have to drop the acting school that she loves and it's all going to start over again, and I just feel so..."

Helpless. This is exactly the place I spend so much time and effort in avoiding.

I wince and swing my eyebrows toward him. "I need to find a job."

Keith snorts, repeating, "Good luck."

"No, I'm serious." I put my cheeks in my palms. Scholarships may get me started in college, but I'm going to need a lot more in savings if I'm going to be able to make my own declaration of independence after college. "I don't want to be the little rich girl who lives off of Daddy's fortune."

"Well, you can make money around here," Keith says, "but you have to be willing to take a lot of small gigs. A lot of people work two or three different jobs, and when you're a teen, it's more like something different every day. I mow one day, work the lunch tables two others, and pick up whatever odd jobs come along. You might be able to get something babysitting or cleaning houses."

When I envision myself working, I know I'll start at the bottom. But the bottom for me is always somewhere in the secretarial department before I work my way up to an executive, complete with briefcase and suit pants.

Or putting in long hours to start my own company, wearing different hats until it makes enough to hire others for the tasks I don't want. I spend a lot of time thinking about this, though I can never decide what kind of work I want to do. But not once has that plan included cleaning somebody's toilet.

So I try to sound smart about it, instead of just admitting that I am a little prouder and pickier than he is when it comes to jobs. "The problem with hourly jobs is they pay so little when you're a teen," I say. "And you only have so many hours that you can work before school or whatever gets in the way. You probably won't get much of a raise. So you can only make so much and nothing more. I need something that doesn't have a limit. That can just build on itself and make more and more. That's how people become rich."

He's squirming, and I realize I've lost his attention. I can't really expect him to understand. He mows lawns. He gets paid. He goes home. He's good with that. I can't afford to be good with that. But he's also the one who's gently waving two twenties and a ten in front of my face.

I straighten, feeling my cheeks flush. "Oh...no that wasn't a...I can't take that."

"You're going to come up with a job with no monetary limit within two days?" he asks.

"I just..."

Well. I'm going to have to borrow from Dad. Or Keith. But this isn't being independent. This is compromising, depending on a man to get me out of a bind. I blow a breath, racking my brain.

"It's just money," Keith says. "You can always make money if you want it enough. Besides, I've been homeless, and it sucks."

This isn't for me. It really isn't about me. It's for Kate. I take the money. "I'll pay you back, I swear."

Keith almost grins. "With interest?"

"Maybe," I say. "That would be one way to grow your money."

"Kind of a crappy way," he says. "It's not really my style."

But I have money in hand. I even have a real card and envelope to mail it in. Disaster temporarily avoided.

I eye Keith, then offer half a smile. "You know. I think you might be like your grandpa after all."

9

CLARA CASTLE
Summer, 1911

ADJUSTING MY HAT TO SLANT SIDEWAYS, I SKEWER IT WITH A HAT PIN.
My white gloves are going to be miserable in this heat, but I pull them on
to complete the illusion of a cultured young lady. I hardly recognize myself.
I certainly don't look like anyone capable of keeping the peace in a family
of competing men. I'm playing all sorts of roles today: sister welcoming
brother home, beautiful woman on a picnic as though I go out every day,
and detective solving a hundred-year-old mystery to report back to two
other time travelers. The last terrifies me, but if I make it into a game like
I'm part of a book, I can keep my head about me.

I hope.

"You look lovely, darling."

Father stalls in the doorway behind me, cutting quite a fine figure in
his suit. It's hard to believe he's the same man who huddled for an entire
evening in the hallway until the rain let up. He's been perfectly normal ever
since.

I feel very grown up, but I also feel like the wide brim of this hat is going
to vex me before long. But the dress is new, tailored for me by Hannah so
that the hem falls perfectly. Father offers his arm and I accept it, feeling the
wave of affection that has randomly hit me ever since I discovered he'll be
in danger within a year.

Simon has shined up the carriage and brushed down the horse, even
though the railroad station is only two blocks. It looks quite nice, especially
compared to the wagons around us. I count several automobiles as well and
watch Father flinch as they pass.

"What are those?" I ask, pointing to the wires strung between poles
outside the newspaper office.

Father glances over, then replies, "Telephone lines."

"Really?" After meeting Scarlet, nothing seems beyond my capacity to comprehend, but I still peer at the swooping lines. "So, if we ever have a telephone, my voice would travel through those wires all the way to Galveston where Vincent could hear it?"

Father chuckles. "Or to New York if you wanted."

"That is extraordinary," I blurt. Between that and the four electric lights that have been erected in the square, I really feel as though I live in the most exciting time in history. It's a pity I see so little of it.

Father only chuckles and turns the horses into the depot. "It'll be a while before we have a telephone. You'd be better off continuing to develop your handwriting and composition skills."

I want to tell him that compared to people in the future, my handwriting is very elegant and just this morning I posted a letter to 2012 by way of the chest. But I can't, so I watch the wooden wheels crush against the shell as the road curves toward the station.

There aren't many trees on our coast and most of the transplants are still young, so we spy the train when it is far down the track. There is so much going on around me that I want to look at everything at once, but I know Vincent will be peering out of the window and I want to see him the moment that he sees me. I suspect that he might jump from the train before it's at a full stop, but I hope, for the sake of peace, that he makes the effort of properly descending like a gentleman.

"Mr. Castle!"

Father and I turn simultaneously as Billy and his father stride toward our carriage.

Father's face brightens, looking truly happy to see Mr. Meyers. They greet each other with a hearty handshake as Billy rounds the carriage to my side.

"Good morning, Miss Castle. You look quite lovely today."

"Thank you," I respond, pleased at my own response. At Christmas when Andrew helped me with my coat, he said very softly that I 'looked pretty.' I was so stunned that I couldn't manage a reply. Then Vincent came, and Andrew hardly said another word for the entire evening.

Today, the only prickling that comes into my cheeks is the worry that Billy is kissing my hand in front of so many people, and I'm not sure if that's proper or not. I suddenly wonder if gloves weren't invented for this very purpose by some woman who didn't particularly want her hand being kissed.

Father says nothing about it, and I resolve to try and make sure I do not repeat the social blunders of my last encounter with this family. I stay quiet, smiling and following Billy's lead, answering that yes, we're all quite well and yes, it is a very fine day.

Then Billy runs out of things to say so we're left looking at each other in uncomfortable silence, and I can tell he's trying very hard to think of conversation or, at the least, a polite way to end it. The train rumbles into the station as Vincent comes to my rescue again, jumping from the train onto the grass with a suitcase and a package tucked under his arm. He runs a few steps, regaining his balance and then grins as he strides to us.

"Hallo, there, Meyers! How are you?"

"Oh, fine. Fine," Billy says. "I was just speaking to your lovely sister here."

Vincent's eyebrows lift as suddenly as a seagull goes into flight. He keeps his grin as he tosses his luggage onto the back of the carriage. "Well, careful what you say. Clara is our one and only, and we're quite protective of her."

His teasing turns Billy's skin a brighter shade, and I can't decide if Vincent is teasing me or mocking him. Normally, I would dwell on the question, but I'm too distracted studying Vincent's face for features that match Keith. Their expressions most resemble each other.

I hardly hear Billy's next sentence until I realize he's saying, "Goodbye."

I smile at him, not coyly, but striving to act like a social girl. "It was lovely to see you. Have a good day."

He hurries away so quickly that I wonder if he's going to have a good day at all or spend it fretting over the encounter.

Vincent cuts his eyes from Billy to me and raises one eyebrow like he suspects someone else is residing in my body. I shrug. I cannot tell him about the dinner party, and I've resisted in the letters because I don't know what to make of it myself.

Father leans forward next to me and calls, "Hello, Son."

"Hallo, Father!" Vincent swings into the back, sending such a cheery greeting that it seems impossible to believe they will ever disagree to the point of abandonment.

"We're going on a picnic," I say.

"Splendid," Vincent answers.

"How was school?" Father asks.

"Boring." Vincent stretches his legs until they hit the back of my seat. "But you'll be pleased to know that I passed every class."

'Passed' doesn't mean 'excelled,' but Vincent did so poorly last year that the answer thrills Father. I suspect he doesn't inquire further because he doesn't want to know the tiny margin involved with Vincent's success.

"Well done," he says.

The streets are rather crowded with tourists coming in for a day on the water. They'll be gone by dark, but afternoons are always a bustle. We pass the Hotel Palacios, and I peer down the porch that runs the length of the building. Vincent told me once that it's the longest porch in Texas. The orchestra plays for the lunch guests taking up a portion of the porch, but tonight they will play for the dances on the pavilion.

The music floats across the yard toward the sea bathers on the shore. Father thinks their swimsuits are vulgar, but I do enjoy watching them, especially when they whoosh down the slide on the second story of the pavilion straight into the water. A young boy hollers particularly loudly, and I laugh as he disappears into the sea. I do love people, even if I don't know what to say to them.

Father unharnesses the horse to tether. Vincent and I carry the luncheon toward the grass near the shore. When Vincent shakes the blanket, it unfurls like a sail. Most of his attention is on Father, who is chatting with a man in a Model T.

"Hannah and Simon are not coming?" Vincent asks.

"Father gave them the day off," I say.

"That's peculiar," Vincent responds.

"He's happy," I argue.

"I know. That's what's peculiar. It makes me wonder what's wrong."

"Perhaps things are finally right," I say. "Stop being Sherlock and enjoy it."

"It won't last." Vincent lowers himself beside me, draping his forearms over his knees as I set out a dish of cheese. "The good spells never do."

And then we both quiet because Father approaches. Picnics are queer things if you think about it. Father, Vincent, and I all sitting on the ground with our food spread across the blanket strikes me as almost comical, but I'm too happy to be in the sunshine to dwell on it.

"How did Andrew do with his studies?" I ask, when I have an excuse to keep my eyes on the cloth I'm unwrapping from a loaf of bread.

Vincent hesitates. "Better than the first semester, but he hardly took a break, except on Sundays. His tutor is good at his job, but he's notoriously brutal. Still, Andrew pulled through like a saint."

Father frowns, brushing a bug from his sleeve. "Your Grandfather shouldn't set him up for that sort of failure. He'll ruin that boy if he doesn't take care. You can't expect an uneducated boy to thrive in a secondary school, even with the best of tutors."

"I don't know. During the first semester, Andrew relied heavily on his memory," Vincent said. "He's very good at working out sums and retaining facts in his head."

"Of course he is," Father snaps. The words burst out as he slices a dull knife through the cheese. "He couldn't write anything down. You learn to use your memory when it's all you have. But the best memory can't cover for ten years of missing knowledge."

Vincent shrugged. "Andrew's like a weed. If he has the tiniest amount to survive on, he'll manage it. He barely scraped by, but he made considerable progress, seeing as he couldn't tell 'A' apart from 'B' when he first arrived. Between Grandfather's influence and his determination, I think he'll actually make it with the rest of us."

"Well, good for him," Father says. "I'm sure his family is counting on it. And your grandfather, no doubt, expects a return on his investment."

I frown. I don't know much about investments, but it makes Andrew sound like some sort of commodity.

"No doubt," Vincent replies. "But Grandfather picked well. Slums or no, Andrew is honorable to a fault."

Father actually smiles at that. "I know. It makes me wonder why your grandfather picked him at all."

"What do you mean?" I ask.

But Father only shakes his head. "Never mind, darling. I'm sure Andrew will do very well for himself."

It's all rather confusing. I realize, if Vincent will suspect that Grandfather is in Europe and James will be here to escort me to Galveston, I have no idea where Andrew will be a year from now. I don't like that thought at all.

"Has anyone heard anything about James McMinn lately?" I ask, before I can lose my nerve to inquire.

"No," Vincent answers. "But I'd love to see him while I'm down. You should come along."

"Last I saw him, he was stitching up a boy who got caught up in the oyster beds," Father says, frowning at the sea. "His mother's been in poor health lately. It might not be a bad idea to go along as long as you're with Vincent. You might cheer Mrs. McMinn a bit."

Vincent frowns. "I hope she gets better. He'll be completely alone in the world once she goes."

"I can't imagine," I say, though I am imagining it, and it's a horrid thought.

"I can't either," Vincent says. "I'd hate to be all alone."

I glance back in the direction of our house. From now on, I must make sure Vincent and Father continue to bond. I must pursue a friendship with James, knowing he'll play some sort of important role later. And Andrew . . . that's the part of the story that must change. He mustn't disappear.

For now, I push future thoughts away. For now, Father's eyes sparkle as he laughs at Vincent's recounting of spending the night in a store when the clerk accidentally locked him inside. The sun glints off the rippling waves as sailboats travel past the strollers on the seawall. We lack only Mother, to be completely happy.

But as we pack up, the melancholy returns. This moment is over and can never be retrieved. Traveling by music box hasn't worked for the last few days, but when we reach the house I try it again. I can't redirect choices unless I know which to avoid. I swallow and wind the box, letting it play muffled in my bedroom. I feel the lurch, like a pole when a fish has taken the bait. But this time there are four hands covering the box and Scarlet fades into view. We're still in my bedroom, surrounded by clothing, papers, and things I don't recognize.

"Clara!" Scarlet cries. "There you are! How long has it been?"

"It's July," I reply. "What about you?"

"Three days," she says. "We've carried that music box all over town in case you played it."

"But I have played it," I say. "Never mind. It doesn't matter. We can't force it, but we must accept the idea that my time is going to pass very quickly."

"Which is why you need to stay here as long as you can," Scarlet says. "That gives you more time to figure out what's going on, without time passing in your world. Any news?"

"None," I say. "Everything is going extraordinarily well. Vincent and Father are getting along for the moment. What about you?"

"We have looked through the Internet," Scarlet says. "We've tried to track down old newspapers, but they're all recorded on these tiny slides that are hard to read. We've found birth certificates for all of you, but only your father's death record. There is little on Vincent, and there are no further records for you at all."

"I wonder why," I say.

"I don't know. All of your letters stop this spring," Scarlet says, "so there is no personal writing. Does your father have any enemies? Anyone who would want to destroy your family?"

"No. Not that I know of," I say. "The only person I've ever seen him crossways with is Grandfather, but Grandfather would never harm Father because he knows it would hurt us." I cock my eyebrow, eyeing her with rising fear. "Why? You know something. Tell me!"

Scarlet swallows. When he doesn't speak, she takes a breath. "It could really be anything. But..." She falters, her breath hovering with effort. "Your father dies from a blow to the head."

I cringe, feeling myself sag. I knew whatever took him wasn't old age. I don't know what I was expecting, but I picture Father's face, adding damage to the skull. My hand goes to the side of my cheek, and I glimpse the panic in my companions' expressions. I can't cry. Not yet.

"But you don't know how?" I ask.

"No. We're still working on that," Scarlet says. "So let's focus on what we know and not waste time on what we don't." She holds up two fingers. "One: you must do everything you can to keep your father and Vincent from fighting. Whatever the danger turns out to be, if Vincent doesn't leave, you won't be facing it alone. Two: There is a James somehow involved in this. Do everything you can to cultivate a friendship with him, because you're going to need him."

"That's James McMinn," I say. "He and Vincent grew up together, though he's twenty-five. He's a physician."

"A physician is a good person to know," Scarlet says. "When are you going to see him again?"

"I don't know," I answer. "He has only been to our house a few times when Hannah had a stroke. Vincent and I may call on him and his mother soon, but I don't know when or if Father will change his mind about allowing me to go."

"Then he must come to your home," Scarlet says. "Try to find every reason to invite him over if your father won't let you go."

I can't think of a good reason to summon anyone to the house, but Scarlet has already left the subject. She eyes me, forgetting the third thing. "First of all," she says, "we have to get you out of that dress and into something modern before someone sees you."

I flinch at the idea, but now there are far greater things to fret over than wearing a skirt that reaches to my knees. Scarlet's clothes are larger than I am, but we secure the jeans with a belt, rolling the hems and pulling them over my boots. She knots the shirt on one side, taking up most of the slack.

She pulls the pins out of my hair, loosening it before running a brush through the length.

"Your hair is so long," she mutters. "I have no idea how we're going to make it look modern."

I watch her in the reflection of my vanity as she chews her lip, twisting my locks one way, then another. She finally brushes it into a side part. "Just leave it."

"Just leave it down?" I glance upward to look directly at her.

"Yeah." She tosses the brush onto the bed. "Only grandmas wear their hair up now. And most of them have short hair."

I consider going downstairs looking like I just brushed out my hair without doing anything to it. Then it strikes me that I'm 115 years old, and I grin. "I could be a grandma."

She snorts and tosses the brush onto the vanity. "Come on, old lady. Your great-nephew is waiting. We need to have a crash course in modern living and slang before you give yourself away."

My heart speeds as I look through the window to a view I no longer recognize. "We're going out?"

"You don't want to stay in my room all day, do you?"

I turn, cocking my head. "My room."

Scarlet plants a hand on her hip. "Mine."

"It was mine first." I remind her with a smile.

"Well, it's mine now." She draws out the sentence but grins anyway.

Now. Now when everyone I know and love from my world is dead and forgotten. I swallow and look back into the mirror, asking the question that has haunted me. "Scarlet? If Vincent is leaving penniless and alone, and Father is dead, where am I?"

She blinks, dropping her eyes. "I don't know. Maybe by then you're with Andrew."

"What?"

"Well, you like him, don't you?" she asks.

I glance toward the doorway as though Andrew is downstairs and can hear me. "Well, of course I do, but..."

"You like him. He likes you. I'm telling you. That boy is meant for you."

I flinch. Of course I must marry someone and Andrew has crossed my mind more times than I care to admit. But marriage to anyone is so terrifying, and it's unlikely he'd ever consider it with everything that stands between. Besides, I'm not sure my father ever plans on allowing me to marry or if he intends to keep me with him for the rest of his life.

"Andrew hardly speaks to me when we are together," I say, because I don't want to think about Father.

Scarlet shrugs. "That's because he's shy. But trust me. He likes you."

"But..." I squash that thought before it takes too deep of a root. "Vincent tells me to go to James, not Andrew. I don't even know if Andrew will still be part of my life a year from now."

"Which is why we have to make sure that he is," Scarlet says. She faces me squarely. "Just answer this. If Andrew expressed any interest whatsoever in dating you, would you say yes?"

"I don't know what you mean."

She huffs a breath, irritated at my ignorance.

"You mean court?" I ask.

"Yes!" She snaps her finger and points at me. "Court. Come sit in your parlor, whisper sweet nothings, whatever it is you guys do."

I see her mouth moving, but I cannot respond. Andrew has been in my parlor when he came with Vincent, but just the two of us... I can't imagine that either Father or Grandfather would approve.

"Oh gosh, well don't cry," Scarlet says quickly. "Dating's fun. I mean, honestly, if you lived in my world, I wouldn't really push it. But you need a guy, and he's a good one."

"You've never met him," I protest.

"Yeah, well, I sort of read your letters, before I knew I could meet you," Scarlet says.

I watch her, again feeling my mind receive so many thoughts that it empties itself. Anger swells but I cannot keep it long. If Scarlet hadn't read my letters, she never would have known that I saw her. She never would have tried to write me. And we wouldn't be able to change the letters that Vincent and Anne have yet to write. But none of that prevents my face from turning a bright shade of red.

"Hello?" Keith's voice floats upstairs as he knocks on the door.

"Upstairs!" Scarlet bellows.

I wince and grin at the same time. Father would scold us so terribly if we greeted our friends so, calling them through the door like dogs into a gate. But Keith doesn't seem to mind and he comes up the stairs nearly as quickly as Vincent descends them. He grabs the doorway, hanging forward from his fingers as he greets us. "Hello! I'm free for the day! Oh, hi, Clara! I wondered if you'd be here."

I spread my arms. "I'm here."

"We're not sure how long she'll be here," Scarlet says. "We're going to the bay. Want to come?"

"Yeah," Keith says, as though his answer should be obvious. "We can take my car."

Scarlet's phone rings. She snatches it from my bed, glancing at the screen before she says, "It's my step-mom. I'll be back." Before either of us can agree, she runs past Keith shouting into the phone. "Hang on! I have to find a signal!"

Keith scoots into the room, then looks to me and we both laugh.

"The telephone worked better when it was hooked to our wall," I say.

Keith sticks out his lip and shakes his head. "Nah. The cell just doesn't work in this house. Mine works great everywhere else."

"I wonder why that is," I say.

"I don't know." His eyes snag on me, then go up and down my face. "Are you okay?"

"Yes," I say. "Flustered is all." I rub my arm for a moment before I go on. "Scarlet read my letters."

"I thought you knew that," Keith says.

"I did," I answer quickly. "It's only that I didn't realize that she read every one of them. I never meant some of those to be read, not even by Andrew. I was so careful to keep them hidden in my time that it never occurred to me that they would outlast my care and be read by someone a hundred years into the future."

Keith nods. "Well, I'm sorry she did. But look at it this way. She knows almost everything about you and she still likes you."

I laugh, more to please him than from merriment, and glance around the room at my things which no longer belong to me. It's strange to think that I am the only thing that I will ever truly own, and that isn't saying much since Father currently makes my decision for me and he'll only stop when I have a husband who will have the final word. I think I could trust Andrew with my future, or perhaps someone who is as thoughtful as Keith. But what if I marry someone like Billy or Scarlet's father? Then what?

I fidget with the pendent at my neck before asking, "Keith. Would you tell a girl that she was pretty if you didn't care for her?"

"You mean if I didn't like her?" Keith asked. "Maybe. But I'd be careful about it. Why?"

"I was just wondering," I answer. "I'm not very good at discerning whether a man is being kind for its own sake."

Keith watches me like he's trying to guess what I'm referring to. Then he says, "If he goes out of his way to say it, he probably likes you. Or if he clams up and stutters all over himself, he probably likes you, too."

I laugh, but if that is flipped around, then every man I ever speak to probably thinks I like him. The laughter doesn't stay and I squeeze my fingers together, forcing myself to go on. "If you cared for a girl who you thought was above your station, would you tell her?"

Keith juts his mouth to one side, pushing against his teeth with his tongue. "You mean like a girl whose father drives a Jaguar?"

"I suppose that will do," I answer, though I'm not sure what a Jaguar is.

"I might," he said. "If she gave me any indication that I had a shot with her." He sits on the bed beside me. "Do you think you like Andrew? We are talking about Andrew, aren't we?"

I feel my face burning again, but all I can do is look away from him. "I'm not sure," I say. "But it doesn't matter. I don't think he cares for me." If he does, I don't think he'll speak up about it. He knows just as well as I do that circumstance dictates a marriage far more often than feelings, so those feelings should be carefully monitored and not allowed to run wild.

But Keith just sighs. "Sucks, doesn't it?"

And just like that, we're not talking about Andrew anymore. I glance toward him. "Scarlet just told me that dating is fun."

Keith's eyes lift, fixing on the wall in front of us before he asks, "She did?"

"Yes," I say. "You should ask her sometime."

"I don't think that's a good idea," Keith answers.

"Why not?" I shouldn't meddle, and even I'm not ignorant enough to ignore the gaps between Keith's situation and Scarlet's lifestyle, though people don't seem to care about that sort of thing anymore.

The front door slams and Scarlet stomps up the stairs so heavily that we both rise as she enters the room.

"How'd it go?" Keith asks.

She flings the phone onto the side table. "I do not know why Sherri married Dad to begin with, and I sure don't know why she's crying about him leaving her. She can do so much better. Even nobody is better." The air pulsates as she grabs a towel she's set out on the bed. "Come on. Let's just go to the bay. No talk of fathers today. We'll solve the mystery tomorrow."

She's gone nearly as quickly as she came and Keith arches an eyebrow at me. He doesn't say anything, because it's not required. I step toward him, wrapping him in a hug.

He huffs a laugh. "That's why, Clara. That's why."

10

SCARLET BELDON
Summer, 2012

DAD'S TIRES CRUNCH THE PARKING LOT, A MIXTURE OF WHITE DUST, crushed shell and some pebbles thrown in. It sinks beneath my heels as I slide out of the car. The heat has just about ruined my fashion sense, but today I'm sporting a power dress, a layer of lipstick and eyeshadow. Yes, it's overkill, but I've spent the morning at the library researching scholarship options for Keith. If Mower Man wants to go to college, I'm going to make sure he can. I have a few things lined up and even more questions for Keith, such as what are the chances that he has even a tiny percentage of Native American in his bloodline.

But Dad interrupted just when I was getting on a roll to see if I wanted to have lunch with him. So now we're at the grill that looks like it wants to be a seafood restaurant, and I'm overdressed but feeling satisfyingly confident. My dad can take me from a city to a shrimping village. The boys can stare as I walk through the door. And my heels can catch between the boards on the ramp. None of that has the power to keep me from getting exactly where I want to go when I'm on my own.

Inside, the walls are littered with old nets, signs from the 40s and photographs of country musicians. A man carries a fish through the door to the counter and greets the woman behind it. "Can you cook this up for me?"

"Sure," she answers.

As the fish is toted to the kitchen, I lean in toward Dad. "They weren't kidding with that 'you catch it, we cook it' sign."

He smirks. "I told you this place would be awesome."

I smile at the hostess when she seats us and hands me a menu; one laminated sheet of choices.

"You're happy today," Dad says.

"I am," I reply. "I've had a good day."

I'm feeling somewhat in control of my life again.

"Good." Dad tilts his head. "What are you dressed up for?"

"You can take the girl out of the city..." I start.

Dad pushes his lips to the side. "Sure you didn't meet somebody?"

"No, Dad." I set the menu down. "Sometimes I like to dress up entirely for myself."

"Well, you picked an interesting day to do it," Dad says. "I'm going deep sea fishing later. I was hoping you'd come. We could have some family time."

"On a boat?" I ask. I'm already picturing the cramped space, the sun burning my skin, and spending the day within speaking distance of Dad surrounded by water and sharks.

"Well, yeah," Dad says. "Deep sea fishing normally requires a boat."

"I actually still have a lot of research," I reply, like my morning's work is a mandatory job.

"Okay," Dad says.

He's not buying it, but I'm not really expecting him to. It's just easier to say than, 'I'd rather die.'

"Hey there." I hear Keith's voice, but I never saw him come through the door. Trust me. I scanned the room when we arrived and he wasn't in it. I swing in my chair, and there he is, wearing a black smock and holding a notepad.

"Seriously?" I grin, then shake my finger at him as I remember. "You serve tables twice a week."

"Yeah, I do." He squints at me. "Are you stalking me?"

"I promise you, I'm not," I say.

"Yeah, she is," Dad says. "She got all dressed up and everything."

"Why do you men think everything's about you?" I sigh.

Keith laughs softly. "Well, can I get you a drink?"

"She knows better than to let the boys buy her a drink," Dad says, shaking his finger at Keith.

I moan, dropping my face into my hands. "Just bring me a water," I beg.

Keith rearranges his face into what I'm assuming he's supposed to look like when serving. "You, sir?"

"Ice tea," Dad says. "Wait. Is it sweet?"

"You can add sugar," Keith says.

Dad's eyes lift to him. "Let me tell you something about sugar. When you add sugar to ice tea, it doesn't mix. It just swirls around and sinks to the bottom."

Keith glances back to the kitchen. "I'll see if I can catch the next batch right after it brews."

Dad spreads his hands. "I like the way you think." As Keith turns, he calls, "Can you just bring out a whole pitcher?"

"Yes, sir," Keith says.

I wipe my face. "Why do I take you into public?"

"Just saving your boyfriend some steps."

"Do not drink out of that pitcher." I lift my eyebrows to glare at him like I actually have a shot of scaring him into compliance. "And he's not my boyfriend."

He just chuckles, and I realize he's going to pull out every trick he knows just because Keith is serving us.

I shake my head and wag a finger. "You better tip him well."

Dad keeps laughing, and I remember him teasing me at the amusement park when I little. I was the only kid whose dad would play hide and seek and wear balloon animals on his head and sneak me onto rides when I wasn't quite tall enough. It pangs, and I swallow and look away.

Sometimes I miss the comradeship we had before I woke up and realized how manipulative Dad actually is.

"You better be nice to me," I say. "When you get older, I can put your butt in a nursing home."

Dad smirks. "I can send you off to a boarding school right now."

I don't really like that idea, but I straighten. "What kind of threat is that? I'd be good at boarding school."

I fold my hands and set my chin on to them, smiling smugly as he flounders for a comeback.

"There's games here." Dad points to the collection of board games on the separator. "Want to play checkers?"

No.

I catch the word before it escapes, feeling my competitive spirit already perking.

"Sure," I say.

Dad swings out of his seat to go for the game as Keith comes from the back.

"Water, and one well-mixed, iced sweet tea," he says, sliding the tea in front of me. "Oh wait..."

He switches the drinks as I snort.

"So, uh." Keith peeks over my shoulder, putting his face closer to my level. "What are you dressed up for?"

I shrug. "It makes me feel more in control of my life. What are *you* dressed up for?"

"Work," Keith says. "Don't worry. I've got tennis shoes in the back. But, I was thinking about seeing a movie tonight if you're up for a completely string-free, platonic outing.

"My such big words," I say. "Impressive." Then I cock my head. "Wait. There's a movie theater here?"

"There's a movie theater thirty miles from here," Keith says.

"What are you watching?" I ask.

"I'm not sure, actually," Keith says. "It's only one screen. Changes films every Friday, so it's always kind of a surprise."

"Of course it does." I laugh.

"Come on. Get in touch with your spontaneous side," Keith says.

"Fine," I say. "But are you allowed to ask guests for dates?"

"Not a date," Keith shook his head. "I'm going to see a movie. If you would like to ride along and save gas, you can."

"Okay," I say.

"This afternoon?" he asks. "Tickets are cheaper, and I get off at four."

And Dad's going to be somewhere in the bay. "Sure," I say.

Dad grins as he comes back. "Is that tea sweet?"

"It's sweet," Keith says.

"Good boy."

"Dad," I whisper.

And that's when she enters.

I'm not sure how I know she's there to meet us. Maybe it's the way her eyes swing straight to Dad. Maybe its because she looks like Sherri with blonde hair and a slightly pudgy but pretty face. But I realize, it's the look of adoration that tips me off. Dad has two kinds of women: really hot women, sometimes on the young side. The kind that show up when he's spending money like it's Christmas. And this kind: Middle aged blondes, usually a bit insecure, who look at him like he's God and will do anything for him.

"Hi!" She smiles so warmly that I can't bring myself to be rude to her. My mouth is hanging, and I turn an incredulous look to my father who failed to warn me that "family time" involved a new woman.

"Hey, there you are!" Dad rises, reaching to hug her before he pulls out her chair. "Have a seat. This is my daughter, Scarlet. Scarlet, this is Melinda."

"Hi, Scarlet." Melinda shakes my hand with a warm grasp that's a bit too eager. "I've heard so many wonderful things about you."

"Really?" I ask through a smile, because inside I'm wondering what Dad told her to imply he thought I was wonderful.

"Hi, Keith," Melinda says.

"Hey, Mindy," Keith says. "You want the normal?"

"You know me well," Melinda replies.

"And I'll take the bacon cheeseburger," Dad says. "But don't ruin it with anything green."

Keith looks to me, quirking an eyebrow, but it looks more like he's asking if I'm okay than what I want.

"I . . ." I completely forgot what I wanted and I circle a hand helplessly, begging, "Just bring me something."

"Catfish is good," Keith says.

"That's great," I reply. "Thanks."

He goes back to the kitchen, leaving me stuck at the table. Well. At least I'm dressed up.

"So are you going on the boat with us?" Melinda asks. Her voice is super bubbly like Barbie, and she looks like a mother who's asking for details about prom night.

"Uh no," I say. "I have a date." I sputter the sentence, closing my mouth as I realize it's out. "Just a friend date," I add.

"I knew it!" Dad claps and points to me.

"Oh, really? With who?" Melinda asks. "Anybody I know?"

"The cute waiter," Dad answers.

"His name is Keith, Dad," I say. "And we're just friends."

"Oh, Keith?" She flips her wrist to point to the door that I really hope Keith can't hear us behind. "I know Keith. He's a great guy. You should keep him."

"I don't think people should be kept," I say. "They're not pets or toys."

She tries to reply to that, but then trails off like she has no idea what I just said.

"Scarlet is a liberated woman." Dad digs his pinky into his ear as he talks, making me wonder how any woman is attracted to him.

"Oh." Melinda tries again, but she's faltering.

It's so freaking hard. She actually seems like someone I could like, and I want to stand and shout for her to run. Because I know my dad, and he's going to use her and leave her as soon as someone else catches his attention.

"In my observations," I say carefully, "dating usually ends badly."

She misses the double meaning, but Dad cocks his head slightly, looking unimpressed. I unroll my silverware, dropping the napkin in my lap. I will not apologize for bucking this system. I am a woman. I am on earth to contribute, to hone and present my skills. I was not put on earth as eye candy for men's personal pleasure.

Dad reaches for her hand, resting it on the table. I rub my temples, then set the checker box on the only free chair.

"So do you own this boat you're going on?" I ask.

"Oh no," Melinda says. "But I know the captain, so I made some calls for your dad."

"That was nice," I reply.

"Yeah, I think it's going to be fun," she says. "It's too bad your date is at the same time. Maybe we can take it back out sometime."

"I'm not really a boat person," I reply quickly.

"She's boring," Dad says. "She spent all morning doing paperwork in the library."

I perk when I see Keith again. He's got two plates in each hand and one balanced on his arm.

"Did you know," he says as he slides my plate in front of me, "that there used to be a lumber yard where this building stands?"

I tip my head toward him. "Really?"

"So the story goes." He gives a short smile. "Enjoy."

And then he leaves and I can't even focus on food because I'm too busy glancing into the corners like if I stare hard enough, I'll see translucent versions of Vincent or Edmund doing whatever lumber yard owners do. Has Clara ever been here?

The fish is good, but it begins to taste sour as I listen to Melinda laugh at all of Dad's jokes. By the time that Keith stops to see if we'd like dessert, I'm contemplating the most effective way of excusing myself. But Dad orders chocolate cake for all of us, subjecting me to another ten minutes of heartfelt but invasive questions by a woman I've just met.

I stab my fork into the cake, biting my tongue as Dad excuses himself to take the bill to the counter. It's now or never.

I interrupt Melinda with a burst of determination.

"Don't date him," I say.

"What?" She laughs like I'm a little girl.

"He will cheat on you," I say. "He will use you and dump you."

Again her mouth moves, again nothing comes out. She touches the earring that dangles and catches the light, making me wonder if Dad gave them to her.

Her eyes waver across my face, then flash to him as he returns.

"So, are we ready?" Dad grabs the back of the chair, leaning forward with his best charming smile.

Melinda looks a bit lost, first to him, then to me. Then she shuts her mouth, gives a crooked nod and stands. "Yes, I think we are. Are we dropping your daughter off first?"

I smile tightly like I haven't just undermined my father's romantic endeavors. I can't tell if she just doesn't know how to get out of this and plans to later, or if she's chalked this up to a daughter who doesn't want a woman in her father's life. But I warned her. Maybe she'll bolt when she sees the first clues that I'm right. Or maybe she figures a little while with a rich guy is better than nothing.

He looks rich now, despite the unrefined manners. He throws a twenty on the table, then adds a five. I want to roll my eyes at the display but the money's going to Keith, which is a great way to spend it.

"Scarlet's got to have a good date," he winks. "Might even be able to afford popcorn."

I stand, but we're out before I get to watch Keith's face when he sees the tip. It's not a date, and I'm buying my own ticket, but I am excited. It's the first normal teenager thing I've done in a while. The power dress is not comfortable so I decide that my official work day is over and change into jeans and the softest shirt I own. It's teal, sort of a classy casual look that doesn't give away how much effort I put into not looking like I tried.

I wind the music box a few times, but Clara doesn't answer, so I pacify myself with scribbling a note.

Keith and I are going to the movies. Wish you were here.

And then I glance at the clock, wondering what I'm going to do until 4:30, and repeating to myself that this isn't a date. It's an outing, between friends, to save gas.

CLARA CASTLE
Summer, 1911

"WHAT IS IT?" I ASK, PEERING INTO THE LARGEST CRATE I'VE EVER seen, only to find a cast iron tub with two silver faucets at the end. Father is too busy prying the boards free with a crowbar to answer, but Vincent does.

"It's a bathtub, silly."

"What's it for?" Hannah asks, as the full thing comes into view. It looks like a boat with clawed feet.

"To bathe in," Vincent says.

"Well, I know that," Hannah says. "But why is it so large? We're not all going to bathe at once. You could fit three people in that! And just think of the water."

"Well, that's the whole idea," Father says, touching the faucet. "It will fill with both cold and hot water. We won't have to pump or boil the water anymore."

I knock lightly on the side, listening to the ring. "How in the world are you going to get it upstairs?"

I know they will, because the tub is still there in Scarlet's time in the room across from Father's.

"We're going to wait until Andrew gets here so he can help carry it," Vincent says.

I peek inside the screened door at the short railing guarding the stairs, trying to imagine three men lugging the contraption upstairs. "Good heavens, someone is going to fall over."

A new bathtub. Andrew's and Grandfather's visit. I haven't seen Scarlet lately, but at least I'll have plenty to fill my next letter.

"And for now it's just going to stay on the front porch for God and everybody to see when they drive by?" I ask.

"It'll have to," Father says.

Hannah shakes her head as she returns to the kitchen with her lips pushed together. She worries when Father's mood swings into the benevolent humor that usually results in one or two extravagant purchases.

I know little about finances, so perhaps he makes rash decisions, but I can't help enjoying the spells when he feels we are doing well enough to buy new and exciting things. Besides, I've never been in this much water in my life.

"It looks like a boat," I say. "Like we could float it around the harbor."

Vincent laughs. "I doubt it would float."

"Your mother would have liked it," Father says. He's smiling into the porcelain like it's a picture of her.

It's true, of course. From what I know of Mother, she was as fascinated by new innovations and luxury as Grandfather. Before I can decide whether to take advantage of the moment and ask about her, or change the subject so Father doesn't grow sad, he puts his hand on my shoulder and nudges me toward the house. "Come inside, darling. We'll move it later."

I glance toward the sunlight brightening the field and glinting off the water. It's a beautiful day, and I don't want to spend it inside.

"Can't she stay out with me, Father?" Vincent asks. He shrugs a shoulder, attempting to add a joke to counteract the tinge of irritation in his voice. "Someone must guard the tub, right? The neighbors might carry it off."

Father doesn't smile. The flash in his eyes causes me to reach for the door handle. "I need to help Hannah anyway."

I doubt Hannah really needs my help, but I hope my obedience will disarm both of them. I glance back toward Vincent, prepared to send an imploring look that he not protest, but his face is already turned away. He grips the railing with white knuckles as the screen shuts. Hannah informs me, rather sharply, that she does not need help and to please refrain from being underfoot. I feel like a child again, which makes my eyes water as though I really am one.

"What in the world is that?" The iceman calls from his delivery cart. He stalls, letting his ice block drip onto the porch.

I peek through the curtain as Vincent explains, and the man says, "Well, I'll be!"

For the rest of the afternoon, there is a steady trickle of automobiles and carts meandering past the house. Each motor car disappoints me because I think it is Grandfather and Andrew, only to find another pair of curious eyes peeping at the porch. Father calls me away from the window, finally ordering me not to get up again. By the time they really do arrive, I've lost myself in a book.

This time it's Vincent who peeks from the window, then laughs. "Ho! Andrew's driving. That scoundrel."

Vincent hits the screen door so hard that Father winces as it bangs. He peers out of the window, his eyebrows drawing in curiosity before he folds the paper, tucks it onto his chair, and pushes the entire thing beneath the table. Then he catches me watching and says, "What's the matter? Don't you want to see your grandfather?"

I do want to see Grandfather, but I don't want to leave Father alone. We've had such a lovely time together for the last week. Father has even joked a few times, which always startles Vincent. I cannot feel quite excited to see Grandfather, for I would rather have Father in a good mood than be all together. We go to the porch arm in arm.

But it's not Grandfather that I see. It's Andrew.

He's gotten even taller since Christmas, but his face has drastically changed. It's filled out and a healthy color, though his skin is a bit blue beneath his eyes. His quiet nature has gone nowhere, but he swings out of the car with loose movements. He sees me, smiles a bit, then turns his attention toward helping Simon retrieve the luggage on the back.

Oh, what's the use of analyzing what I can't understand myself? I feel as though Andrew is wearing a magnet and every time he's nearby, I just want him to look at me. It seemed quite exciting in the novels to be drawn to a man, but it isn't. It makes me want to hide. I feel just the sort of silly ignorant girl that Father doesn't want me associating with.

Even now I feel Father watching me, so I drop my eyes. Grandfather abandons his car, coming to wrap me in a hug. "Clara! You look very well."

This time he seems to mean it.

After that, there isn't time to feel awkward, for a gale rushes across the bay creating a mad scramble to bring in the traveling trunks and stow the car safely in the carriage house. Inside, Vincent peels off his coat, then flaps it at me to spray me with the drops.

I'm laughing, but not too hard to notice that Father takes Andrew's hand, greeting him with, "Hello, Mr. Callaghan. It's good to see you."

"Hello, sir." Andrew responds with a smile, though he looks a bit startled.

I linger, unsure whether to follow Vincent to the dining room or say hello to Andrew. It's different between us now. We've only spent the Christmas holiday together and were only alone once when we spent an hour on the balcony as Andrew described Christmas Eve Mass. But we've written for an entire year now. I know things about him that I doubt he's told anyone else, and I cannot imagine him saying while he's here at my home. It should be easier to talk to him, but I cannot breathe.

He speaks first after Father steps into the parlor, leaving us alone in the hall. "Hello, Miss Clara."

"Hello, Andrew," I say.

"Andrew." Grandfather steps back into the doorway. "Did you unload the green trunk? Simon says he didn't see it."

"Yes, sir. It's in the parlor by the window," Andrew answers.

I frown at the difference in his voice. It's lost its melodious lilt, the unique flip. He's not stuttering, but he doesn't sound like himself.

"Vincent said you were driving," I say, hoping to spur him to speak again.

"I was," he answers, still speaking methodically. His accent still leaks through his vowels, but the words are carefully honed through a filter. "Mr. Mordaunt wished me to practice on the way over."

That's when I realize, he's not trying to avoid stuttering around me. He's trying to sound like an American. I want to pull him onto the front porch and ask him why he feels the need to cover his accent, and if he's struggling in school as much as Vincent implied.

But I can't, so I only smile. "Well, come in and tell us all about the year. Hannah's been cooking treats all day."

"Good god, it's hot in here," Grandfather says, loosening his tie. "Even on the water, I don't understand how you stay here all summer."

"It's only bad in August when the breeze stops," I say, straightening Vincent's coat on the rack.

"Only because you don't know any better, my dear," Grandfather says. "I wish you all would let me take you to England for the summer."

"England!" I blurt before I mean to. I've rarely traveled outside of Palacios, but to travel across the sea sounds terribly exciting.

Father shakes his head. "You'd hate England, Clara. The sun never shines there."

"Well, if you won't allow Clara, I must at least take Vincent," Grandfather says, "for Andrew has decided he'd rather see his family this summer."

"I'm game," Vincent says, which creates a frown from Father.

"Good for you, Andrew," I try to turn the conversation. "A year is a long time to be away."

"It would only be the second half of the summer," Andrew says. "The hotel here asked me to play in their orchestra, so I'll be working in Palacios for two months. It would be easier than acquiring a job in New York, and I can send more home."

Now Grandfather frowns, shifting in his seat as Father speaks up. "There's no need to board at the hotel, Andrew. You can stay with us, help out here, and send as much home as you like."

The offer startles all of us, eliciting different emotions. Vincent looks confused, Grandfather's eyebrows tuck a bit, and only the greatest effort keeps me from bouncing in my seat.

Andrew could be here for several weeks, though I do feel badly for Grandfather. I suppose traveling alone would grow dreary, but my heart is slamming so hard it's a wonder everyone can't hear it.

"Yes, do," I add. "We've never had anyone stay with us before." Perhaps I am a bit too enthusiastic, because everyone grows a bit tense.

Grandfather recovers first. "Well, next year, perhaps. I plan to introduce Andrew there, and you may all go."

Next year. My stomach lurches as I glance to Father, wondering where any of us will be next year.

"Thank you, sir," Andrew says to Father, oblivious to the future only I know.

I can't even look forward to this summer because every day takes me closer to the day I can no longer undo the collision we're heading toward.

"Well," says Grandfather, "I suppose that settles it. Perhaps when Andrew is out of school we can all go together. Rose always wanted you children to see England. Who knows? You may have grown up there if your Father hadn't insisted on staying in Galveston."

Grandfather crosses his ankle over his knee and sips his tea as the rest of us stare at the steam rising from our cups. Even Andrew gives a surprised glance toward Grandfather. I study the pattern on the carpet, trying to see Father without actually looking at him. Vincent's nails dig into his palms. Father's breath grows shallow with long pauses between.

Where am I to take the conversation from here? A hurricane is responsible for Mother's death, not Father's place of business. Grandfather lived there, still lives there, and was hit as hard as the rest of us so it's not as though Mother were a prisoner. My teacup rattles until Andrew gently tugs it from my hand and sets it on the table. I suppose spilling hot tea into my lap would have effectively changed the direction of the visit, but I'm grateful he noticed the danger.

"Well." Grandfather speaks again, apparently realizing that his barb for Father actually speared everyone in the room. "I promised to meet Mr. Lipscomb this afternoon. Thank Hannah for the tea. I'll be back this evening."

He takes up his cane, flourishing it a bit on his way out the door. Freed from his obligation to play host, Father stands, digging through his pockets for a cigar before he even reaches his study.

Vincent blows a slow breath, then lifts his eyes toward Andrew. "What did I tell you?" He points to Father's study, then the front door. "Gunpowder. Match."

"What's between them?" Andrew asks.

"My mother," Vincent replies.

"But it isn't Father's fault!" I snap. "He told Mother to stay inside our house. She's the one who left!"

Vincent held up his hand. "It's no one's fault, except God's, if there is one."

Andrew flinches, and I blow out a breath, give up all pretense of formality and reach for the abandoned teacups. "I wish Grandfather wouldn't come at all if he's going to keep blaming Father."

"Do you want me to try and keep him away next time?" Andrew asks. "I could probably distract him."

"I want them to get along," I say. "I don't like choosing between them all the time."

"Don't let it spoil your day," Vincent says. "They're grown men. They can work it out."

Except they won't. I sigh and carry the cups to Hannah. "Tea's over."

The door to Father's study is closed and I stall in front, trying to decide whether to return to the parlor or venture inside. I grip the handle, pulling in a slow breath before I push open the door.

The study is dark with the curtains drawn, but Father hasn't bothered even to light a lamp. The only light in the room is the glow of his cigar releasing its scented smoke. Father sits in his high-backed chair, staring out the window. I brush the cold leather of the headrest before I touch his hair.

"Father?"

When he doesn't respond, I force myself to step to the side of the chair. I knew this would happen the moment Grandfather said Mother's name. Father is rigid, his spine so stiff that it looks painful. One hand clamps the chair arm, the other the cigar that releases a steady stream of smoke like it's leaking out Father's life. His eyes are glazed, fixed on the wall. His brows draw toward each other, contorted in a way that makes him look like a scared little boy trapped inside a body that's braced for war.

"Father," I repeat, though I know he won't hear me.

His cigar butt glows, threatening to drop a wad of ashes, endangering not only his trousers and leg, but the carpet below. It's very hard to move Father when he is trapped like this. If you managed to force his body into another position, it will stay like a human doll. I gasp for breath and blink back tears as I glance around the room for the ashtray.

I haven't told Scarlet about this. I haven't told anyone about this, though Hannah and Vincent have seen the spells. It's another thing we don't talk about, except to warn each other to leave him alone. He'll come out of it and probably won't remember it at all. The first time I found him like this

I thought he was dead, but Hannah says it happened even before the Great Storm.

I tap the ashes into the tray and hold it beneath as I wiggle the cigar in his hand. "Let go, Father. You're going to burn the house down."

I'm not sure if he can hear me or not, but I keep talking to make things feel a little more normal. "It isn't your fault, you know. You told her to stay in the house. And you tried to save her. I know you did." But assuring Father seems a sort of betrayal to Mother so I add, "But the walls were swaying. She really did think the house was going to fall."

I bite my lip and force the tears back. I can't remember the order of events and most of it is blurry, but other images are so sharp, they may as well have come from Father's mind instead of mine.

Mother was brave to venture into the water with her skirt wadded in one hand and hanging onto me with the other. It was that skirt that filled with water, tripping her and taking us both under. She'd tied me to a rope and wrapped it around her waist. Hannah said it cracked one of my ribs when the water swept me away, but Mother pulled me back up, keeping both of us in place by using a post to hold the rope.

I have no idea what Father shouted, but I still remember clinging to that pole and squinting past the wind to see him wading toward us. Perhaps that's the worst part. Remembering how harshly he scolded her for leaving the house, and all the horrible names that she shouted back. It was the only time I ever heard them argue and the last conversation they ever had.

I'm remembering far more than I want to, so I shake my head to send the images away. I'm not in a flooding house and the only thing wrong now is that Father's mind has flown from his body. I move closer, stroking his arm and calling, "Father?"

His fingers curl around the gap where his cigar should be.

"Father," I call a little louder.

He shudders, pulls in a breath and blinks a few times, then swings his eyes toward me. Bewilderment plays across his face.

"Rose?" he asks.

It hurts, really hurts to be called by Mother's pet name. I try to convince myself that he's only referring to my middle name, but I know it isn't true.

"Clara, Father."

"Clara," he repeats, then blinks again.

I let him look around, reorienting himself on his own—and remembering in his own time.

"Of course," he says, and shakes his head. He squeezes his eyes shut and I can't tell if he's confused or covering tears, but I drop my eyes until he touches my cheek. "What are you doing in here, darling?"

I want to bang my fists against his chest and demand that he tell me whether he realizes that he's been unresponsive for ten minutes. But I'm a coward, so I only say, "I came to check on you. You were so quiet."

He sucks in a breath and reaches for that loathsome cigar, relighting it. I fix my eyes on the bookshelf, clenching my jaw while he smokes the entire thing. But his hands stop trembling and his breath deepens.

A thousand questions go through my mind, but I'm afraid asking him will send him into another spell. He stands and offers me a hand to help me to my feet. He doesn't let go, and I shrink beneath the displeased glint in his eyes.

"You mustn't come in here again," he says. "When I'm in here or my room, it is because I want to be alone. Do you understand?"

Has he any idea? I'm hurt and angry all at the same time. It's the sort of response that would send Vincent into a rage. But Father doesn't know what happened, and I know better than to cross him.

I swallow, drop my eyes and reply, "Yes, sir."

12

SCARLET BELDON

Summer, 1911

"OW!" I FLINCH AND LEAN AWAY FROM THE HAIRPIN THAT CLARA JABS into my bun. I thought getting ready for an outing in my time was difficult. Preparation for a summer dance in 1911 feels next to impossible.

It's only been three days since Keith and I went to the movies, which ended up being a film about superheroes. I've been storing up the stories to tell Clara, but she waylaid me with her own updates as soon as I managed to bring her forward.

Another month has passed. Andrew has been staying with them, playing from noon to midnight in the orchestra at the hotel. Her father gave her permission to attend a dance at the pavilion with Vincent, and she's so excited she can hardly finish a sentence. So I set the night of superheroes in a ridiculously tiny but somehow charming theater, on the back burner.

Inspired by the futuristic movie, Keith came up with a dozen theories about how the music box worked, though the only one we proved was that song has to match in both times almost exactly for anyone to travel. But we've decided to use it to explore more than just Clara's mystery.

Dressing up for the dance at the pavilion seemed fun when Keith first suggested it, but teasing my hair into an Edwardian style isn't easy, even with the online tutorials. I'm starting to miss my jeans and loose locks.

"I'm sorry." Clara flinches behind me and glances toward the doorway, probably wondering where Keith is.

It's a good thing she was ready when I got here, because we're spending most of the afternoon on me. Hannah helped her with her hair, and her father even bought material for a new dress. I can't imagine sewing my own dress, but Clara is actually a decent little seamstress.

My gown, on the other hand, is a castoff prom dress we found at a resale shop with an empire waist and a black overlay that flows over cranberry silk. It wouldn't work in Clara's time since it's entirely sleeveless, but no one except Keith is going to see me. We're going as moral support because this isn't just a dance.

"And you're sure that James is going to be there?" I ask, glancing toward her.

She nods. "Vincent asked if he was going, and he said yes."

I tilt my head, trying to see what in the world she's done in the back of this elaborate do. "Good. Make sure you dance with him. Just ask him if he knows what would cause someone to go into a catatonic state. If he says 'no,' don't push it. If he asks questions, he might be able to help your father.

Clara pushes her fingers into her eyes. "It's not an illness. It goes away."

"Your father still needs help. We only have a year and whatever is causing this could contribute to the accident."

Clara turns to her dresser, rummaging for longer than she needs to find a hatpin, especially because there is one sitting on the vanity in front of me. I know she's not being stubborn. Leaving the house is a big step all on its own.

A regular party would be overwhelming, but this is a dance where she has to entice an older man to ask her onto the floor, ignore the boy playing the violin, and get answers about her father's illness without actually admitting that he is ill. James is going to figure it out. Who else does Clara see? But I keep acting like she can be sneaky about it, so she doesn't feel like she's stepping into an outright betrayal — however necessary it is.

For now, I spin with an overenthusiastic grin like we're dressing up for the prom with our favorite crushes. "How do I look?"

"Lovely," she answers. She actually smiles as she carries a black hat and lifts it to my hair. It's going to look stupid with the dress, and I wince.

Clara tilts her head. "Now, if you're going to be authentic, you must wear a hat when you leave the house. You may take it off when you arrive at the dance, but decency demands that if you won't cover your shoulders, you must at least cover your head. Besides," her voice mimics Hannah's, "you must protect that porcelain skin."

I snort, adjusting the hat myself. I demanded that she don flip-flops in my world, so I can't refuse a hat now. "Are you kidding? Tomorrow, after I sleep off my punch-induced hangover, I have a tanning date with the UV rays at the bay."

She pauses again. "What's a hangover?"

"A headache and nausea after a night of too much alcohol," I say.

Now she snorts nearly identical to me, and I realize my bad habits are rubbing off. "Alcohol is prohibited."

I've never actually drank because I'm concerned for the welfare of my brain cells, but I can't resist dropping my head to grin at her. "I'll bet Vincent knows where to find some."

Her eyes widen before she hits my shoulder. I slouch in my laughter until I spy a book beneath Clara's bed and pounce on it, pulling it out with exaggerated curiosity. "Ooh, what's this? Naughty novels?"

I'm teasing, but Clara blushes a deep shade of red as she says, "I stopped reading it. One moment he was eating chicken with paprika and the next he was a prisoner in a castle with a man who climbs walls like a lizard, and these women that materialize out of nowhere, and I think they're planning on eating him."

"Wait! Are you reading 'Dracula'?" I flip open the cloth cover to verify, then bark a laugh.

"I don't know what Vincent was thinking to leave it here," Clara answered. "Here I thought it was a travel story, and then I couldn't sleep for a week!"

I smirk and return the novel to its hiding place. "Well, don't worry. In a hundred years vampires will be sparkly and relatively harmless."

The music box begins to tinkle on the shelf.

And even though we're talking about the supernatural world, we respond by rushing over as eagerly as if it's a doorbell. Which it essentially is.

We both take it for good measure, and this time it's Keith that fades into Clara's world. He looks — well, different — with his hair slicked back into a 1911 style. He scrounged up a suit from somewhere, again not time-period but close enough. But he completely ignores us, breaking past our little group, thrilled with the surroundings he's heard about, but just now seen.

He cusses in awe, making Clara flinch, but he's oblivious to everything except the decor. He grips his hair. "Look at this house. Look at that lamp!"

I chuckle and glance to Clara. "You had no idea your house was so interesting, did you?"

"Says the girl who carries a telephone in her pocket," Clara responds, almost in an accent that matches mine.

"Clara!" We all jump as the door shakes with a light knock.

"Come in!" Clara calls.

The guy looks enough like Keith that it must be Vincent poking his head through the door. Keith's eyes widen, his jaw dropping as he doubles over mouthing, "Oh my gosh!"

"He can't hear you," I whisper.

And as amusing as Keith is, now that's he's sitting on the ground in a sheer effort to contain himself, it's hard to keep my eyes on him. I mean, I could live without the wave in the hair, but for an Edwardian guy, Vincent is pretty hot.

"Father is getting antsy," he says. "We need to leave before he changes his mind."

"He can't change his mind!" Clara says quickly.

"I know. That's why we need to leave. Besides, I have someone I need to meet."

Clara's head snaps up. "A girl?"

Vincent sends her a closed-lip smile and turns, leaving all of us without an answer. "Get a move on it," he calls. "Grandfather said we could take the car."

"Is he leaving it for the entire summer?" Clara asks, running to the doorway. "I supposed he'd want to ship it to England to show it off."

"Apparently." Vincent throws the answer back casually, though his excitement betrays him. "I think he's trying to spoil Andrew, so he'll decide he doesn't want to go home after all."

Keith bounds to the window to check out the car. "I don't even know what kind that is," he says, "but it's awesome!"

"It's a Lozier," Clara says.

"And it's going to leave you if you don't hurry and get into it!" I grab Keith's shoulders, pushing him toward the door and we clamber to the bottom of the stairs. Keith slips through the door as Vincent lets it close, but I'm not quick enough so I'm trapped until Clara comes to let me out.

One of the beads on my dress hangs loosely and I finger it, trying to decide if I can tighten the thread or just pull the thing off without damaging the dress. I feel the floor vibrate and look back up, feeling my heart squeeze.

I'd know it was Andrew, even if the house held a hundred more people and he wasn't holding a violin. His face reflects the unique mixture of humility and dogged determination that his letters imply. He's smaller than Vincent, even a little smaller than Keith. His nose is straight, his eyes a light blue that reflect a somber tone, like he's grown so used to putting one foot in front of the other that the dogged concentration stays even when he's happy. I imagine he writes like that too, using the same amount of effort on one letter, then the next, then the next, until he manages to pen what he's trying to say.

I step back as he sets his free hand on the ball at the bottom of the stair rail, calling softly, "Miss Clara?"

"I'm coming!" Clara calls back.

I grin as Andrew steps back, still watching the top of the stairs. He's adorable, and they're going to have adorable children. Clara is deluding herself if she still thinks he doesn't like her.

"Slow, slow!" I call as Clara rushes to the top of the stairs. "Give him a chance to see the new dress!"

Clara obeys, but her excitement bubbles over her attempt at a regal descent. Andrew offers a hand at the bottom of the stairs, but he doesn't kiss it. I'm not sure if he was planning on saying anything because Clara's eyes move from him to the door. I glance into the yard to see why her face turned so pale, but I only see Vincent cranking the car with his great-grandson hovering nearby.

"Are you well?" Andrew asks.

Clara's eyes mist as her chest pumps slightly. Her voice cracks as she replies, "I don't know what to do at a party."

Andrew flinches, then offers a commiserating smile. "Just watch the others. That's what I do."

She laughs a little, but I worry that she might turn and bolt back upstairs. Maybe Andrew does too, because he tugs her hand, guiding her down the final step and then they're so close I wonder if he's going to kiss her.

They stand for a moment, before he steps back, shifting his violin to his left hand and reaching to open the screen door.

Clara sucks in a breath so shaky, I wonder if she's going to collapse, but she raises her chin and steps through. The screen hits me before I clear the door, but no one notices the bounce, except Keith who only laughs.

"I get shotgun!" I call, scrambling into the car and leaving poor Keith to squeeze into the backseat. Clara scoots to the middle, which puts her even closer to Andrew. She glances back to the house as Vincent pulls the car onto the road.

Andrew senses her discomfort and leans away, but Vincent counters the move by swerving straight into a pothole. I grab the back of the seat to keep from tumbling out as the entire car jolts to the right. Keith clings to the side, managing to avoid sliding into Clara, but Clara pitches toward Andrew's knees. She might have even landed on the floorboard, except she grabs the first thing she encounters — which ends up being Andrew's suit.

He grabs her arms, snapping, "Lord, Vincent!"

"Sorry," Vincent says. He keeps his face forward, twitching the corner of his mouth and missing the commotion in the back.

He doesn't see the slight widening of Andrew's eyes as his eyebrows dip in that universal, do-not-embarrass-me-in-front-of-my-crush look, but I do. I'm pretty sure I might fall for Vincent if he wasn't Keith's great-grandfather.

I snicker, but look away for Clara's sake.

"Are you all right?" Andrew asks softly.

"Yes," Clara answers.

I rub my face. Somebody needs to push them into a shrimp boat and shove it out to sea with no engine, paddles, or easy access to civilization, before they're going to overcome enough formalities to kiss.

"Say something, Clara," I whisper.

Clara's eyes flicker in my direction, then back to the seat in front of her. Her mouth closes as her breath grows shaky, and I wonder if she isn't going to do the same thing her dad does and close off the world.

When we reach the bay, parking between the hotel and the pavilion, Andrew shoves open the door and swings out, balancing both violin and bow in one hand.

"I'll see you when you get back," he says, though it's hard to tell if he's addressing Vincent or Clara.

"From where?" Clara asks.

Vincent turns in his seat with a grin. "Well, if you must know, I like to dance at dances, so I'm fetching a girl who is a phenomenally good dancer."

"Who?" Clara and I shout in unison.

"Her name is Anne, and that's all I'm going to tell you until you meet her."

"Anne," Clara echoes. She blinks, pushes a smile, and I can't decide if she's excited or horrified at the first tangible piece of the future falling into place. If she's trying to appear happy, she's a terrible actress.

"Do you want to stay here with Andrew or go with me?" Vincent asks.

Keith and I poise on the edge of barreling out as Andrew stands holding the door open, waiting to hear if he should close it.

"I'd like to stay," Clara says.

Andrew helps her out of the car, and Vincent winks when her back is turned. "Be good. Do anything I would do."

Andrew's eyes flicker toward the pavilion and back, though I catch the edge of his mouth twitch. I jump out of the back as softly as I can so I don't distract Clara.

"I'm going with him," Keith whispers, pointing toward Vincent.

I give him a thumbs up. Clara lets go of Andrew's hand, walking a few steps like she's looking at the pavilion.

Andrew shuts the door, lifting only his eyes to Vincent in a reproach.

"You did that on purpose," he whispers.

"If I did that on purpose, she'd have landed in your lap," Vincent responds.

Andrew huffs out a breath and turns to walk without a word.

"You're welcome!" Vincent whispers after him.

I smirk at Keith, realizing he's got the same dimples as his grandfather when they're both snickering. Then I scramble out of the way because Vincent shifts gears again and the car lurches unnervingly close to me.

Andrew takes Clara's arm and says something that she answers. I trail them, hoping she'll momentarily forget that I'm here and focus on romancing Andrew. Even though Andrew doesn't know I'm here, Clara does, so I stay in my place until a Model T nearly mows me down.

Then I take a deep breath and smooth out my dress like people are actually going to see me. It's 1911. The pavilion is humongous, forming a T that stretches over the water. Sailboats are tied to one side and a water slide descends from the second story. It's so weird to think that these people in suits and sweeping gowns also swim in the bay.

I've always said I'm not going to prom, but this is a real dance. The dresses aren't as extravagant as those I've seen in the movies about this era, but for a small town, they're nicer than anything I've seen in the modern world. I wish I had asked Clara what James looks like, but I just scan for any men that look like young physicians. Then I get distracted because another car pulls onto the wooden pier, driving straight up to the pavilion and forcing me to scramble near another couple so my invisible self doesn't get run over. The weirdest part is that, Model T and all, I actually know these people. Mr. Meyers shifts to talk to Billy in the backseat as they pull to a stop.

"Oh, there's the Castle girl. Be sure you look after her tonight. The poor thing will need some guidance. I don't imagine she's been to a lot of parties. Oh, but she does look lovely, doesn't she?"

But Billy's not looking at Clara's loveliness. He's zeroed in on Andrew, who sways toward Clara and the hand he hasn't quite released yet and back toward the orchestra as they begin to tune up, like the violin he holds is pulling him toward his job.

Dang it.

I forgot he was going to play all night. No wonder Clara looked at me funny when I teased her about dancing with him.

"Who's that with her?" Billy asks.

"Oh darling, he's dressed like one of the musicians. He's probably just saying hello."

"If he's a musician, he shouldn't be talking to her," Billy says.

My jaw drops before I sputter like he can actually hear me, "Oh, no you didn't."

"As we said," Mr. Meyers says. "Look after her, son. I don't imagine she knows much of the ways of the world."

Billy nods, then slides from the car. I follow him, trying to think of a sneaky way to circumvent his intrusion, but he smiles as he approaches so I relax a bit. Andrew does need to go to work tonight, and I already know Clara's not in danger of being wooed by this boy.

"Miss Castle. Just the girl I was looking for!" Billy holds out both hands like he's arrived on the scene and expects her to swoon.

Andrew drops Clara's hand, looking as confused as she looks startled.

"Were you?" Clara asks.

I stick out my tongue and give her both thumbs down behind Billy, but it backfires because she sees me and laughs, which makes her look flustered, which makes Billy perk a bit and Andrew's eyes fall.

"Mr. Meyers." Clara recovers, sweeping her newly freed hand toward Andrew. "I don't believe you've met Mr. Callaghan."

"Hello, Mr. Meyers," Andrew answers, in an accent that mimics an American tone as he extends his hand.

It's hard to believe these are high school guys. I try to picture the boys at my school all suited up, shaking hands and calling each other by their last names. The effort hurts my brain.

"Oh! No, I haven't." Billy smiles like he's recognized the name. "I've heard wonderful things about your playing, Mr. Callaghan. We're fortunate to have such talented staff tonight."

I don't have to say anything because even Clara has caught the drift and blushes harder than Andrew. Billy eyes him, raising his chin like he's backstage security and Andrew doesn't have a pass.

Andrew drops his hand, making me hope that he'll punch the guy with his liberated fist. Instead, he nods toward Clara. "Let me know if you need anything." He keeps a split second of eye contact before he adds, "Clara."

Clara's eyes snap back to his face, smiling with something that can't be called anything less than adoration. "I'll see you tonight, Andrew."

Sass. My grin is tight because my jaw is too busy hanging.

"Good job, Clara," I say.

All merriment leaves Billy's face, even when Andrew leaves them to join the other musicians.

"Please be careful, Miss Castle," Billy says. "He's very forward, calling you by your first name, especially while working in public."

Again the smile returns as Clara glances back toward Andrew. "I asked him to use my first name, but he doesn't normally."

"Well, he shouldn't." Billy's tone turns disapproving. "You are a lady. Such informality is highly improper, especially from a worker. He ought to be let go for that. You can't be expected to know what he means, but I do."

The little speech works to gain 100% of Clara's attention.

"I know what it means," she says. "I am not wholly ignorant of the world. Andrew is a very dear friend and always will be, and he may call me by my Christian name anytime he so wishes."

"Please be careful, Miss Castle," Billy says. "Men can be very deceptive.

Some will tell you anything you wish to hear if they think they can gain a fortune by you."

"Mr. Callaghan knows me well enough to know that would be a silly endeavor," Clara says. She takes a breath, then stutters forbidden words. "Because I haven't any fortune."

"But your grandfather has," Billy continues. "And Mr. Callaghan has placed himself in a prime location between your affections and your grandfather's esteem." Clara sucks in a breath, but Billy holds up his finger. "Forgive me for upsetting you. I mean only well. But tonight is not for warnings. I do want you to have a lovely evening and for the memory not to be spoiled. Talk to him if you'd like, but don't be blind."

If he's trying not to spoil her evening, he's doing a terrible job. Clara has closed her mouth and looked past him at the wooden railing like she's blocking out everything so she won't cry.

And then Billy's shoulders collapse as remorse and frustration wrinkle his face. "Oh god, I'm blundering. Miss Castle, please. I was only concerned. I'd hate to see you harmed, truly. Let me make it up to you with a dance."

"Tell him your life is none of his business," I snap. "You're a smart girl. You can make up your own mind."

But Clara does look like a damsel in distress. Her eyes swirl with confusion and fear. She's out of her element, and I glimpse the naivety that he's implying.

"Right now is not a good time to ask me for a dance, Mr. Meyers," she replies softly.

"Walk away," I say. "You don't owe him anything. Walk away."

But she doesn't. She sucks in shaky breaths, standing miserably until Billy sputters, "Please, forgive me. I'll leave you if you wish."

She gives no response at all. Billy lifts her hand to his lips, then walks away with as much dignity as he can muster, though when he reaches the far side of the pavilion and greets someone, I see him look back. Andrew's watching too, plucking the violin strings while adjusting the tuning with habitual accuracy.

"Hey." I turn my attention back to Clara, waiting until she looks at me before saying, "You're okay. He doesn't know Andrew like we do."

She can't respond, but her eyes wander away, reddening around the rim. This is not how I wanted this night to go.

"Remember what we're here for," I say. "Do you see Dr. McMinn?"

She searches the crowd, then turns to lean on the railing, looking back toward the land and the hotel. "He isn't here yet," she answers.

She glances back to Billy, who is talking to a young couple with a smile that looks very forced.

"You did fine," I say. "You're going to be okay."

"I think I was cruel," she responds softly, barely moving her lips. "He was in earnest, even if he was very wrong."

"Billy is not in charge of you," I say. "He has no right dictating anything about your life."

"Father's not going to allow me to attend another party if he finds out that I've upset Billy," Clara says.

I open my mouth to tell her that her father has no right to dictate her life either, but she has a point. For whatever reason Edmund's decided that this family needs to be involved in their life, it's important to him. And he can and will force Clara to obey his whims.

I stall, pushing my tongue against my teeth. It's not fair that she can't tell any guy she wants to buzz off and go sit with Andrew for the party if that's who she wants to be near. But she can't. Even my modern, freed, roaring self knows that Clara's world is stuck in a bad system and the only way out is for her to work it.

"He's not going to tell," I say, and it's the truth. I think. "If he told anyone that you didn't want to dance, he'd have to admit that he insulted you. He messed up, not you."

"He doesn't have to admit anything," Clara says softly. "He can tell them whatever he wishes."

"Don't let him bully you," I say. "Even if he thinks he has good intentions, you know Andrew better than anyone in the world. And no matter who you marry, you are the one who will have to live with that choice, so that choice should be yours and yours alone. You can dance with any man here that you want. Except for Andrew," I falter at the last of my little speech. "Which sucks."

Clara's not listening. She grips the railing, lifting her chin toward a figure in the distance. "There's Mr. McMinn there on the boardwalk."

"It's now or never," I say. "Talk to him. We'll plan your wedding later."

She huffs a short laugh, then steps back, smoothing out her dress. I wish I asked her whether me following makes things better or worse, but I stay at my post as she moves toward James.

He sees her, sending a genuine smile as he tips his hat. She looks so young next to him, and it strikes me that if she lived in my world, she'd be sharing my lunch table, discussing cute boys and complaining that teachers are too strict.

But she's not. Clara Castle, for all her sheltered blunders, has far surpassed me in certain areas of growing up. She's a girl, completely new to crushing, much less love. She can't express feelings to the guy she likes. But she can care for a grown man who has lapsed into a terrified child state. She can keep a house impeccably clean, even if she stays awake peering at shadows in the corners because she read a book about vampires. She's never been to school a day in her life, but she's cultivated the ability to ask questions without embarrassment and taught herself to grasp every bit of knowledge that comes her way. And I realize that she doesn't need my help to ask James how best to help her father.

13

CLARA CASTLE
Summer, 1911

"WHY, CLARA CASTLE!"

James relieves me with his greeting, for I had no idea how I should approach him. He takes my hand, kisses it, and says, "You look lovely tonight."

"Thank you," I reply.

"Are you here with your father?" James asks, already searching the crowd.

"Vincent, actually. Though he's left me in Andrew's care while he's gone to fetch a friend."

"That's unfortunate," James says. "I suppose Andrew will be engaged all night. Do you think he'll manage one dance?"

"I don't expect him to," I say, though I very much wish that he could. "But I'm happy enough just being here."

James will understand the implication. Unlike half the town, he knows that I exist, that I don't go to boarding school, and the reason that no one ever sees me is that Father doesn't often allow me outdoors. I wonder if he understands other things about Father too, but tonight he seems more concerned about my social life. "Well, you must have one dance, at least," he says. "Allow me one, and then you can decide who else you'd like to partner with and I'll introduce you. Billy Meyers, perhaps?"

I flinch. He must have talked to Vincent. Or he's as curious as everyone else why the reclusive Castle family invited the Meyers for a dinner party. Even knowing he's eying me for a reaction, I can't keep from grimacing.

"Perhaps not tonight," I say. "But I will accept your dance. I was actually hoping to speak to you. I have a medical question."

"A medical question?" he echoes, looking concerned and intrigued at the same time.

"I know it's not a customary topic for a dance," I say, "but I don't know when I will see you again."

"Is it something you can speak of here?"

I feel my face flush and shake my head. "Oh, it isn't me. It's more about . . . your mother."

I'm not sure it's the best way to start this conversation, but I'm not sure how to proceed in general. James offers his arm. "Walk down the seawall a little ways and I'll see if I can help you."

I glance back toward the pavilion, but Scarlet and Keith aren't watching. James' arm is surprisingly strong beneath his coat, but it feels odd to walk so close to anyone.

"Now what's this about?" he asks.

"Well, I know she suffers from lapses of memory," I begin. "I was wondering if it is possible for a person to have a complete but momentary loss of memory — to the point where they forget how to move or respond in any way."

It's a terrible start. I thought the presentation was good in my head, but now that I'm saying it, it seems absurd. Then again, everything about Father's situation is absurd.

James frowns before replying slowly, "It is possible for a person to stop responding, but I would have to know more to determine the cause."

I knew he would, but I still haven't come up with a good explanation. But I need to know, and I've already perked his curiosity, so I continue, "It would be like if you were speaking to me and something you said upset me. If I suddenly just stood here and didn't respond to anything you did or said, didn't even blink or move, what would you think?"

James laughs a bit. "I would think that you were being overly sensitive and childish, or that I had just been a complete cad and ought to leave you alone." He eyes me, then the pavilion, before adding softly, "And if it happened here, I should think such a reaction would be a response to an insensitivity on my part."

Oh dear. He must suspect I'm somehow referring to Billy. I swallow and try again. "But what if you only made me sad?" I ask. "What if I wanted to respond, but couldn't because I truly couldn't move?"

"Oh," he says in a different voice. "Well, there is a vast difference between a refusal to respond and an inability to do so."

The waves lap against the shore pushing bits of shell forward, then tugging it back into the sea like a cat tormenting its prey.

I watch the bits glint in the sunlight as James continues, "Now, in this scenario where you cannot respond to me, how long would I have to wait before you remembered that I was there?"

"It could be a while," I admit. "Anywhere from three minutes to . . ." I consider every time Father has done this, searching for the longest of his spells, "A few hours?"

"And in all this time, do I see any change in you?"

"No," I answer. "If I were holding anything, I'd still grip it, but wouldn't react if you took it from my hand. You'd have to pry it though. But if you lifted my arms they would very gradually sink."

I've never spoken about this to anyone and the more I describe it, the odder I realize it must be. I want to tell the entire story, but I feel as though if I begin to describe the little quirks about life with Father, I would never stop, for he does act so very odd at times and I know it can't possibly be normal. I know this even before I glimpse the growing puzzlement on James' face, but it's disconcerting all the same.

"And when you did remember me, what would you do?" he asks.

"Nothing," I reply. "I might answer the last question you asked, and then wonder why the hour has gone so late. I might just excuse myself and mope. Or I might just shut myself up again and . . ."

Here I stop because I have no idea what Father does when he shuts himself into his study and orders us to leave him alone. But I suppose it satisfies James because he walks for several minutes before asking, "Coming out or going in — would you ever hurt me?"

I stop, feeling my heart stall. He knows. He must know whom I'm speaking of. But he's gone a completely wrong direction. "Oh no! No, I would never, ever hurt you!"

I say it louder than I intended, and a couple glance over as they pass.

"But would I be afraid of you?" James asks. "Even a little?"

It's not a fair question. I'm afraid of everything, and I'm not here to discuss my feelings toward my father. But I swallow. I'm not afraid of Father. He would never intentionally hurt me but, in some ways, he is damaging my chances of a normal life, of knowing how to navigate people and places out-side the four walls of my home, or even answering this question.

"No," I say. "He's never hurt me." I realize I've replaced myself in this scenario with Father, but it doesn't matter. James knows.

We stand, watching each other's eyes for clues, before he responds slowly. "In that scenario," he says. "I would make a very careful account of when it happens, how often, and the events around it. There is a type of stroke that could cause such a phenomenon, but it would not be my first guess. My first guess — without knowing anything more — would be that it is your mind, not your body, which is troubled."

I told Scarlet that it wasn't an illness, but his words are hardly comforting. I turn my eyes as he continues, "Sometimes when a person has very traumatic memories, they can bring on spells — in this case, overwhelming the mind until it stops all observations of reality because it cannot handle anything more. This, of course, is a theory. It's not really my place to say, since I'm only trained for ailments of the body."

Even with the simplified explanation, I'm glad when he stops talking. Of course, I know that Father's thoughts are sometimes irrational, and he cannot seem to fully control them. I know that his memories drive him to unresponsive stupors, but to hear the scenarios explained by someone who has never witnessed it is frightening

I grip the seawall to keep myself from shaking and just so he won't think that I stopped responding myself, I ask, "So, if you discovered you couldn't help me, what would you do?"

James sighs like he's suddenly debating talking to me at all. "I would watch you and ascertain where else your thoughts were affected. If you showed excessive fear or anger. I would observe how you impact my own life or impair your own. And, because I'm a very young doctor with newfangled ideas, I might have you psychoanalyzed by someone who could help you and possibly take you somewhere where you can receive treatment and live until you were well again."

I asked him to speak, and now I must resist waving at him until he quiets. He can't know the details. Father isn't that ill. But this conversation is confirming what I haven't been willing to consider before now. There is something very wrong and things aren't going to right themselves unless changes are made.

Still, my imagination begins to scold me for telling, imaging James showing up on our doorstep and hauling Father off to an asylum, when it's really only fear that a thunderstorm will turn into another disaster. But these secrets are bubbling up inside of me, and I must speak to someone. Vincent knows, but I cannot tell him how many times it's happened without increasing the tension between him and Father. If Father is to be healed, I must be the one to initiate it.

"One thing I've learned about troubles," James says after a moment, "is that they will steal every moment they can." He holds out his hand with a smile. "Enjoy tonight. Things will keep until morning."

I force a smile and take his hand. I do want to enjoy tonight, without worrying about secrets and a looming catastrophe. But every morning is one day closer to the day I'm dreading. One year, and this man offering his hand will be my lifeline unless I can discover what the danger is and stop it.

14

SCARLET BELDON

Summer, 1911

ANDREW SITS IN THE CENTER OF THE PAVILION, UNAWARE THAT HE'S MY NEXT project. For a guy who just got insulted by a snotty rich kid in front of a girl he likes but can't seem to talk to, he looks remarkably competent. He's turned his attention to the guy in charge, undaunted by the number of song titles being launched at him.

"...starting with Merry Widow's Waltz, then going into the Castle Walk we'll play..."

"What about dancing the Bear?" another guy asks. "There's already been a few requests."

A few of the men's mouths perk at the reddening of the conductor's face. He eyes the boy before stating, "Only traditional dances here."

I settle myself very close to Andrew's feet so I don't trip anyone. Life would be much easier if I could talk to him, but from down here I can see his violin. It's... well, it's old. The other instruments shine with some sort of gloss coating, but Andrew's violin looks like it was carved out of a tree and fixed with strings with only the dullest sheens. In fact, I can see A. C. carved into the back of it, and I wonder if Andrew marked it or if that's his father's initials.

But then he lifts it to his chin, scoots his foot forward, and rams his shoe into my thigh. We both jump and some of the guys laugh as Andrew looks through me, then leans to the side.

"What? Did you sit on a bee?" the cellist teases.

"No, I just..." Andrew trails off, better at covering than I expected him to be. "Just lost my balance."

I scoot forward somewhere where I hope no one will kick me or dance over me.

116

"Miller did that," the cellist continues.

"What?" Andrew asks.

"Sat on a bee." The man waves his bow toward the tables in the lawn of the hotel. "Right in the middle of proposing at that table."

"Well, I hope she said yes," Andrew returns.

"She didn't." The cellist chuckled. "Your girl was pretty. Who is she?"

"That's Clara Castle."

"Is she from Galveston?"

"No. She lives here. She's Edmund Castle's daughter."

The man stares lightly. "Edmund Castle. He lives on Silver Stocking road?"

"He lives on Harbor Avenue," Andrew returns.

"Silver Stocking road," the man replies like they're the same place. "I didn't know he had a daughter. How come I've never seen her?"

"I don't believe they socialize often," Andrew replies.

"They don't," the man replies. "Mr. Castle is an odd man. One day he's as smart as a whip and the next he acts like he's forgotten why he was dropped on this earth. How's the girl? She as addled as her father?"

Andrew glances over. His fingers tighten on the neck of his violin, but his voice doesn't change its controlled, slightly Irishized American accent. "No. Miss Castle is young but very bright."

"Well, she's brightly got her eyes on you," the man counters. "And that Meyers boy's got his eyes brightly on her, so if you're aiming, you'd better shoot soon."

"Yeah, buddy," I add, but Clara's already told off Billy, at least for tonight. Andrew doesn't know that though, and we both swing our eyes toward the boardwalk where she's walking with James. Their steps are sober, and she's got that glazed look like she's warring between acting on whatever she has heard and pretending she never heard it.

Andrew swallows, but the conductor taps his stand and the first dance is underway. I start to get up, then sit back down as James smiles toward Clara, apparently asking her to dance. I'm not sure what this dance is called, but it's structured with no one calling out steps, so I guess you just have to know what you're doing.

Clara looks a bit lost as well, but she's good at following his leading, only laughing when she misjudges James's next step. Better her than me. I'd be a bumbling idiot out there.

I'd half hoped to dance but as the dancers sweep by, I pull my heels onto the platform, feeling like I'm stuck in the middle of a racetrack, and content myself with waving as Clara goes by.

Vincent must be back, because I see Keith darting through twirling couples, trying to make his way to me.

He plops beside me, panting. "So what's the medical term for 'trampled by waltzers?'"

I shrug. "I have no idea, but welcome to the oasis. Stay away from feet. Andrew's already kicked me once."

He throws me a side glance. "Clara's boyfriend is playing footsy with you, huh?"

I huff a laugh. "Shut up." Then watch another pair sweep by. "Can you imagine people still dancing like this?"

"No." He shakes his head. "The only thing people do on this pier anymore is fish. "

I meant in general, but somehow I know my morning runs on the seawall are always going to be overshadowed by the ghosts of dancers over this spot.

"Where is Vincent?" I ask.

Keith snorts a laugh. "He's kissing in the car. I didn't really want to watch the 1911 make out session, so I came ahead."

"Grandma and Grandpa getting it on, huh?" I ask.

"We don't know that they end up together," Keith reminds me.

"With that letter, I'd say the chances are pretty high," I reply, pointing at Clara sweeping by with the doctor. "That's James. They already talked, and she looked pretty upset. What are we going to do if we can't save her father?"

Keith lets out a slow breath. "Well, I mean, I don't want him to die but..."

"But what?"

He watches his hands as he speaks because he doesn't have the guts to look at either me or Clara. "Worst case scenario, he dies. Maybe Clara loses her home. But then she's free. I mean, her dad does need help, but Clara needs out, especially if we really are dealing with some sort of mental illness."

"But Vincent says he was alone," I say.

"He said he was coming alone. If a fallout with his dad is the only reason that he leaves in the first place, what's going to keep them from reuniting with each other?"

I nod. "Our long-term answer is sitting behind us. We need to focus on getting her with Andrew."

"Why?" Keith asks, like an idiot.

"Because they love each other," I say. "And Andrew's — good. He's not going to let her struggle on her own. He's not like the guys now."

"Wow, ouch?" Keith says. "Don't lump us all together."

"Sorry," I say, rubbing my arms. "I was five when I saw Dad kissing another woman. I told Mom, and she said it didn't mean anything. That sometimes men kissed women just to remember that they'd married the right one, and he'd always be my daddy."

"Hmm," Keith says, because there isn't really a good response for that kind of confession.

"I never told anybody that," I say. "Don't share."

"Who would I share with?" Keith asks. "I'm not exactly teeming with friends." After a moment when all we can hear is the cheerful melody behind us, he asks, "How's Kate doing?"

I shrug. "She has a roof over her head. I still need to pay you back for that."

"Don't worry about it," Keith says. "Some of us 'guys now' still like taking care of girls when they let us."

The song ends, and I duck as Andrew lowers his bow, nearly clobbering me and saving me from having to respond to Keith's barb.

"We need to move," Keith says, but as we stand, he points to the entrance where Vincent is walking in with a girl on his arm. She looks like a princess with feathers set against gleaming dark hair, but her movements are free, swinging her free arm.

"Clara!" Vincent calls as James releases her.

Clara turns toward them, smiling though her eyes waver a bit.

"This is Anne," Vincent says.

He barely gets her name out before Anne pulls Clara into a hug.

"Clara! I'm so glad to meet finally you. I wasn't sure I'd get a chance after all. Vincent drives like a bat out of Hell."

"It's true," Keith says.

I drop my head back and laugh. "He's probably trying to get her into his lap."

Vincent tugs at his suit coat like a boy admitting to a broken window. "Couldn't help it. I was distracted."

"You'll be more distracted if you ruin Grandfather's car," Clara chides.

"It's true," Anne says. "Not to worry, darling. Next time I'll drive and make sure we arrive safely."

"You can't drive, can you?" Clara asks.

"I can," Anne says. "I've got a license and everything."

"It's gone to her head," Vincent replies. "Now she thinks she can vote like a man too."

Anne slaps his arm. "No 'think.' I'm going to."

Clara laughs a little bewilderingly, like she's not sure if the girl is joking or not.

Vincent huffs a sigh, though his eyes are sparkling too much to make his despair believable. "Well, what in the world are you going to need me for if you can do it all yourself?"

"Not much," Anne pats his arm. "Just stand there and look pretty. That's what we do."

"And so it begins," Keith whispers, and I slap his arm.

"I guess we know why Vincent hasn't introduced her to daddy yet," I whisper back.

Clara hears and raises her eyebrows in agreement.

"Say," says Vincent, wrapping his arm around Anne's waist. "What are the chances we can bribe the orchestra into playing a Tango? Maybe you can get Andrew to put in a good word."

"A what?" Clara laughs, again out of her element.

"Don't worry," Vincent says. "I'll teach it to you later, and then you can teach Andrew."

"Does he always tease you like this?" Anne asks.

"Fairly often," Clara eyes Vincent who's still chuckling at his own joke. "But I usually know what he's talking about."

"The Tango is a new dance, currently forbidden," Anne says, throwing a side look at Vincent. "Tell me, which dances do you know? The Bunny Hug?"

Clara shakes her head.

"Grasshopper? Cakewalk?"

When Clara continues to wince and shake her head, Anne sighs. "Oh dear. We do need to catch you up. What about the waltz?"

"I know that one!" Clara replies quickly.

"I don't," I mumble. "I don't know any of those."

"I've never heard of most of them. What's with the animal names?" Keith whispers.

I shrug as another, livelier song starts.

"This is the Castle Walk," Anne says. "Watch it. We'll teach it to you soon, and you'll be dancing every dance."

Clara nods and steps toward us as the couple join the others in a stately dance that looks like they're just walking to the music.

I step closer to Clara so she can see me without turning her head. "How's the punch?"

She laughs. "I haven't tasted it."

"You should do that," I say.

I want to ask about her dad, but I don't want to make her sad again right in the middle of the party and that's too much talking for her to pull off to an invisible friend anyway.

She moves toward the refreshment table, turning her back to the majority of the room where we can speak a little easier The punch looks like lemonade with added oranges. I watch her mouth turn down as she takes a glass.

Since she's frowning anyway, I ask, "What's wrong?"

I'm expecting something about her dad, but she stalls with the ladle. "I don't like being ignorant."

I know what she means, and worse, I can't even tell her it's not true. "It's not really your fault," I say. "You'll learn. You have a lot of people looking out for you. That means a lot."

Clara glares at the liquid streaming into a crystal cup. "That only means they think I don't know any better and can't do things for myself."

"So prove them wrong," I counter. "Decide on something you want and make it happen."

She swallows and eyes her cup so long that I wonder if she's going to throw it, drink it, or cry. But when the song ends, she turns on her heels and carries it toward the orchestra. Keith and I pull away from each other as we exchanged amused wide-eyes.

"Well...that works," I say. I take a step, but Keith grabs my hand.

"No, leave them alone," he says.

"But..."

"Scarlet." He steps in front to block me. "Nobody wants to kiss on their first date while their parents are watching."

He has a point, but I really, really want to see how this goes down. "But..."

"You just told her to prove that she doesn't need help. Don't turn around and act like she does."

I sigh. "Fine."

I'll ask the juicy details later. Or snoop in her journal. I haven't found it in my time, but I know she keeps one. And looking at her future to make sure all is well gives me the perfect excuse to catch up on her past.

"We're not really people," I say. "We're like their guardian angels." When Keith raises a skeptical brow, I shrug with a smile. "It's true."

"You know what I think?" he asks after a moment. "I think you're so focused on getting Clara to fall in love because you're afraid to do it yourself."

Excuse me, what does he know about my love life?

I step away so I can glare at him better. "I don't need to fall in love. Clara does. It's not fair that she can't live life on her own if she wants to, but she can't. So she needs someone who is kind and gentle and loyal."

"But you don't?" Keith asks.

"No," I say. "I'd like that, and maybe someday I will fall in love. But I'm not banking on it. It's possible to live a perfectly happy life as a single woman, and I'm going to do it until I meet somebody whom I feel would be an asset. But so far..."

I trail off, but Keith presses. "So far what?"

I know what he's pushing, and it isn't fair. If I say "So far all I've met are irresponsible jerks," he's going to remind me that I can't go lumping all men together just because my dad believes that all women live in a giant revolving door.

I feel my jaw clench to one side before I shrug to cover my twitching throat. "So far I'm okay being alone."

"Fair enough," he says. "But we came to a dance. So I think we ought to dance at least once just to say we did. And you can't dance alone." He holds out his hand. "I promise not to kiss you."

I eye him, letting suspicions show clearly on my face.

"I've got a 'maybe' back home," I say, though Blake can hardly be called that. I haven't written or heard from him in weeks.

Keith shrugs, then looks around at the dancers. "I don't think anyone here is going to tell."

"Just so we're clear," I say.

But dancing sounds fun and I think we were planning on doing that all along, so I take his hand. We keep to the outskirts, spinning in awkward steps that keep halting as we try to find the beat again. We step on each other's feet way too much for any inkling of romantic hope to stay.

Halfway through, we're collapsing against each other in laughter. We're back to being friends, and that's exactly how things should be.

"I suck at this," Keith moans.

"Yeah, you do," I say.

And Clara, who is currently sitting without a partner, bursts into a laugh and looks away, chewing her lip in an effort to look sane.

"It's not your fault," Keith says. "Something is in the punch."

Billy's suit brushes Keith's tuxedo as the guy passes with determined strides toward Clara.

"He's going to ask her to dance," Keith says.

"Seriously?" I spin, then growl. "Oh no, he's not."

The dude is walking fast, but I dodge Vincent and Anne spinning in a circuit and stick my foot in Billy's path. It hurts like nobody's business, but it works. Billy sprawls onto the floor, landing in a series of thuds that attracts glances from all over the room.

"Scarlet, what was that?" Keith calls. He jerks me away as Clara gasps and jumps to her feet. "Gah, you are a man-hater, aren't you?"

"Trust me, he deserves it," I growl. "He's awful."

He's also red-faced. Clara sits down as quickly as he scrambles onto his feet, glancing around as he straightens his coat. Clara, being the nice girl that she is, grips her hands and pretends she didn't see anything.

Billy takes one step toward her, then stops and sways. I see his breath shake and remind myself of what he said about Andrew so I don't feel sorry for him. But Clara throws a monkey wrench into the 'fix her up with Andrew and only Andrew' plan and stands, approaching Billy on her own.

"I'm sorry about what I said earlier," she says, as I slap my forehead. "I know you meant well."

Billy's shoulders collapse in relief. "I didn't realize you knew him."

"Yeah, you did," I say.

It's like a slow motion moment in a horrible movie when he holds out his hand. "Let me make it up to you?"

Clara hesitates, then takes his hand with a brave smile. I collapse, folding my arms. "He had to pick a slow dance to make it up to her?"

"Scarlet," Keith says. "Why are you so worried?"

"I'm not worried, I'm just mad," I snap. "I'm mad that she doesn't have her own voice. That she can't just tell them all to jump in the bay and become an astronaut."

"Why does she have to?" Keith asked. "I mean, if Clara wants to go to school or take a career, she should be able to. Anne should be able to vote. But what if she doesn't want to? What if she really does just want to marry and have a family? Isn't that okay too?"

"If that's what she wants," I say. "I don't care what she does, as long as she chooses it."

"Then why don't you let her make up her own mind?" Keith asks.

"Doesn't mean I can't be mad that she's dancing with a guy she doesn't like," I say.

Keith chuckles. "Why not? You did."

And then we look away from each other while I try to decide whether or not I actually do like Keith. I turn toward him. "So what do you want to do? Since we're plotting out life goals here. You don't want to mow lawns. What do you want to do?"

Keith takes a breath. "Honestly? I kind of want to go into architecture."

"Why don't you?"

He glances across to Andrew. "You got to mow a lot of lawns to go to college. We don't all have wealthy benefactors show up out of nowhere."

"But I found scholarships you could get," I say.

Keith winces. "Scholarships are for smart people. So is architecture for that matter."

"You're smart," I say. "You just have to decide what you want to do and stick to it."

"You know what's really weird to think?" Keith asks.

"What?"

"That every choice you make, everything you decide to stand or not stand for, every person you marry or don't marry, affects generations of people that you will never, ever know."

"True," I say, watching Clara and Billy part on better terms than they started. It also makes me worry just a bit about changing history.

"I'm going to go," Keith says.

"Why?" I ask. "No time is passing."

"I know. But they don't need me here."

By 'me,' I know he means 'us,' but I'm not ready to go. I want to see Clara after the party. But Keith's right. Clara doesn't need moral support or even guardian angels. She needs room to breathe. So I stand as she curtsies. Keith and I wave as I mouth, "See you tomorrow."

Tomorrow—which could be next week for her—when we're going to see what James said about Edmund. But for tonight, she catches my wave from the corner of her eye. She smiles, sends us a short nod and then turns back to the party to fly solo.

CLARA CASTLE
Summer, 1911

Dear Scarlet,

I am well. I have become so worried of late that your father decided to leave the house and I may never see you again. There is so much to tell you, but I don't trust it to writing. It's morning. These days, both Vincent and Andrew drag themselves down to a late breakfast. Poor Andrew doesn't even arrive home until after midnight. Sometimes when I can't sleep, I'll hear the screen door slam and him trudge up the stairs.

I hope when he returns home, he'll be able to go to sleep far earlier. He talks more of his family these days, funny things his siblings do and how hard his father works. He won't say it, but I know he's becoming excited to return home, though I must admit I'm dreading it. I'm going to miss him and haven't any idea when I will see him again. It could be Christmas. At least Vincent is finished with school, so I won't be alone anymore. Will I?

We have nine months left. I keep telling myself that history can be changed since it hasn't happened yet. Just because you saw something horrible, doesn't mean I have to live it. Father is only stressed, but things will get better. Vincent is struggling with the transition home again, but he can adapt. Andrew can prove to Grandfather that his family won't hold him back. That there is no shame in being Irish.

I'm worried though, Scarlet. Was it a mistake, do you think, for Andrew to choose returning to visit his family instead of traveling with Grandfather? Suppose Grandfather decides not to let him *return to school? He wouldn't do that, surely, simply because Andrew wants to visit his family? Even if he did, Andrew could continue working here. So what happens to him, Scarlet? Why isn't he mentioned in Vincent's letter?*

I set down the pen and blow against the ink, unsure I want the writing to stay. Having Scarlet read my letters has made me second-guess what I write now, wondering who will end up seeing it. I sigh and walk to the stove, shoving the paper into the coals. Scarlet is not the only snoop. Vincent is worse and there is no way to explain this letter, should he discover it. And then I feel very glad I did, for Andrew walks into the room, shrugging one arm through his coat, though his free hand is restricted by the mail.

"Clara, there is a letter for you," he says.

"A letter!" Scarlet flashes into my mind first, but it's Grandfather's hand-writing. It would be silly to receive a letter from her in the post anyway. When I take the envelope, my fingers brush Andrew's and I back up quickly.

"Thank you. Did he send you one?"

"Yes." He smiles, but it looks strained. Or perhaps he's only tired.

"He's in England now?" I ask, trying to draw out the conversation.

Andrew nods. "He says he's already made arrangements for me to play on winter break. That he'd just as soon get me a tutor if our stay should exceed the beginning of school, especially now that Vincent has returned here."

"Oh," I say.

England. Vincent didn't mention Andrew because he's traveling in England with Grandfather. Surely, that must be it.

I let out my breath. "To play around Europe? Your father's going to be so proud."

Andrew flinches before he tucks the letter into his pocket. "I hope so," he whispers.

"You're going to become a musician," I say. "You'll be able to arrange to see them. You'll probably end up playing in New York as well, and then they could come to the performance."

Andrew stills with his hand on the glass. "They wouldn't let my family in, Clara."

"But, surely if you were..." I trail off, because he's already shaking his head. "No?"

"No," he says. But then he smiles and steps back. "I must go. Enjoy your letter."

"Andrew," I speak as he reaches the door. "Your father would still be proud of you."

"Thank you," he whispers.

I wait until I hear the front screen slam, wondering why Andrew feels it's more important to play on a hotel porch for pay, than travel and create a reputation. But how can I possibly come to any conclusion? Even with Andrew's descriptions of New York, I cannot picture it in my head. And I think he's left a lot out, the way that Father omits me from any financial talk, and Vincent won't tell me what's gotten him out of sorts. I truly make the worst sort of detective and it's no wonder we haven't made any progress on diverting unknown disasters.

I set my face in my hand, wishing I hadn't burned the letter to Scarlet. Grandfather's letter is identical to almost every other he's sent in the past. I used to read them over and over, trying to imagine traveling with him and seeing all the things he describes. But I frown at the animated, cheerful language. I'm sure he is having a nice time, but I feel the sting of being protected when what I really want to know is how he's feeling about traveling alone while we are all together here.

Vincent's footsteps are quicker than I have heard them in a while when he pops into the kitchen. "Anything for me?"

I shake my head. "Why? Are you waiting for a love letter?"

"Good heavens, no, though I wouldn't mind one. But Anne hates writing as much as I do. I wish we had a telephone," he says.

I shouldn't tease him, but I can't resist. "Can you imagine," I ask, "what would happen if you had a tiny telephone that fit into your pocket?"

Vincent stalls with his hand on the pump, throwing me an inquisitive glance. "You have been inside too long, my dear." But then he thinks about it and replies, "It would be a useless contraption without being hooked to a line."

"What if it didn't have to be hooked to a line?" I ask. "What if your voice could travel through the air?"

"Where do you come up with these ideas?" Vincent asks.

I giggle. "Just curious."

"Vincent!" Father's voice bleeds anger, making both of us jump. Vincent swings bewildered eyes toward me, then steps to the door where Father practically plows into him. They stumble away from each other, but Father hardly notices before he demands, "What boards did you order for Mr. Harris?"

"Two by six, center match like Mr. Harris wrote," Vincent replies. "Why?"

Father stares lightly. "What was Mr. Harris building?"

"An outhouse," Vincent says.

"And where on an outhouse are you going to find an entire wagonload of center matched floorboards?"

"Oh," Vincent says. He brushes his hair back and blows out a breath. "But it said center, so that was the only thing I could think of that..."

"It said 'cinder,' Vincent," Father says. "Not 'center.' Twelve years in school, and you still can't read? What have they been teaching you all this time?"

"You know I'm terrible filling out orders, Father!" Vincent's voice is rising, and I can't tell if the color in his face is humiliation or anger.

"Well, you'd better become good at it!" Father snaps, shoving a handful of papers into Vincent's chest. "You're going to sit down and check these orders and recalculate all of the numbers until you are sure they are right, and God help you if any more deliveries are botched. And when you find someone who's building a house, let me know so I can sell these."

I watch the color from my tea swirl around the bottom of the cup, afraid to move or breath. From the corner of my eye, I see Hannah hover near the doorway, then step out of sight. Vincent's eyes stay on Father's buttons, but his jaw is tightening.

Don't argue. Don't argue. I chant silently as if I think hard enough, my thoughts will transfer to Vincent's head. Perhaps it works, because his eyes move toward me.

His body is rigid, but he wets his lips, then steps back. It was a mistake, but he must understand the magnitude of the implications.

"Yes, sir," he says. "But maybe you'd better put me somewhere else in your company."

"You'll be taking over the company," Father says. "You have to learn every aspect of it. You can't be sloppy, and you can't be lazy!"

"I don't want it!" Vincent snaps. "I don't want to work with numbers and wood. I want to work with words and people!"

I glance over, but neither man notices me. Father's glaring, though I see a glimmer of hurt in his eyes.

"What are you saying?" he asks, though I feel sure that he knows exactly what Vincent is saying.

Vincent raises his chin. "I've applied for a position at the paper."

"The paper?" Father echoes and for a moment, he's too bewildered to stay angry. "A paper coming out once a week? How do you expect to make a living from that?"

"Here would just be a start," Vincent says. "I don't want to stay here forever. I'd like to go back to Galveston and work as a journalist."

Father's lips grow as white as his face, and my own heart slams.

"You can't leave!" I blurt.

Vincent turns his head to soberly appraise me. "That's why I applied here. To start."

He isn't going to stay. If he ever owns the lumber mill, it will be little more than a business investment. And a reporter? He'd be good at the job with his love of people and places, but a reporter doesn't seem a very respectful sort of job. He's staying for me, I know, but why hasn't he told me any of this? How am I to stop him from leaving when he's already planning on it?

"Well, who in blazes am I building up the mill for?" Father shouts.

"I don't know, Father," Vincent says. "You, I suppose. You could leave it to Clara, since you clearly intend to keep her caged here her entire life. Lord knows she has nothing else to do."

Father's hand flashes out so quickly that I hear the slap before I even realize it happened. Vincent stumbles back, covering his cheek with his hand as I stand. Their eyes are locked and the only movement comes from heaving chests and shaking breaths.

Father has never hit us, not like this. He drops his eyes, perhaps as startled as us, but instead of apologizing, he says in the calculating tone that I hate so much, "You are my son. Even if you work for a paper, you will not back down from the mill. And you will never, never speak to me that way again. Do you understand?"

"Vincent," I whisper.

Vincent ignores me, ignores that if he estranges himself from Father, he'll cut all ties with me. "If you ever hit me again," he says, "I will never speak to you at all."

The threat switches the emotions in the room. The rage drains from Father's eyes, leaving a dull light of pain. His hand clenches loosely at his side.

"Please, stop," I repeat, loudly enough that it gains both of their attention. "We need each other. We all need each other. Father's right. The newspaper won't be enough work, but you could do both."

Vincent's shoulders sink as he lets out a silent breath that tells me that I'm missing the entire point. But I'm not. This is the start of the path none of us can afford to take and there's no reason why they can't compromise.

"I want those orders finished by morning," Father says, before he retreats to his study.

I let my head fall against my fingers, blowing out a slow breath. Vincent crushes the papers, storming away with enough muttering that I feel he's going to spend a good portion of the next hour simply calming down enough to see straight.

And that's when I hear the music I've been listening for all week. Forgetting to grasp the railing, I rush upstairs to quiet the music box before someone realizes it's playing on its own will.

"Please work, please work," I whisper, and this time the box yields to prayer. I've never been so glad to see the other version of my house with the creaking floorboards and faded walls.

"You!" Scarlet calls. "I've been dying to know all night. How was it? Did you dance anymore?"

Dance? The dance was a week ago, currently so far from my mind that I blink in confusion, but my face must look as tight as it feels because Scarlet pulls back and loses her grin.

"What's the matter?" she asks.

I've never been very good at talking when I want to cry, and the moment I even take a breath to respond, the tears begin and I'm sobbing into my hands.

"Clara!" She rubs my shoulder, asking over and over, "What's the matter?"

I shake my head, trying to convey that I cannot answer yet. But what do I tell her? She doesn't know our story — not our full story — and she'll jump to conclusions that aren't true.

"You're in my time now," she says. "You're safe."

I don't feel safe.

"They're fighting," I choke. "They're already arguing."

"Hey." Her voice becomes firmer as she shakes my shoulder. "Look at me." When I do, she continues, "My dad and I fight all the time, okay? I call him all kinds of horrible names and tell him I want to leave, but I haven't. We make up. We move on."

I've never fought with my father. Not once. I can't imagine even protesting, much less provoking him.

"Does he hit you?" I ask.

"Uh, no." Scarlet frowns. "Why? Did he hit you?"

I shake my head, flinching because I really wanted to know if that was normal, but it's apparently not.

"Vincent?" she asks.

I've never been slapped. I have no idea how badly it hurts, but I know how loud it was and how quickly Vincent's face changed colors. He's planning on slipping out to see Anne tonight. I wonder if he's going to have fingerprints on his face.

I nod, trying to shake the memory from my head before it embeds itself there. "He should have stayed quiet. He knows better."

Scarlet stares. "What happened?"

"He told Father that he didn't want to inherit the mill. He wants to be a reporter."

"So your father slapped him?" Scarlet asked.

"No. Father slapped him because..."

Because Vincent accused him of keeping me locked up. I drop my eyes. "It wasn't what he said, it was how he said it. Father wouldn't have punished him if he hadn't been so belligerent."

"Whoa, whoa," Scarlet waves her hands between us. "Stop there. Okay. Clara. If your dad is hitting your brother, there is a problem."

There is a problem. Vincent knows better than to push Father past his patience. He also knows that Father has been struggling, both with the mill and with his mind lately. He has no excuse to so suddenly crush every dream Father's ever had of working with him and then announce that he's going to leave us for a job that isn't even respectable.

"He didn't hit him, he slapped him," I mumble. "It was just discipline."

"Slapping isn't discipline," Scarlet repeats.

I realize I'm clenching my skirt, but I simply watch the material fold between my fingers. "But it's never right to disobey your father."

She stares at me. "How do you figure?"

I sigh, realizing again how drastically different our worlds are. I don't think there is any way that I could explain that Scarlet could understand. I glance toward the door, wondering if her father is close enough to hear us.

Scarlet reaches for my hand, climbing to her feet. "Come on. Let's go to the bay."

I'm not allowed to go to the bay. I keep telling her I can't leave the house. But Father's not here, and I don't want her accusing him of keeping me caged as Vincent has. It isn't true. I'm not locked up anywhere. I choose to stay in because Father prefers it.

But today I choose to prove that I can leave so I follow her downstairs, wincing at the mess on the dining room table. It only takes a few minutes to walk to the bay, but it's stressful with the automobiles driving by at much greater speeds, pounding out music that vibrates the ground.

An arm extends from the window as a man calls to us as they pass. I can't understand what he says over the music, but Scarlet sends a black glare after him, hissing, "Oh, come on!"

I realize that I'm still in my day dress, the one Hannah and I made from gray material that Father picked out. She had her doubts that it would make a nice garment, but I rather like it. I suppose Scarlet gives up on me talking, because as we near the jetties and pick our way across the rocks, she restarts the conversation on her own.

"Sometimes people make mistakes," she says carefully. "If they do, you have the right to stand up for yourself and protest."

"You can, but you are to respect your father," I say. "He is the head of the household and has the final word."

"Well, if you're going with that logic, you're gonna be miserable," Scarlet says. "Are you going to spend the rest of your life doing stuff you don't want to, just because Daddy says so?"

I rub my eye. "I don't know."

"No." Scarlet jolts and takes my shoulders. "You're not. You're going to marry Andrew, and you're going to end up living happily ever after and whatever happens to your father and brother is up to them."

I'm trying to listen, but I'm still caught up in thoughts of marrying Andrew. Ahead of us, seagulls run a few steps, lifting their wings in preparation for flight. Poor things, they have no idea they're not in any sort of danger from us.

"Andrew's already taking care of his family," I say.

From here I can see the porch of the hotel where, sometime in 1911, Andrew is probably playing. The hotel has changed its name to the Luther Hotel, but it still stands with palm trees that line a circular drive. The porch has shrunk, seating guests with no idea that 100 years is the only barrier that separates them from beautiful music.

Talking about Andrew's family feels like a betrayal, but Scarlet already knows his situation, so I continue, "His family can scarcely make ends meet as it is. Even if they could, Father would never consent to a marriage."

"Andrew could manage," Scarlet says. "And you can help him. If he's really taking care of all these people, who's taking care of him?"

I flinch. I don't even like to think about that. Andrew is the type to run himself into the ground, taking on far more responsibility than belongs to him. But Scarlet truly doesn't understand my culture.

"Every man marrying the daughter of a gentleman is expected to bring money into the marriage. He must prove that he can support her," I say. "Father would be considered cruel to let me marry a man who might let me starve."

"What are you talking about? Andrew won't let you starve!" Scarlet stares, like starving isn't a very real danger. Perhaps not in her world, and perhaps not yet in mine. But I remember Andrew when I first met him and somewhere in New York, there are at least eleven other people who are still as gaunt as he was then.

"You and I know he would deny himself before he let me go hungry," I say. "But Father doesn't. Father thinks that Andrew is only living well because he's in Grandfather's good graces and, once Grandfather grows weary or irritated with him, he'll be right back to where he started." She looks away. "Honestly, I'm not sure it's not true. Grandfather can be very thoughtless when things don't go the way he wants. If Andrew does choose to retain his family's name, I'm not sure Grandfather will forgive him."

"Why not?" Scarlet mutters. "He forgave your mother for marrying your father. Did your father come with loads of money to buy his permission?"

I flinch. "My mother had plenty of money on her own. The Great Storm took my father's business, but he was doing quite well for himself. Even now, Father's business is struggling, but that's only because of the fire. The lumberyard is always in demand and if Vincent insists on walking away from it, he is being very foolish, for in a few years, it should do very well."

"I'm sure your father means well," Scarlet says quietly. "Maybe he really does think he's protecting you by keeping you inside all day and bullying Vincent into a job that he doesn't want. But why can't he teach Vincent to run his own business if he knows so much about it? Why won't he let you learn the skills you need to create your own life, instead of trying to keep you in the one he makes for you?"

How can I explain to her that my life is not so different than other girls? Many girls in my world don't attend school. Perhaps they leave the house more than I do, but they don't run alone to the beach to lay mostly naked on the sand like some of the girls we are passing. I avert my eyes to the cut rocks beneath my boots.

"I know he seems strict to you, but my father is a gentleman," I begin. "Perhaps his mind is not quite normal, but his expectations for us are not so very different than any other gentleman. Any gentleman guides his family, looking out for their best interest and welfare. He is firm and kind. He demands respect and does not condone disorderly behavior, but that does not mean that he is cruel."

Scarlet plops onto a rock at the end of the jetties. "So in other words, he's the big boss everyone obeys while he does whatever he wants."

"No." I lower myself onto the edge beside her, choosing my words carefully. "In being in authority, he has a greater responsibility to monitor his own behavior and see that his family is happy."

She glances toward me as I sit on the cleanest rock I can see. "Are you happy, Clara?"

"No," I answer, honestly. "But if my father did not suffer from his mind, I think I could be."

"But there is something wrong with his mind," Scarlet says. "And even if there wasn't, nobody should be given complete control over anyone."

"And yet, you try to control everyone," I say softly. "You show your father no respect. You order him around like a spoiled child. You tell him what you are doing and where you are going, instead of requesting his permission."

Scarlet turns her head to stare at me, but I see anger glimmer in her eyes. "My dad can be cool and he can be a jerk, but I'm not gonna act like he's the greatest thing since cheesecake, just because he's my dad. People have to be accountable to other people and treat them well."

But that's my entire point. I'm not sure I want to risk angering her, but in some ways, Scarlet is as controlling as my father, even to Keith and I. But she has brought up her father, so I continue, "You don't treat him well. You act as though he is the child, and you are the parent."

"Well, sometimes I feel like that." Scarlet huffs a breath and looks away. "I'm the responsible one and he's goofing off, but guess what? He'd still be goofing off, no matter what I did. I'm not going to run and kiss him when he gets home from work just because he decided to jack around with mom."

I shrink a little, swallowing as her voice rises. I don't say anything, but she continues anyway.

"You're stupid, Clara," she says, "and you can't even see it. How can you treat anyone with respect when they're controlling you? You've made your father into a tyrant. If he can get away with treating people like crap, he's going to treat them like crap until somebody forces him to deal with his mental issues. That's all there is to it."

Now tears spill, and a fisherman glances over at us. I think about Father dragging that piano through the door just because he thought it would please me. About when he kisses my forehead and every night he used to tuck me beneath the covers because Mother wasn't there to do it. I remember his clumsy attempts at retelling the stories she had entertained us with each night. And sometimes when I cried for her, he would hold me and he cried too.

"Father's not a tyrant," I say. "He really is trying. It's only the strain that's bringing out his worst side."

"No," Scarlet answers firmly. "Either your father can control his actions and he's making awful decisions, or he truly can't control himself and he's desperately sick. You can't put the responsibility for his actions onto you or Vincent."

I forget about our disagreement, Vincent's anger; everything, except the conversation I've been trying to avoid all week. "He's sick, Scarlet," I whisper, pulling my knees to my chest and watching a pelican dive into the water. "Even James said that the trouble is with his mind, and there is nothing a physician can do about it."

I don't want to tell her the rest. That he thinks Father ought to be psychoanalyzed and perhaps locked away. Father has spells, even drastic moods, but he's not incapacitated. And he's not the tyrant Scarlet makes him out to be. I don't want to keep talking about him until she lets go of this silly idea that he's some sort of monster, but the words and worry spill out anyway.

"But how could he be treated?" I ask. "When he's back to normal, he won't believe that he is ill. And he's not going to pay for his own treatment for something he doesn't realize he's doing. I haven't any money. We can't ask Grandfather, even if he did offer to help. I don't believe he would anyway because he and Father had never liked each other to begin with."

Scarlet sighs. We're never going to agree about Father, but even so, for all her cleverness and education and pluck, she doesn't have any better answer than I do. So we sit quietly, watching the sun sink behind the water and end another day of the future.

16

SCARLET BELDON

Summer, 2012

"I WAS JUST CALLING TO SEE HOW YOU WERE," SHERRI SAYS. HER VOICE sounds a little like a video game over the phone. She'd freak out so bad if she could see me right now. I've discovered two places in the house where the phone won't drop. The first is sitting in the bathtub, which ends up being a little awkward when Dad has guests over. The second is sitting on the loft outside of Edmund's old bedroom with my legs dangling over the edge and the phone tilted at a precise angle.

I peer at the ground a story below as I answer, "I'm okay. Pissed at Dad, but that's nothing new."

I'm really pissed at the moment because Melinda stopped by with a bucket of bait ten minutes ago, and her car is still running on the edge of the front road.

"Well, try to get along with him," Sherri says, because she's oblivious to the make out session on the lawn. "Being angry only makes you miserable. It won't change things."

"I know. I just don't like thinking of you struggling," I say.

"We're fine. We've been on our own before. We can do it again." Sherri's voice trembles before it grows falsely bright. "So, Kate told me you went to the movies with someone."

"Yeah," I answer easily, already feeling my inner shield lifting. "I have a friend. Imagine that."

"Tell me about him."

"Mmm." I lean forward to peer along the side of the house where Melinda's taillights still glow. "His name is Keith, and he mows our lawn. He wants to be an architect, and he likes old buildings, and history, and weird stuff."

"Sounds like a nice boy," she says, before adding the universally important question. "Is he cute?"

"Yeah, kinda," I admit.

"Do you like him?" Sherri pries.

"I don't know," I answer truthfully. "I don't *dislike* him."

Sherri laughs. "Well, that's a promising start, coming from you."

"Ouch," I say, though I have been wondering if I'm not a bit too hard on men in general.

When I hear the music box, it almost startles me. I glance back toward the screen that I used as a door. "Mom, I have to go. I'll call you later, okay?"

"Okay," she answers, like she thinks I'm just avoiding admitting to a crush. "I love you, sweetie."

"I love you, too." I close my eyes because the words make my heart hurt.

I hang up, then clamber through the window to run down the hall. I reach the box when it's around three notes away from winding down, only glimpsing Clara before the music wavers and stops. I wind it again, letting it play, but Clara doesn't come forward. I hold it while it plays, frowning at the wall as it turns into her world, then mine, then blends in sort of a compromise. I see Clara's wallpaper, but I can also see a translucent outline of Melinda's car.

"Weird," I whisper.

The hall is empty, but I still sneak to peek into Clara's room. The bed stands in the same place. My things are strewn across her quilted bedspread in a blurred collage. I hear the car ding as Melinda lingers near her open door, keeping her keys in like she's intending to leave. But I also hear voices downstairs and the clink of china.

I start to call Clara's name before I catch my own words, clamping them back into my mouth. The hallway is darker than it should be with that sunlight coming through the window. I peer outside, glimpsing Clara's moon trailing my sun.

Her little tree is shivering in the wind, bent double by random gusts of wind, while its older and wiser self sits stoically shading Dad as he presses Melinda against her car with his lips locked across hers.

I close my eyes and turn away, willing myself to go fully into Clara's time, but when I turn into the kitchen she's literally walking through my stove to set the kettle onto hers. She smooths her nightdress before she kneels down to open the side door and stoke the coals.

"I'm sure he'll be fine, Father," she says. "He's probably still waiting for the rain to stop. Or perhaps he stopped by to hear Andrew play. They wouldn't continue playing if there were truly any danger, even under the pavilion."

Edmund shifts from one foot to another as he looks out the window. "Vincent isn't afraid of storms," he says. "He should be, but he's not."

"No, but he might be very much afraid of ruining Grandfather's car," Clara says. "The roads will be swamped and he wouldn't want to slide into a ditch. Truly, I feel that he's all right." When her father doesn't move, she sighs and walks to the table, passing me like I'm not there.

"Clara?" I whisper.

Clara spoons dried leaves from a tin into an infuser, adding water and watching it turn colors. She blinks quickly, then turns back. "Please sit down. We can wait up together until the boys return."

She can't see me. Panic swells. I'm halfway in my world and halfway in hers. Can Dad see me? I want to run out to the car just to assure myself I haven't literally disappeared off of the earth, but a flash of lightning sends Edmund stumbling away from the window.

"Father, please!" Clara flings the kettle back onto the stove and steps toward the man, taking his arm. "Please, come sit down and don't work yourself into a stew."

Or a freeze, I think.

But Edmund takes her arm, and when his eyes fall he looks completely sane—and sad. "I'm all right," he says, then jolts. "I need to wind the clock."

He passes Clara, who closes her eyes. I reach for her shoulder, but the screen door slams behind me, and I spin without making contact.

"Scar?" Dad's voice bellows through the hall.

I jump, but Clara doesn't react. Rushing into the dining room, I hold my breath as Dad brushes within an inch of Edmund, who is winding the clock with a key. Thunder booms, shaking the house beneath everyone except Dad. Edmund's hands clamp across his ears.

Dad cocks his head. "You okay?"

I snap my eyes from Edmund, who's hunching like his brain is exploding, to Dad's amused grin. I know my eyes are wide, but this is so bizarre that I can't even pretend normalcy.

"Yeah," I huff in a voice that's anything except convincing.

Dad frowns now. "You mad about Melinda?"

"Father." Clara pleads as she hurries past me. I hear her breath shake, and a sucking noise as her feet sticking to the floor glazed by the summer humidity. Edmund turns, wrapping her in a hug that's almost tender.

"He's going to leave us," he whispers. He can't see her eyes scrunch, because he's buried his face into her shoulder.

"No, he's not," Clara says. Tears leak from her eyelids as she whispers, "Just don't...don't run him off."

"Yeah." I remember I'm supposed to be answering Dad and turn my attention back toward him. "I'm mad about Melinda.

Dad huffs a breath like it's not what he wants to hear. "We're not looking for anything serious. So don't run her off, kay? She knows where we stand."

I stare. "We are not having this conversation right now." My brain is swamped by the image of Edmund crying. By worrying about where Vincent went or if he really will leave. Clara's distressed. Melinda is stupid, if what Dad says is true. And I can't fix everybody all at the same time.

I turn on my heels, stomping toward the kitchen to make sure Clara's kettle doesn't burn down the house while everyone inside is falling apart. Dad follows me, which I hate, but at least I know he's not going to smack into Edmund.

I sit at the table, pressing my fingers against my temples and willing this double-vision to go away, feeling like a mother with a teenage son as Dad's sighs.

"Come on, Scarlet," he says. "Some people are made to stay together forever and some just want a good time. She's got her life. I've got mine. We have each other, without strings or entanglement."

I glance up at him. "This is why I'm never getting a boyfriend."

"Oh, get the boyfriend," Dad says, opening the refrigerator to pull out a soda can. "Just keep your personal life separate. Trust me, it's a lot easier."

"Really? That's where you're going to take this?" I ask.

Clara steps into the kitchen, just ahead of her father, hovering like he might fall, though his steps are steady.

Edmund pulls out a chair, sitting and pressing his fist against his mouth. "I really thought he'd want it," he says, as Clara pours tea into two cups on the service tray. "When he was little, he always begged to ride out with me when he was on break."

Clara wets her lips, then slides into the chair next to me. "Vincent loves you, Father. You're going to be around for years and years. There's time for him to explore other careers and decide what he wants to do."

Edmund lifts the teacup two inches, then sets it down again, shaking his head. "When I was a boy, I wanted my father's store. And when he died, it was stolen from me. I promised, I *promised* that my son would have something."

"He does have something," Clara whispers. "Perhaps not what you intended, but Vincent is happy. Isn't that all that matters?"

Edmund drops his face into his fingers, then replies softly, "It's all that matters when you're twenty." His voice drops to a whisper, changing into a hiss. "But he has no head for business. He could inherit your grandfather's fortune, and he'd lose it in five years unless he learns. And he won't learn!"

His teeth grit but he speaks through them. "He won't learn because he's an idiot and your grandfather has ruined him."

Clara and I straighten at the same time, sensing the change. She pulls back slowly, eyeing Edmund like he's a rattlesnake. "Father?" she asks, like she's checking to see if he's still there.

"He's trying to ruin all of us," Edmund whispers, fixing his eyes on the teacup. Every sentence from his mouth comes a little faster. "He's turning Vincent against me."

"That's not true," Clara says.

"Scarlet?" Dad's watching me watch the two at the table. "Honey, what's wrong?"

"I told you, I don't want to talk right now," I say. I don't want to leave the table either, because Edmund's face is morphing into something dark and ugly.

Clara is staring as hard as I am like she's never seen this. Fear swells in her eyes. She needs to leave, but she can't hear me. Dad can. And that's a problem.

Dad slides into the chair across from me, right next to Edmund and he looks just as pissed. He sets his arms across the table.

"Look at me," Dad says. "I am sick of your attitude. You don't have to agree with my decision for leaving Madison..."

"Sherri, Dad," I correct. "Her name is Sherri. You're still with Melinda, and I don't have a freaking clue who Madison is."

"This is my life!" Dad snaps. "Your mother left me. And I have raised you. And I have taken care of you, and you will not—"

Edmund slams his hands at the table, covering the rest of whatever Dad is saying with his own rant. "He's doing it all for spite! Isn't it enough that he has that boy dancing to his tune! He can't have my son, too. I won't let him have my son!"

"Oh my god, just shut up!" I scream at both of them, pressing my hands to my ears.

"Do not tell me to shut up!" Dad yells. "I am your father!"

"Father, please," Clara wails. "I don't think Grandfather's trying to hurt anyone."

Edmund stands, growling something that sounds animalistic. He hurls the teacup, smashing it against the wall.

"Get out!" I yell, partly to my father, partly to Clara.

Dad reaches for my chair, almost yanking it from beneath me. "Go to your room! Just go to your room! I'm sick of talking to you."

"Dad, what?" I spin to face him. "Why are you freaking out?"

Clara pushes back her chair, smacking into me, but stepping around without noticing. Her eyes are on her father and she dances around him, like a puppy unsure if she should bark and herd or retreat.

"He is, Clara," Edmund says. "He's been trying to control my life ever since we met. He can't have my son. He can't have you!" He wraps Clara in a hug as Dad shoves my shoulders.

"I said go!" Dad snaps.

"You can't leave me," Edmund says. "Promise me, Rose. Promise me you won't leave."

Clara stares, then sputters, "I'm Clara, Father."

"Oh my god." I panic, shoving Dad back away. Edmund's eyes have this weird glint that's freaking me as bad as Clara.

"Clara?" Edmund asks. He spins, glancing first to the tree branches banging against the window, then shouts, "Where is Clara?"

"I'm Clara!" Clara shouts.

"The children . . . find the children! The storm." Edmund's feet shake the entire house as he runs from the kitchen and pounds up the stairs.

Clara stumbles back, gripping her hair, her eyes as wild and wide as her father's. Her voice is high, her breath so shaky that it's busting each word into syllables.

"Fa-ther," she moans. Every word becomes trapped in panic. "You're al-right. You're al-right."

"Let me go!" I scream.

I try to step around Dad to get to Clara. But she stays rooted to the ground as Dad wrestles me toward the door. She needs to get out. Her father has snapped and for the first time, I hope he'll freeze up.

"Hannah." Clara sputters. "Hannah!"

I don't think Hannah can hear her from the cottage. I wonder if I can create enough commotion to wake them, but Dad's face blocks out everything else as he shouts.

"Scarlet, I mean it! Upstairs, now!"

Edmund pounds back down the stairs. "Rose, I can't find them!" He reaches for his coat on the rack.

"I'll go, I'll go!" I shout. "Just leave me alone!"

Dad lets go of me as Clara rushes past to grab her father's jacket arm. "Father, don't go! They're fine! The children are fine!"

My dad points to the stairs like I'm a dog. "Up!"

Edmund turns, steering Clara away from the door. "No, stay inside! Stay inside. Take Clara upstairs and stay there. I'm going for Vincent."

"Vincent's upstairs!" Clara screams. She grips the cloth at her father's arms, whispering and nodding. "He's all right. He's all right. The children are sleeping and they're fine."

I stumble toward the stairs, reaching to grab Clara and drag her with me, but she steps out of reach, forgetting that she's trying to play along with this delusion. "Father, please let's just—"

Edmund opens the door and a gust of wind-driven rain sprays the hallway. It hits his face and he slams the door again. His entire body heaves with every breath as his hands clamp onto Clara's shoulders, shoving her back as he shouts. "The winds. Go, go! They'll knock in the walls."

"No!" I shout.

Dad's entire frame presses against me, herding me back onto the steps. I lurch for Clara's hand as Edmund steers her past me, but I only manage to catch her sleeve.

She sidesteps, wrenching against him, unable to break free. Her eyes are as wild as his, her pleadings turn into frantic repeats. "Father, stop! Listen to me! Listen to me!"

I kick Dad, adding my own yells to the pandemonium. "Let me go!"

Dad blocks the stairs, gripping both railings glaring at me. "Scarlet, do not make me tell you again!"

I consider jumping over the railing, but I hear a door slam in the kitchen. I can't help Clara until I'm fully in her world. I turn and rush up the stairs to get back to the music box. Dad must assume I'm going to my room because he doesn't follow.

Clara's pleas become muffled, like he's shut her up in a cabinet or something. "Father, stop! Stop, please!"

"Stay inside! Stay inside!"

I pant as I wind the music box, shaking so hard I can hardly turn the key. Don't panic. Focus. But the music winds down and she's not near the box to match the notes.

I hear her beating against a door, but her voice has changed directions, coming through the grate at the end of the hallway. I abandon the music box, rushing down the hall to drop onto my knees and pull the cover away from the slats. Clara and I are separated by boards, a wire screen, the shelves stacked with taped shoe boxes and neat lines of canned jars, and about a hundred years.

"Father!"

I can barely see Clara's outline and probably wouldn't at all if she wasn't hitting the door with a flat hand. She looks like she's drowning in gray ink and then I realize. Clara's trapped in her world. She can't see my light above her. She can't hear me if I call.

She's alone in the dark.

And she's still banging, still screaming when she fades.

CLARA CASTLE
Summer, 1911

KNEES DRAWN TO MY CHEST, I TRY NOT TO PANIC. I SHOULD GO BACK to sleep until Father returns to sanity and lets me out. Vincent truly must have decided to sleep at wherever Anne is staying. One moment I'm angry at him for not being here to help me, and the next I'm relieved that he didn't see Father like that.

I've never seen Father like that. Perhaps panic from the storms, perhaps even a momentary confusion coming out of his spells. But for him to go so long not knowing where he is, who I am; this is what will kill him if we do not intervene, and I have no idea how to help him.

My shoulder is stiff from sleeping on the floor, wedged between the jars of apple cider and the broom. I adjust my back against the flour sack, wiping my face. Hannah can't hear my shouts from their cottage. Father might, but will he know it is the daughter he locked in the kitchen pantry, or will he think I'm my mother calling for help during a storm? I just spoke to him at the wrong time, becoming part of his memory instead of pulling him from it. Perhaps if I'd been quiet, he'd have gone into the spell instead of panicking about his endangered children.

I close my eyes. I wound the music box, but only one turn before I had to go down to Father. Scarlet didn't come and I cannot summon her now.

If Vincent finds me — or even discovers that I've been here — this whole thing will escalate far beyond what it should. Hannah will discover me first. She should be coming any moment to start breakfast. That would be best. She won't be happy with Father but, like me, she knows when to speak and when to hold her tongue. As frightening as this is, I won't die in here. And I suppose there could be worse places to be trapped than a pantry.

At the moment, I can't think of any. I can't think of much more than the panic swelling in my chest, irrational thoughts that make me feel as delusional as Father. How? How can we spend the evening having a perfectly logical conversation, speculating Andrew's return to New York tomorrow, and then a few hours later, he's flinching every time the lightning cracks across the sky?

My eyes glisten, but it's not because of the rain. Father says that he suspects once Andrew returns to New York tomorrow, that will be the last of it and we'll never see him again. Father says he was bound to end up there anyway. That one not born a gentleman could never become one. That even one who is born a gentleman can scarcely manage to stay one. I think that is what sent him down the road to his panic, imagining all sorts of horrible things for Vincent's future.

I sigh and try the door one more time, but Father must have braced it, because it sticks fast. Oh, why did I insist on speaking when I knew better? I knew Father was growing unwell. I'm growing as bad as Vincent. Scarlet is wrong. Arguing doesn't work.

I hear the screen door shut, followed by soft footsteps that can't possibly belong to Vincent. I need to knock, need to call, but I can't make a sound. How can I explain this?

"Father?" I squeak, but I suspect it's my light palming of the door that carries into the kitchen.

The footsteps stop. That's not Father.

"Hannah?" My voice trembles, threatening to break, though I had thought that I had finished crying.

"Clara?"

My name comes with that familiar flip of the "r." My voice catches in my throat, and I clamp my hand against my mouth. Andrew. Of course, it's Andrew. It's not early morning. It's near midnight, and he's returning from the hotel.

"Clara?" He takes a step toward the pantry, before he stops to listen.

I scoot away from the door, knocking into the broom that betrays me with a clatter. A chair scrapes against the far side of the door, and I try to blend in with the jars and boxes as soft candlelight spills into my prison. It lights Andrew's face, the surprised lift of his eyebrows, and the lines that form on his forehead.

"Clara!" Andrew sets the candle aside and kneels next to me. He grabs my arms to steady me as I push onto my knees. "What happened?"

My mind flies for an answer. I open my mouth, but no words come. I didn't realize how much I was trembling until I feel how steady his hands are.

"Are you hurt?" Andrew asks.

"No," I answer quickly, palming tears away. "Andrew, don't..."

Don't tell. Don't ask questions.

Andrew takes my hand, tugging me to my feet. He's still in uniform, and I blush as the hem of my nightdress brushes the tops of my feet. I fix my eyes on the counter behind him, feeling him search my face. He's formulating questions that I don't want him to ask.

"I sleepwalk," I say quickly, drawing from something I read in *Dracula.*

Andrew cocks an eyebrow. "And place a chair against the door behind you?"

Is that what Father did? I flush, rubbing my face with one hand and clinging to him with the other. I'm a terrible liar.

"Who put you in there?" Andrew asks. "Your Father?"

I want to tell him. I want him to hold me, but the very idea shocks me. I numbly shake my head and try to step around him.

He steps backwards, like we're dancing, grabbing my waist as he blocks my path. "Were you in there all night?"

I cannot look him in the eye. My own eyes flutter to the buttons on his shirt and then to the wall.

"Are you harmed?" His fingers tighten as I try to pull away.

"Yes." Panic creeps into my voice. I brush his hand aside. "I — " I drop my voice to a whisper. "Please forget it happened. Andrew. Please."

His eyes darken into concern, but his voice grows firm. "Clara, if someone is hurting you— "

"It isn't what it looks like." I'm not sure what I expect him to believe that it is, but I give it with a stony voice that leaves no room for discussion. I step past him, smoothing my sleeping gown. "Please, I am not in any state to be in the kitchen with you in the middle of the night."

And he's leaving in the morning, back to New York, back to a family with their own needs and troubles. I hurry to my room, shutting the door behind me. Glancing into the vanity mirror, I wince. My hair is tangled, nightdress crumpled and dirty. I sit at the vanity, hunching forward.

What should I do? He won't ask me about it, not tomorrow, not in front of everyone. If I plan it correctly, he won't have a chance before he boards the train. But I don't want that encounter to be how he remembers me. And I didn't even thank him for unbarring the door.

I rub my face, grateful that the redness is only humiliation and not a hand print. I owe no explanations to Andrew. He is not part of this family. I hold my breath as I hear his footsteps in the hall between my room and Vincent's.

Don't knock. Don't pursue. I won't answer. Even if he knocks, I won't answer. I bite my lip, scrunching my eyes and steeling myself for the inevitable, but he doesn't knock. I hear his feet shift, then the light swish of his coat sliding down the wall. He told me once that he always slept in front of the door at his home to block the cold and wake if anyone forced entry.

As relieved as I am that he's not going to demand answers and guilty because I won't give him any, I close my eyes against tears of relief. Even if Father hasn't come out of his delusions, nothing else will happen tonight, because Andrew's watching my door.

When the sun rises, I take extra care to dress, striving to look better than I feel. I even manage to pin up my hair. There's not much I can do to cover the blue shadows beneath my eyes, but I pinch my cheeks until some color returns. I wish I could speak to Scarlet. I wish that I could cover my face with her powder that pales everything and then draw the color back in. Even Anne has a bit of powder, but I don't. Father doesn't know that I need to cover his shame.

I stick two crystal combs into both sides of my hair, then add a locket that Hannah gifted to me when I was little. I hear Grandfather's car and peek from the window, worrying that Andrew will say something to Vincent. I must reach him first. If Vincent notices anything amiss, I'll play it off as sadness that Andrew is leaving. Father won't ask. He'll simply revert to feeding me 'simple food' to cure my insomnia.

And Andrew... well, hopefully Andrew won't.

But he does, though not out loud. He takes my hand at the bottom of the stairs and says, "Good morning."

But his eyes almost plead, *What happened?*

"Good morning," I answer.

I can't tell you.

We stand a moment, both bleary eyed. My chest barely moves, squeezing slight breaths in and out as though anything deeper will loosen everything I'm holding in. Andrew's jaw tightens. I watch him swallow, but he drops his eyes and steps to the side to let me continue on to breakfast.

Father's already in his seat, twisting his fork round and round like he's contemplating its shine. His eyes snap to us, though I can't tell if he's trying to remember what happened or wondering why Andrew and I are entering the room at the same time.

"Morning, Sleeping Beauty," Vincent calls with the ignorance of someone who just arrived for breakfast. "Are you ill?"

"No," I answer.

Father's shoulders relax. Andrew pulls out my chair with hands that tremble a bit. I sit, glancing at the clock. Five hours are all I have left with him. It's far too long to avoid his questions, and too soon to say goodbye for the summer or forever. I serve myself without glancing toward Father for his approval of any of my choices. It's one of the quietest meals we've had in a while, and even Vincent doesn't try to alleviate the silence beyond explaining that his wheels sank in the Millers' front lawn.

Andrew's frown increases throughout the meal. His luggage is waiting by the door, a small carpet bag with his clothing and two violin cases. The sight makes my heart sink as we pass.

When Andrew opens his mouth, I speak up first. "Two?" I ask, indicating the instruments.

He nods. "Mr. Mordaunt bought me one. I thought...I could return Da's to him. Not that I don't want it," he adds quickly as though his father is standing with us. "But he used to play every night for us and when he sent it with me, he didn't have another."

I try to imagine my father playing music for us every night, or having any sort of ritual, but I can't. The only habit my father has is smoking a pipe after dinner. When he does speak, it feels more like he's asking for a report of the day.

"Tell me more about your family sometime?" I ask.

Andrew nods.

"You'll write me, won't you?" I ask again. "From New York or England or wherever you end up going?"

"I'll always write you." Andrew finds my eyes as he answers. "No matter what happens. I'll find a way."

I wonder what he means, that he'd have to work to find a way, but I've discovered that life outside of my house is a lot more complicated than I realize and sometimes it's better not to show my ignorance. Like me, there is something that he's not saying. I don't like it, but it somehow makes me feel connected. Like the very people who feel we must be sheltered are the people we're actually going to great lengths to protect.

I maintain the eye contact long enough to realize that there are tiny bits of dark blue flecked in with the lighter color of his eyes. Then I remember that we're having a conversation and think back to the last thing he said —his promise to find a way to write.

"Good," I say. "So will I. No matter what."

Perhaps when he's back at school and not busy helping his own family, I'll pen him the truth about mine.

Perhaps.

"Clara..." Andrew speaks with a sudden resolve that makes my heart pound, but Hannah interrupts.

"Clara?" She stands in the doorway with her head cocked. "Did you make tea last night?"

"Yes," I answer. "We were waiting for Vincent to return."

She eyes Andrew like she suspects he was the one having a midnight tea party, but she says, "You should have woken me."

"I tried," I say, then add quickly, "But I really didn't need help boiling water."

"Well, you boiled the kettle dry," she says gently. "Just be careful next time. There was ash on the floor."

"I'm sorry," I say.

"Well, it's cast iron," she says. "I think I can mend it."

Andrew's still watching me and I feel compelled to give some sort of explanation. "I'm sorry," I repeat to Hannah. "I don't think anything like last night will happen again."

Andrew still looks confused, but at least now he'll know that being locked in the pantry is not a regular occurrence. I only give him a glance before I find Vincent and we spend the next few hours chatting on the front porch like we haven't any cares in the world.

As the boys are loading Andrew's few belongings into Grandfather's car, Father steps onto the porch behind me, setting his hand on my shoulder. "I want you to stay here," he says.

The station is only a few blocks, but my heart sinks. "I thought I might ride with Vincent," I sputter. "Please, let me?"

Father's fingers tighten on my shoulder. "I want you to stay here," he repeats.

The boys glance toward us from the car. Father raises one hand while I force a smile that I'm sure doesn't look real. All I can really think of is Father's fingers on my shoulder and how it doesn't feel safe anymore. Does he even remember last night?

Andrew and Vincent exchange glances before Andrew swings down from the car. He returns to the porch and offers a hand to Father. "Goodbye, sir. Thank you for allowing me to stay with you."

"My pleasure," Father says in his most professional tone.

Undeterred, Andrew offers his hand to me, and I hold it a bit tighter than I mean to. I don't want him to leave. I should have told him last night. I should have pulled him onto the balcony and let him hold me, instead of pushing him away. For an hour or so we could have been like Scarlet and Keith, free to talk without the restrictions and protocols that keep us smiling politely at each other.

Andrew's hand is warm and slightly sweaty, contrasting something cold and stiff that pokes into my palm. I curl my fingers as naturally as I can as he draws his hand away. He steps back, smiles, and then returns to the car to swing back into the passenger seat. I wave with my free hand until they've turned the corner.

"Clara?" Father asks.

When I look at him, his eyes rove my face and the worry has returned. He takes three short breaths, pausing each time like he's trying to ask something he can't formulate. The pressure builds in my chest. I cannot remain angry with him, not when he looks like this, like the lost little boy that lives inside the man's body.

Finally, he sighs. "We'll be fine," he says. His voice changes, lowering into a matter of factual tone. "I've left your list inside, along with one for Vincent. Please make sure everything is finished before I return tonight."

"Yes, Father," I answer.

He watches me, then says, "Stay inside today. I'll see you this evening."

"Yes, sir," I repeat.

I step into the doorway, watching through the screen as he saddles the horse, weaving it through the motor cars that he claims are a nuisance. Then I uncurl my fingers just enough to catch the glint of sunlight off a silver ring. Instead of a stone, it has a small pearl.

I close my fingers, feeling confusion lace each heartbeat as Hannah speaks from behind me. "I'm going to miss that boy."

"Me too," I whisper.

It's not an engagement ring, but what does it mean? Does he think that he'll never see me again? Was it meant as a birthday gift he was too afraid to give me? It was bought for me, that's for certain, for it couldn't be a heirloom. My chest warms, but my temples pound. I've seen this ring before. Vincent left it for me in the attic.

18

SCARLET BELDON

Summer, 2012

Dec. 31, 1911

Dear Scarlet,
I cannot find the music box. It was on my dresser last night
when I fell asleep, but missing when I woke. Did you move it?
Clara

I find the letter, frowning at the music box in the chest. If Clara doesn't have access to it, can I even get a letter to travel back? I pull out my pen, jotting beneath her handwriting.

Nope. It's safely here in the chest. Did you check your trunk?

It's been almost a month since I've seen her, so there's no telling how much time has passed in her world. Keith and I have sent out four applications for scholarships. He's been driving me around in this banged up car but at least it gets me out of town. Yesterday we went bowling, and we've hit the movies twice. Dad thinks he's my boyfriend (which isn't true), and that's the reason I've suddenly decided that I don't want to move away from this house (which is true, but not for that reason).

It's a good thing Clara's time is passing more quickly than mine. I only have until the end of summer to get her through half of a year, though I don't worry about her as much now that Vincent is home. I grilled her about the night in the pantry, the only time I've seen her since.

She cried but insisted that it never happened before and so far, it hasn't happened again. She says that Andrew is still writing, though she must be hiding the letters now, because I can't find any besides Andrew's lament over whether or not to become a Mordaunt.

Personally, I think it's a terrible idea. Even if Andrew did decide to be officially adopted by this guy who could be his grandpa, that would legally make him Clara's uncle, which throws all kinds of monkey wrenches into my plans for them.

If that's occurred to Clara, she hasn't mentioned it, only the rage upon receiving the letter that her grandfather would ask such a thing of him.

What did he decide?

We don't know. He's never mentioned it again, though he did write that he won't be returning to school in Galveston. He spent the summer with his family, but he's gone to Europe for the winter with Mr. Mordaunt. Clara seems good with the arrangement, only talking about her relief that her grandfather won't come to the house to agitate Edmund until after we've had time to change the events that marred her former life. I glance at the letter, then jolt because she's replied.

I've looked everywhere. Even Hannah hasn't seen it.

Heedless of the concern of a missing time-travel device, I snatch my pen, smearing the ink from her flourishing letters as I scratch out a reply, hoping she hasn't left yet.

Wait. Can you see this?

The ink looks like it's drawing itself, and I squeal as the curvy letters spell.

Yes.

I'd prefer to talk to her, but this 19th century instant messaging is good enough for now. I write again.

Look for it later. Catch me up on your life. What month is it?

New Years Eve, 1911.

How's your father?

His spells are still coming, but are relatively harmless. Nothing delusional. However, his list of chores for Vincent and I grow daily. I don't know if he's simply trying to keep us busy, or if things are becoming more imperative that we do as much of the work ourselves as we can. I suspect we are in financial difficulties, for even Vincent does not complain about the work.

Look through your father's papers. His desk should have clues.

I couldn't.

You're a detective. It's okay to snoop if you're helping.

But I haven't the key.

Do you know where your father keeps it?

In his pocket.

That is an issue. The world is full of pickpockets, but Clara isn't one of them. I suck on a tooth, slitting my eyes at the car that is rounding the curve, pounding out music. Then I write what's probably going to give her a small heart attack.

Next time he has a spell, get it.

She takes so long to reply, I wonder if I've scared her off, or if she's contemplating that. But I watch the ink scroll across the page.

Very well.

My eyebrows fly up as I scribble.

Good for you.

Father is at the mill. I suppose I could look now.

Do it.

I try to be patient. I really do, but the rest of the letter ends up looking something like this:

Did you find it? I'm trying to guess how much time has

passed in your world.
Are you there?
Earth to Clara.
Oh great, now I'm going to worry. At least let me know
you're okay.
HELLO??????!!!!

My knees are killing me. I'm afraid if I take the letter from its spot, I'm going to lose whatever the heck made it connect and run parallel to Clara's time. I pass the stretching moments by researching the Castle family by a slow Internet connection I pick up from a neighboring house. I'm still coming up with nothing when the music box skips a section in the middle of its melody.

"Oh, thank god." I snatch it up, watching the room change, but this time Clara is not holding it, and I'm not in the hallway. The room is dark, the moonlight trapped behind drawn curtains, and only a single lamp gives any light. There is a bed I don't recognize and a writing desk, covered with stacked papers and a neat inkwell. It has a wooden chair that looks like something a mother would sit a kid in for punishment, not the luxurious leather swivel seat of an executive.

And Mr. Castle is sitting in it, with one leg thrown over the other and his fingers clasped beneath his chin. I think he's watching me, waiting to ask why I'm pushing his perfect daughter into sneaking around to pry into his secrets. But his eyes are locked on the music box in my hand and on his desk which has, apparently, pulled me into its imprisonment in Edmund's room.

Even though he brought me forward, he can't see me. I keep still, afraid to bump into the furniture or breathe or do anything that might so much as send a speck of dust into flight. We both watch the music box wind down, slowing until it sputters to a stop.

Edmund's fingers curl into a light fist, then creep free, inching toward it before retreating into his palm again. He lifts his eyes to rove the air around me. He whispers, but the house is so quiet that it may as well be a gunshot.

"Elizabeth?"

We both hold our breath. Then he releases his, wiping his eyes like he's realized he's sunk to a new level of desperation, hoping his dead wife will respond.

Then the man sets his head against the back of the chair, staring at the ceiling with glistening eyes. I'm not sure if this is the glaze that Clara talks about before he goes into catatonia or if he's going to be delusional again, but whatever it is, it's weird.

"Holy cow..." I breathe out, lowering myself to sit right where I'm at. Wherever Clara is right now, the worst thing I can do for her is panic her father.

Despite my efforts, I creak a floorboard. The man's entire head snaps toward me, straining like if he focuses hard enough, he'll be able to sense me. Edmund Castle must have heard the music box playing on its own and thinks I'm Elizabeth Rose, returning to give him a message from the other side. Well. Better me than Clara.

Can I use this to my advantage? Perhaps drop some hints that Clara needs to be free to live her own life? Perhaps putting in a good word for Andrew? Or asking Edmund what he does and doesn't know about his own mental state. Then again, that is an issue, and I'm not sure invisible communication is going help guide the man back onto the road to sanity.

Besides, I'm seeing now the side of Edmund Castle that keeps his daughter so captured. The man looks absolutely miserable. He's staring at the wall now, but he doesn't look unresponsive. I see his eyebrows twitching with emotions that flash from anger to despair.

He fingers the tiny portrait of a woman I can only assume is Clara's mother. It hurts to watch, finally finding a man who truly loves somebody but can't have her, after watching my own dad flit from woman to woman who can't keep him.

For the first time, I worry that Clara won't marry Andrew. This has seemed like some fantastical fairy tale, but it's really not. It's not my reality, but it is Clara's.

And the real world sucks.

"Don't worry," I say softly to the man who can't hear me. "Your daughter's going to be happy."

Even if I don't manage to save Edmund. Even if I have to bring Clara forward to live in my world, I'm going to make sure she gets a happy ending.

"I'm trying, Rose," Edmund whispers to the portrait. "He's not secure, but it's something. Something that is ours, his, and your father hasn't any say in the matter." He puts his fist to his mouth, and I just sit until he says, "But he doesn't want it. He's so much like you. Thinks he can do whatever suits his fancy and somehow the money will just take care of itself."

I wonder where Edmund's fancy would have taken him if he hadn't channeled his efforts into money. Money he apparently still doesn't have if the dashes in front of the numbers on his desk mean anything.

Clara's knock isn't loud, but it scares the crap out of both of us. Edmund jolts, gripping his armrest and sucking a slow breath into his nose as she calls, "Father? It's almost midnight. Are you coming to count down with us?"

Edmund swallows, taking a breath that lifts and collapses his chest. "Yes, darling. I'll be down shortly."

The floorboards creak as she shifts her weight, then ventures another try. "Please come soon. I really want you there."

I scrunch my eyes together, because I realize what she's thinking. If we don't change things, this is the last time she's ever going to greet a new year with her father.

"I'll come," Edmund says, but he doesn't move.

We listen to Clara's boots descend the stairs and you can practically hear them drag. To the guy's credit, Edmund does stand and reach for his suit jacket, though I have no idea why he wants to look so put together in the middle of the night. I'm freezing my tail off, and if I was ringing in 1912, I'd be doing it with a fuzzy blanket wrapped around my shoulders, not some work suit.

Edmund walks to the door but when he touches the knob, he hesitates. I watch him rest his forehead against the door, watch his shoulders heave something between rapid sighs and what I suspect is close to crying. He spins, striding back to the desk to pour himself a glass of wine.

"Father!" Vincent's voice bellows up the stairs and through the doorway. "You're going to miss it!"

And suddenly I want him to open that stupid door because I can't get through it without him seeing the movement, and *I* don't want to miss it. But Edmund sits through the ticking of his clock, watching his breath rise like smoke from a cigar. The church bell begins to ring when he's about halfway through the wine glass.

"Father?" Clara is more polite when she calls up the stairs.

Edmund sets his face into his hands, resting his elbows on the desk, whispering a refrain over and over. "I can't. God, I can't..."

Clara creeps up the stairs in soft, disjointed steps like she's scared to ask again.

"Clara, leave him alone," Vincent's voice comes irritated.

"But he said he was coming," Clara protests.

"Well, he either will or won't come."

"But what if he's—"

She doesn't get to finish her question before Vincent's feet pound halfway up the stair. "Come along. Don't let it ruin your fun. We'll check on him later. It makes no difference either way."

"Go," I whisper, but Edmund's eyes grow duller as he stares into the wine he's swirling slowly.

"Thirty seconds!" Hannah calls. "Come along you two! I didn't spend my hard-earned money on crackers for nothing!"

Edmund's eyes are completely filled, and he brushes his sleeve across them before standing. He stalls in front of the mirror, studying the reflection inside.

"Come on!" I whisper.

He moves to the door, and I follow, ready to slither through. He opens it, just wide enough that I could side-step my way past, but I don't because tears are leaking out of his unblinking eyes. And I can't help it. Maybe I'll freak him out. Maybe I'll push him past his wavering sanity. I reach out and touch his shoulder. His eyes move in the direction of my hand as his breath stops. I step back before he reaches out and finds a solid, invisible teenager in front of him.

He brushes his shoulder, turning back toward the music box, but he looks more confused than excited. Then his eyes completely fill and I mentally cuss myself out, because now I've distracted the man when he's supposed to be going downstairs.

"Ten, nine, eight, seven..."

Clara sounds happy downstairs as her voice rises in pitch with Vincent's, growing louder and louder.

"Six, five, four, three..."

Edmund's eyes fall to the floorboards as he listens to his children bring in the new year just below him. The whole world erupts as more church bells ring, and I can hear the neighbors shouting. There's clanging and clashing and dogs howling and even back then, I see headlights as someone drives by, honking some Henry Ford dinosaur.

There's a scuffle downstairs as Clara and Vincent wrestle over popping the crackers she's told me about. They're little tubes that snap, and Vincent always snatches the surprise inside.

I snort, wanting more than ever to be downstairs to witness it, but I probably shouldn't let Clara see me anyway. As fun as it would be to wish her Happy New Year, showing up would also be a fresh reminder of what the New Year is going to bring. I'd rather leave her to fight over a tiny toy with her brother.

So would Edmund, apparently. He turns slowly, lifting his glass to the picture and putting it to his lips. Before the wine reaches his mouth, he's crying into it, covering his face with his hands and hunching against the door.

Maybe I'm wrong about him. Maybe he is aware of the downward spiral his life is taking. Maybe he knows he needs help and just doesn't know where to find it.

He moves away from the door, sinking into the chair and turning away from the accounts. This time the feet on the steps are heavy and strong and, unlike Clara, Vincent doesn't bother with the protocol of knocking.

He opens the door, peeking inside, but misses Edmund wiping away the tears.

"Father?" he asks.

"I didn't invite you to come in," Edmund says, but his voice lacks firmness.

Vincent shuts the door behind him, then turns to further invade his father's space. I guess he figured he'd find Edmund completely unresponsive, because he looks a bit thrown off. But he's not stupid; he can see the red eyes and knows they're not from the wine.

Edmund stands silently, and they're eye to eye, one looking far older and worn than the other.

"Happy New Year," Edmund says.

"Happy New Year," Vincent responds soberly.

Edmund's eyes move to the wall behind Vincent's shoulder. Vincent steps forward, pulling the man into a hug, and Edmund's shoulders collapse as his arms fold around him. The clanging and shouting continues, but neither man lets go of each other.

Clara peeks in the door, literally showing only half of her face, but it's enough to see her eye widen and flood before it disappears. I step around the men, careful not to creak the floorboards as I join her in the hallway. I reach to squeeze her hand as we press against the wall.

"Hi," I whisper.

"Hi," she mouths, then brushes away a tear.

"See?" I say. "They're going to be okay."

And we stand there silently while the world rings with sound, greeting a year that's already looking brighter.

"Happy New Year," I whisper.

Clara lifts her head and smiles at me through her tears. Then she holds up the unused cracker, before disappearing into the study she doesn't normally dare to enter.

"We saved one," Vincent say. "For you."

And I peek in, giggling unashamed as Edmund grips the other side of the cracker and yanks on it, popping paper and cardboard and this time, nobody seems to care what surprise comes flying out.

CLARA CASTLE
Spring, 1912

March 15, 1912

Dearest Clara,
We are returning to America earlier than planned, as your Grandfather wishes to travel with several other elite families. We'll be leaving on April 10, making the entire journey in one week. There is so much to tell you, too much to commit to paper. I've secured a small farm for my family. They are safe and out of New York. I want you to meet them. When I left you the gift, I didn't know whether I'd be able to give a promise with it. But I can, Clara. I can now. I hope to see you again soon, perhaps as early as mid-May.

"Good heavens, Clara, you've gone pale," Hannah says, pausing with a basket of freshly pressed clothing. "Is the letter bad?"

"No." I mean to answer more forcefully than I do, but I feel too weak and stunned to manage it. "No, it's not bad at all. Grandfather and Andrew are returning to America. I thought they weren't coming until summer, but they're likely already on the ship. They could be here as early as May."

May. The word plays through my mind, forming connections between new information and old. Vincent is wrong that Grandfather will be in Europe. Grandfather may even be in America, which means things have already changed. And Andrew will be part of my life, perhaps a larger part than I realized.

I feel the ring hanging from the chain around my neck, hidden by my clothing. For months I've wondered what it meant. I haven't even told Scarlet, fearing that she would read into things that aren't there.

But they are there. Andrew gave me a ring, and now he's giving me the promise with it. Of course, Father's illness still complicates things, but Andrew's family is out of the tenements and onto the farm they always wanted. I'm not sure how we'll solve my own family problems, but we can find a way. And I won't have to do it alone. I cannot write him a letter. By the time it reached Europe, Andrew would be home. But he's right. Paper is not good enough for this conversation.

Hannah moves on without further inquiry, and I rock gently on the couch. It's been so long since I received good news and this letter is filled with it. Gracious, how am I supposed to hide such joy? Father's going to ask about it, and I'm not sure what to tell him, for a prospective visit from Grandfather isn't going to bring him any pleasure.

But his face is troubled enough when he comes, that concern immediately creeps into my chest.

"Father?" I ask.

He drops a kiss on my head. "Hello, darling."

"What's the matter?" I ask.

Father sighs, looking at me before he turns into the parlor. "Come with me."

I follow him, feeling my heart sink with every step. He sits in the brown chair that's beginning to look worn. I settle into the rocking chair, trying to convert my agitation into a gentle sway. Father lights a pipe, staring at the wall, and I glance toward the empty door.

"Where's Vincent?" I ask.

"He's interviewing for the paper," Father says, then continues dryly, "But don't say anything. It's a secret."

I'm not surprised. Vincent is still working beside Father, but he's published six articles in the paper and received several compliments on them. I suspect that Anne is back in town as well, but I'm sure Vincent's keeping her a secret too. He must tell Father soon. We've already leafed through the Sears and Roebuck catalog, and it wasn't my ring we were looking for.

Father smokes for several minutes, and I hold back a cough, hoping that Andrew never smokes. Though he's not speaking, Father summoned me here for a reason, so I distract myself from the wait by counting clock ticks and imagining what Scarlet and Andrew are doing.

As my foot begins tingling from lack of blood, Father finishes his pipe. He empties it, sets it into his holder and holds out his hand. "Come here, darling."

His face is sober, even a little gray. I know that we are strapped for funds right now, but Father has seemed more cheerful of late and I don't like the turn that this day has taken.

I force a cheerful voice as I creep toward him. "What is it, Father?"

He studies me for a long moment. "Billy Meyers has expressed an interest in courting you."

I had many theories, but this was not one of them. My head goes light as my stomach lurches.

"Billy?" I stutter.

"Yes." Father snuffs his pipe and sets it into the ashtray. "I have given him my permission."

It is the first time that I have ever understood why the heroines in a novel swoon. I take a side step to catch my balance while the world spins, but, unlike the heroines, I know that no one is going to rush through that door to save me.

"Father," I begin.

But what does one say to such an announcement?

"Clara, he is a decent boy from an esteemed family. You'll never get a better offer." Father sighs. "I am out of money, darling, and soon people will know it. The lumber yard is only making enough to pay off the debt of rebuilding from the fire. If you are not married off within a few months, we may not recover in time for you to marry well."

My body grows hot against the ring on my chest. I grasp it for courage. "I'd rather stay with you," I say. "I do not mind being poor."

Father's hand clenches. "You would die, Clara. You are not meant for a hard life of work and cold and hunger. We will not depend on your grandfather's wealth or anyone associated with him."

He means Andrew, and it isn't fair. Andrew is poor, but he is earning his own money. Father was rich, but is losing it. In a few years, they may be on the same ground. Andrew could continue making a living with his music, even without my grandfather's backing. Couldn't he? Or does Father know that Grandfather is pushing Andrew to become his heir? And if he does consent, where does that leave us?

Father sees that I am trembling and takes me into a hug. "Don't fret, darling. People marry for fortune and become quite happy."

Billy. Billy will come here, expecting me to accept his advances. My stomach churns as I try to recall everything Scarlet said about standing up for myself. "I don't..."

Want to marry him. Want to be his wife. Want people knowing we're courting. I don't even want to see him.

"Father..." I try again.

"No more," Father says.

I tremble, but his voice is so firm that it is folly to protest further. He kisses me and leads me to the table where Hannah plunks down the dinner plates a bit harder than necessary.

Tonight, Father fills my plate, and I choke on every bite.

"Eat Clara," he says. "Pouting will not do any good."

He is right, of course, but I am not trying to pout — if that's what I'm doing. My throat is so tight that it's hard to breathe. Andrew cannot even be reached. Even if he could, he could not stop anything. I cannot tell Father that we wish to marry. I certainly cannot marry Billy.

"Clara." His voice grows stern and pulls me out of my thoughts. "Eat."

I force another mouthful, thinking I may as well be eating sand. I wish that Vincent was back, but I don't expect him to return until late. Father does not ask for an account today. Perhaps he knows he has already asked too much of me. After dinner, I hurry upstairs to pen a letter to Scarlet and another desperate letter to Andrew. One so frank that I promptly burn it in the kitchen fire.

Oh, Andrew.

I suck on a fingernail as I watch the sunset. I try to guess what Scarlet would suggest as a solution. Elopement, perhaps, but Father would hunt Andrew down with a rifle. Perhaps Andrew could persuade him, but by then Billy will have had a month to establish himself as my beau and turning him away would insult one of the wealthiest families in town.

Vincent returns too late to talk about it, but the next morning I wake to hear him arguing with Father downstairs. I tremble. I hate it when they argue. Neither of them changes his mind, and it makes everyone cross. Though I'm relieved that Vincent is on my side, I can't afford him to be at odds with Father. Not now. Not when there's less than a week before Father will be endangered.

Breakfast is miserable and no one speaks. After we finish, Father leaves both of us with a list of tasks that run off the page.

Vincent tears his up. "Come along," he says.

"What?" I ask.

He takes my hand. "We're going on a walk. You're too pale."

I'm not sure a walk is going to help my paleness, any more than it will create peace within the family, but I follow him. Vincent shoves his hands into his pockets, taking giant strides that are difficult for me to keep up with, but I don't ask him to slow. Walking is better than yelling, and it's impossible for his eyebrows to dip any lower. My boots sink in the shell, first in the road, then along the edge of the shore. I focus on the waves as they tumble bits of oyster back into the water with a flash of the sun.

"Tell me about Billy," Vincent says. "So far, I've only seen him twice recently, and I'm not impressed."

I take a breath. Billy isn't cruel, and he has made efforts to be pleasing. Father could have easily picked someone much worse. Nothing in me wants to talk to him even for an hour, but it seems wrong to pick apart his character.

"I don't know him well," I say.

"Do you think he's handsome?"

"Not terribly."

"Intelligent?"

"Mmm." I wince. "Not so much."

But then again, neither am I.

Vincent grins. "You can be mean, Clara."

I close my lips, trying to formulate my answer. "I don't want to marry him."

"Then don't," Vincent answers as though the event is entirely beneath my control.

Once I admit my foremost thought, it solidifies into something close to panic. "I can't marry him. I can't. I don't want to. Father must change his mind. I must make him change his mind."

"We'll work on it," Vincent says.

It should be comforting, but it isn't, and I suddenly realize this could be what Vincent and Father split over. If Father is expecting to lose everything within the next few months, enough to make him change his mind about keeping me with him and trying to marry me off to a relative stranger, things must be desperate.

Perhaps Vincent cannot gain access to the house for whatever he wanted, because the house and all the things have been sold. Perhaps that is the reason that I cannot stay. Because if I stay, I'm going to be forced down an aisle to marry someone I hardly know.

"Vincent." I twist my fingers until it hurts. "I cannot marry him. I don't even want to court him, and what if Father forces me to marry him before An . . .'"

I break off. There's no reason to explain everything, but Vincent catches it anyway.

"Before what?" he asks.

"Nothing." I turn my face toward the water.

Vincent cocks his head. "Clara?"

"Never mind."

"Clara." Now Vincent's voice is amused and it disarms me. He jabs me with his elbow, asking, "Before what?"

I take a breath. "Before Andrew returns."

His eyebrows lift and the cloudy look is chased away by an amused sparkle. "And what happens then?"

"I don't know yet," I answer, raising my chin just a tad.

"Well, what do you think is going to happen?"

I bite my bottom lip against a growing smile, then give up and fish the ring into the sunlight. It dangles between us, swaying as though the pearl is drawn back to the waters it came from.

Vincent stares for a full ten seconds, before he exclaims, "Good god!" He throws his head back and laughs. "Clara Castle! All this time I worried you would never make your own decision in anything!"

I huff a guilty laugh. "He hasn't actually asked yet, but..."

"That looks like asking to me," Vincent says. "Why didn't you tell me? Why didn't *he* tell me? That scamp."

"I don't know," I stutter. "I think he was afraid he wasn't going to return after the summer. Even when he gave it to me, I didn't know exactly what it meant."

"But you do now?"

I nod, but if he's hoping for more details, he'll be disappointed. Little memories are falling into place, painting a warm picture I'm not ready to share.

We walk in silence before Vincent shrugs. "Well, we'll just have to make sure you marry Andrew. He can't end up much poorer than Father, even if Grandfather does drop him."

"Are we so poor?" I ask, hoping for confirmation of what I'm already expecting.

He watches a seagull swoop. "We have no ready cash, Clara. Not much. Father would do best to sell the mill and try to pay off the debts, so he can begin afresh. It won't be easy, and we may still lose the house, but the collectors aren't going to give him any more time."

Poor Father. He's built up more than one business from nothing, but the hurricane took the first and the fire destroyed the second. I'd thought we were doing better, but it was either short-lived or an illusion.

"But if we all worked very hard?" I ask.

Vincent shakes his head. "I don't think it's worth it, Clara, honestly. Father's eccentricity is annihilating him from potential business partners, and it's beginning to show enough that even the customers are growing wary. We all need a fresh start. And we can have one. You with Andrew. Me with Anne. We can go to Galveston, and Father can stay with either of us. We can care for him. We can, and perhaps if he's not so stressed about keeping the business running, his mind can rest and heal."

"Perhaps," I say, though it's more likely that another failed business will finish off what's left of Father's spirit.

If he lives that long.

A shattered skull. A fall. Or a jump?

I stop as terrifying images play through my head. Father wouldn't end his own life, surely. Whatever happened must be some sort of accident. Won't it? How can I save him if I don't know what I'm saving him from?

Vincent's idea is more comforting than to think I'll be forced into a marriage with Billy and Father will be left to struggle to keep things afloat. I snag Vincent's hand, suddenly whispering, "Promise me we'll stay together. Promise me!"

Vincent flinches like I've just slapped him. "Clara, I just said that. Unless you marry Andrew, you're going to be with me."

"But you're going to leave," I sputter. "I know you will. You're going to leave, and Father's going to die and..."

"Shh, shh!" Vincent pulls me into his chest, glancing at the people around us.

I shouldn't cry here. Not in public when people already suspect Father of locking away his mysterious daughter like some sort of lunatic. But I don't want to leave my home by the sea. I don't want things to change. I don't even want the roles to reverse, where Vincent is working all the time and Father is left behind at home like a child who can't care for himself.

"Clara." Vincent drops his face near my head, whispering, "We'll be all right. I'm not going to leave you or Father."

I clutch his sleeves. "Promise me! No matter what happens between you and Father in these next few weeks and no matter how much you want to leave. Promise me at least a month before you make any trips at all."

"My word, Clara." Vincent cups his hands around my head, holding me against him. "Look at me. Father doesn't see the world as it is. What he tells you about it, isn't entirely true. It's hard, yes, and some places are unsafe. But there are all kinds of good people. There is music and dancing and work that makes you feel alive. And things may be hard for a while. There won't be much money. We don't know where we'll end up." He turns me to look back over the fields toward our home. "But I promise you, wherever that is, we're going to be together, and it's going to be far better than any of the days you had inside those walls."

I can't think that far ahead. Right now I can't think farther than next week when the letters end. At least now I know why they ended. Perhaps we moved and there is another house with more letters between me and Andrew. Or perhaps not, because we're together, without a need to write.

I swallow, nodding before I pull back. "Just don't leave. Not yet." Later I'll cry, but for now we walk in silence.

When we reach the house, Father's horse is in the field. I stop, freezing as effectively as Father has ever done, remembering that I am supposed to be inside working on the tasks that Father delegated.

"It was my idea," Vincent says.

But it doesn't matter whose idea it was. I slow as Vincent strides toward the door. Father meets us in the hallway, the veins in his temples standing out in blue lines.

"Where have you been?" he bellows.

"We went on a walk," Vincent answers, while I cower between him and the doorway.

Father cuts him off. "You took your sister out?"

"I am quite well, Father," I add feebly.

"You have both disobeyed me!" Father steps toward Vincent. "You will not return to the house and override my commands, is that understood?"

"Yes, sir," Vincent says, but his stance is rigid enough to suggest that that is exactly what he is going to do.

"What?" Father asks, like he didn't hear what he wanted to.

"Yes, sir!" Vincent calls back louder.

"I mean it," Father says. "You fall into line, or you leave."

"Father," I beg, realizing that every time that I feel as though I'm leading our family away from this path, it invariably reverts.

"Clara." Father's eyes blaze at me in a way they never have before. "Go upstairs. Now."

He's angry with me. I've seen him irritated. I've even had a few seconds of terror, feeling like he might shake or hit me, but he never has. But his eyes are blazing the way they did when Vincent was little and about to be caned. I don't know what it means for either of us now.

I squeeze Vincent's hand as I pass, silently begging him not to walk out the door. Father will calm down, but right now he's beyond reasoning and any protest will only make things worse. I am good at obeying, even when I do not want to. I know when to speak and when to be silent. I know when peace in the family is more important than standing up for oneself, and right now is not the time to address Father's need for control.

I try to outrun their voices, but at the top of the stairs, I hear Vincent reply, "We are your children, not your prisoners. You can't just force Clara to marry someone!"

Father is already fighting a losing battle. Vincent is courting a woman who risks imprisonment demanding a right to vote. He's not going to obey a man he doesn't believe can care for himself, much less us. Even if Father is the head of the household.

I slam my door shut, pressing against it like I can further block the noises. How have we come to this? Father is a gentleman. I am a gentleman's daughter. Gentlemen do not shout. But they are shouting so loudly that it is a wonder if the neighbors don't hear.

I sink onto the floor, hoping that Vincent will not tell Father about Andrew. I wish that Andrew would knock on the door and take me away, though that is perhaps the most foolish idea I have ever had. Father would never let us walk out together, especially when I am barely seventeen and

Andrew is so closely identified with Grandfather.

I cover my ears with my hands, rocking back and forth and letting the screaming in my head leak into deep breaths that sound like a suffocating animal.

Vincent's voice drops before Father's, and Father spends a full minute berating him, before the house goes silent. Then I hear Vincent's slow steps on the stairs. I push myself to my feet and meet him in the hall, so that he must talk to me before he can go to his room. His face is drawn. His eyes have turned from anger to hopelessness.

Alone and penniless.

"Vincent…" I move toward him, like he might abandon me in the next moment if I do not detain him.

"No." His arms wrap around me. "Don't cry. It's all right."

"Nothing is all right," I choke.

"Clara." He drawls my name out like he did when we were young and he was trying to make me laugh. Then he tweaks my chin. "Come along. If I were any younger, I'd have gotten licks for that. Nobody ever died from a scolding."

I would die from a scolding.

I follow Vincent to his room, sliding to sit on the bed after he lies down. Books scatter across his dresser; his beloved volumes of Sherlock and novels Father wouldn't approve of, but among those are more somber titles about politics and one or two that look like psychology.

"Vincent?" I ask.

"Hmm?"

I study the embossed patterns on the leather cover. "If someone psychoanalyzed Father, could they cure him?"

Vincent squints one eye at me. "We cannot afford that."

"What if we sold some of our things and had one come?"

Vincent's voice holds so much bitterness that it almost changes as much as Father's. "You stay away from him, Clara. Even when he's normal, try to stay away from him."

"If it's a medical condition, he could be cured."

Vincent sighed. "We can care for him. But it's unlikely he'll ever get better and if you hope for it, you will be disappointed."

"We must try," I whisper. "Things cannot continue on as they are. I can't leave him to spend the rest of his life with no purpose."

"Perhaps he won't. But you can't depend on him either."

Something crashes downstairs. I join Vincent on the bed, leaning against the headboard, listening to Father's laugh or cry. I cannot tell which and neither is comforting. I shiver, edging toward Vincent. Our family seems to be generations of bad luck.

"Vincent?"

"Hmm?"

"Will I be disowned if I marry Andrew?"

"I don't know."

"Will you, if you marry Anne?"

"Probably. But does it matter, really, if Father decides he won't be part of our lives?"

"Why must it come to that at all?" I ask.

"Because the world is unfair." Vincent shifts to place his palms beneath his head.

Vincent knows more of the world than I do, but I don't know what to believe anymore. I rub my arm as I ask, "Do you love her?"

"Yes."

"Then promise me you'll marry her."

He chuckles. "Don't worry. I'll marry her."

"Promise."

"I promise."

"No matter what?"

Vincent laughs. "Clara. I don't need a shove from you!"

I glance at the lamp. Father's story must change, but not at the expense of Vincent's. I owe that much to him, and Keith for that matter.

"We're both going to be happy," I say. "We are going to marry whom we want and be happy."

Though the idea makes me laugh; the reporter and reformer, the musician —and me. I'm honestly not sure what Andrew sees in me, but I'm glad he sees something. "Poor, perhaps," I add. "But happy."

Vincent laughs. "Well said. Especially the poor part. But that's all right. We weren't all cut out for traveling sprees on ships with swimming pools."

I laugh, assuming he can only mean Grandfather, and I can already hear him teasing Andrew about his travels. Then I smile wider because I remember that Andrew is coming home.

"Want to know a secret?" I ask.

"Hmm?" Vincent asks.

"Someday people are going to travel through time."

Vincent snorts. "Clara."

"I mean it," I say. "I've done it."

He cracks open one eyelid. "What?"

"I've done it," I repeat. "I've met a girl who lives a hundred years from now. Oh. And your grandson."

Vincent spews a laugh, and I don't think he believes me. But perhaps he will because Keith's grandmother wanted to know if Vincent had found the passageway yet. But before I open my mouth to convince him I'm not teasing, Father calls my name.

I slip to Vincent's door, glancing back toward him. "Promise me again about Anne."

"In this century or the next?" Vincent throws back.

Father's voice sounds controlled now, but the journey down the staircase still frightens me. He's smoking again. He looks so tired, that I cannot hate him. I feel my resolve to marry Andrew, with or without his consent, crumbling even against the attempts to fortify it.

When Father speaks, his voice hints at depression under the stern tone. "You will accept the attention of Billy tonight, regardless of how you feel. Promise me that you will do as I say," he insists.

I swallow.

Can I explain that I'm already all but officially engaged?

"Father." I start at no louder than a whisper.

"Clara!" Father snuffs his half-smoked cigar into the ashtray. "I will not argue with you over this. You will do as I say. Whether or not you marry the boy, for now you will act as though you shall."

I sway, trying to remember what Scarlet said about standing up for myself. "I don't want to marry him."

"I know," Father whispers. He reaches to stroke my hair. "I am not trying to make you unhappy, Clara. I am trying to secure your future."

I sink down at the side of his chair, tracing the armrest. "I want to stay with you and Vincent."

"Clara, next week I must sell the mill and declare bankruptcy. I don't know what will happen to any of us. Hannah and Simon are already looking for other employment."

"What?" I sputter.

Father huffs a breath, glaring at the wallpaper. "They'll be fine. I dare say your grandfather will rehire Hannah and take on Simon just for spite."

I would never expect to hear these words from my father, and I flush because I have forced him to say them. I crush my eyelids together, reminding myself that things can change. Hannah will live with Vincent and I if we ask her.

But Father continues without regard to the future of our servants. "You are not strong enough to handle hardship. You are not cut out for anything other than the life of a gentleman's daughter." His eyes are sane as he reaches for my hand, whispering, "I've been hungry before, Clara. And without a home. And I don't ever want you to know what that feels like."

I take several breaths. I know bits of my father's past from bits of letters and off-hand comments. Born into wealth and a good family, but growing up under the resentment of a step-mother who left no inheritance for him. I never knew the full extent of his childhood trials, but I see them now, haunting his eyes. I suddenly feel like Andrew, realizing I am the only person in the position to gain the attraction of someone with wealth and knowing that much of my family's future depends on my choices.

I swallow. "I will be nice to him."

"Thank you," Father says, and he truly seems to mean it.

One week. One week of pretending to court. This week, Andrew's ship will reach the harbor. This week my father will declare bankruptcy. This week, I must make sure that my father doesn't die.

20

CLARA CASTLE
Spring, 1912

"YOU LOOK LOVELY TONIGHT, MISS CASTLE," BILLY SAYS.

I focus on my gloves, resisting the urge to pleat the blue gown that Father purchased for me. My mother wore things like this every day, but I can't help feeling like a last-ditch effort to convince the Meyers to merge their family and wealth with ours.

I've never felt so torn in my life. I'm supposed to be acquiring this boy's affection, but all I can think about is Andrew arriving at the harbor only to find I've been offered as a payment for a little more time.

It seems the beginning of a cheap novel with an ending that includes woe for all parties involved. But if I even hint to Billy that my affections lay elsewhere, I am essentially booting my family into the streets. Even Vincent, for all his talk, will be helpless. If neither he, nor Father has any money, how are we supposed to begin afresh in Galveston or anywhere else?

Perhaps this is why Vincent feels it's so imperative to tell Grandfather the truth of what's happening. Grandfather has two houses, one in England and in Galveston and enough money to trot around the globe without using either. Andrew says that his house in England is very fine, and he keeps blundering in his interactions with the servants, which is ironic because we lost ours.

I've seen Hannah every day of my life. She made each meal for today before she hugged me and left to go cook for another family. I've never cried so hard in my life, not even when Mother died. Our family will be lost without her.

Eyes bring me out of my musing. I feel Vincent's glare through the windowpane as he paces the porch. And Billy's inquisitive gaze as he adjusts his tie, waiting for a response to whatever he said.

"I'm sorry," I sputter. "What did you say?"

I'm afraid he might be angry, but his face softens into something close to sympathy. "It doesn't matter," he whispers. "You are preoccupied tonight. I hope my visit hasn't inconvenienced you."

"No, not at all," I reply quickly. If anything, his visit is keeping me from realizing that Hannah is truly gone.

Billy shifts, speaking haltingly, "It's only that—I know I put you off last time we spoke and — and I'm afraid it's haunted me ever since."

For the first time that evening I force myself to look at Billy, really look at him, and I see what Father sees. He's been ending each sentence with a nervous laugh, but just now he looks truly miserable, as though he is as desperate to acquire my good opinion as Father is to garnish his affections for me. If my choice truly was between being turned out into the streets and accepting the affection of Billy, there would be no question. Perhaps he can be thoughtless, but he is not cruel.

"No, it's behind us," I answer.

Andrew forgave him that night, so I suppose there's no use in holding on to past grudges.

Billy opens his mouth to say something, but he looks so nervous that I cut him off with the only question I can come up with on short notice. "Would you like tea or coffee?"

He blinks. "Coffee, please. If you can."

"I can," I say. I have prepared both in silver teapots that show our reflections as tall narrow people, and I watch myself grow as I approach the tea service. I pour him a cup, then one for myself, though I've only had coffee once in the winter when we ran out of everything else. I watch the liquid swirl around the cups, adding sugar without even asking if he prefers it. And cream. Anything to keep my hands busy, to give my mind time to find a way to navigate tonight.

"Miss Castle." Billy rises as I turn, balancing the cups. He takes it without a glance. "I know this is very new to you, and I don't wish to make you uneasy. I realize your social interactions have been limited, and I am prepared to be very, very gracious with your..."

I lift my eyes as he quiets because he can't think of a gracious word for 'ignorance.'

"What I'm trying to say," he continues, "is that I could...I would very much like...to help you fulfill the potential I see in you. You are quite lovely and tolerably bright, and I think you've done astoundingly well considering your circumstances. My parents approve, of course, because of your bloodline, but I...I think we could quite enjoy each other's company."

This is worse than I thought, but I still cannot understand out of all the girls in town, why in the world Billy should choose me. My teacup rattles again, and I set it to the side, wondering if I should have poured coffee into china. Hannah would probably say it was desecrating the tea service.

"Mr. Meyers," I say, then hesitate because I am already imagining the deep disappointment in Father's eyes. But really, could it be worse than watching Billy realize that the girl he just declared to be his beau is completely penniless and disgraced? Somehow I feel that he would keep his word to me —and resent me for it. But he's finally stopped talking and his full attention is on me, so I try to sputter out some sort of compromise. "I know you are honest, and I must be as well. I cannot give you the particulars, but please believe me when I say that you don't understand our family's circumstances as well as you think. I'm afraid... you would be disappointed."

His shoulders soften in a tenderness that somehow still irks. He reaches for my hand, still warm from the coffee. "Clara, darling, you could never disappoint me."

I stiffen at the name. "Darling" is my father's name for me, and what I imagine Andrew will say. I don't like hearing it from Billy's lips.

"But I could," I sputter. "And I will. And I don't want to."

I realize, too late, that it's the wrong thing implied; that I'm hesitant to go into this courtship because I'm afraid I might disappoint him, not that I don't want to court him because I know that I'm deceiving him.

"Well, let's not worry about that," Billy recovers before I do. "Come. We'll talk about other things."

"Clara."

Mrs. Meyers stands in the doorway with a pale face and a smile that doesn't quite reach her eyes. "I'm sorry to interrupt, but where is your brother?"

I glance toward the porch, where Vincent was hovering earlier, but I don't see him anymore. "I'm not sure," I stutter.

"I'm afraid your father..." Her hand circles the air in aimless circles. "Your father is..."

"Where?" I ask. I'm not sure exactly what she's referring to, but it doesn't matter. She's flustered, and my father's life is precarious.

"He's in the study, but dear, he's not..."

Responding. I know what's happened even before I reach the study, but it's still disconcerting to find Father standing instead of sitting. Sitting at least gives some semblance of rest and normalcy. Father is frozen near the window with vacant eyes staring through the glass while Mr. Meyers's hovers nearby in a dance of three steps one way, then the other, poised to catch Father if he should collapse.

"Don't touch him," I say.

"Mr. Castle," Mr. Meyers calls into Father's ear, while Billy stalls in the doorway behind me.

"He can't hear you," I say. "Or if he can, he won't remember anything about it."

"I'll find Vincent," Billy says. He touches my elbow, then dashes for the back door.

"This . . . has this happened before?" Mr. Meyers sputters.

"Yes. He'll come out of it," I reply, calmer than I feel.

Now the two pairs of eyes stare at me, although Mr. Meyers' quickly snap back to Father.

"Father is usually fine when he comes out," I continue. "It's really nothing."

"Darling, this isn't nothing," Mrs. Meyers says.

"Father?" Vincent's voice carries as the screen slams. He strides into the room, bringing the commanding presence I've been hoping for. He shakes Father's rigid arm, calling, "Father."

Father sucks in a deep breath, leaning back and raising his arm, but then he goes right back to his frozen stance and even Vincent looks bewildered. He's seen this, but not often and not for long and he looks a bit desperately toward me. "How long will he stay like this?"

"Probably not more than half an hour," I answer. "But it could be longer. Perhaps closer to three."

Vincent rubs his temples, then turns his attention to the stricken couple. "It's really nothing dangerous. He very occasionally has these spells and comes out quite normal. There is no reason for you to worry, but I am sorry that you will have to continue your visit tomorrow."

"No, no, not at all," Mr. Meyers replies quickly. "If you're quite sure we cannot be of service."

Vincent smiles without mirth. "I'm afraid there is nothing anyone can do, but we would appreciate your discretion."

"Of course," Mr. Meyers replies firmly, though his wide-eyed wife makes no such promises. To my relief, the man reaches for Billy's arm, gently tugging him away from me. "Come. We'll return in the morning. And do send notice if you find you need assistance."

It feels strange to walk the couple to the door with everyone pretending they are calmer than they feel. After they leave, Vincent shuts the door, then turns and puts his back against it to face me.

The house is quiet without Hannah and Simon, and though Vincent is older and talking about marriage, I can't help noticing how young he looks. If this continues to worsen, or Father actually does die tomorrow, this is what life is going to be like. Vincent and I. No money. No home. We're going to be as dependent on Grandfather's good graces as Andrew.

I reach for Vincent's hand as though he might fall out the door and leave me alone. "Don't go to work tomorrow. Please. Let's just keep Father in the house and stay together."

For the first time, I wish that Father would stay in this stupor for an entire day, but all I can think about are Scarlet's warning. A blow to the skull will end my father's life, unless something is changed.

I don't know if the music box will work. Scarlet cannot be aware of exactly what day it is for me, and lately we haven't done well matching the music.

Vincent nods. "I don't suppose work matters anyway if we're going to lose the mill. But I must work at the paper in the morning. I've got the job and I can't afford to loose it before everything goes to pieces. I'll summon James in the morning." He glances at the door. "We must do something, Clara. He can't go on like this. He's already losing everything. He can't rebuild his life if he's going to randomly stop responding to it, and what if he doesn't come out?"

I close my eyes, feeling Vincent's panic. "I don't think that will happen," I whisper.

But a blow to the head could mean a fall. I spin back toward the study. "Let's just see if we can lay him down."

Father's eyes are still vacant, still fixed on the window. His limbs are stiff like he's already dead, resisting Vincent's attempt to remold them. We lower him to the floor, pivoting his body like it's a board, but he moves only once. I retrieve the pillow from the bed, working it beneath his head, though he can't be comfortable when his forearms are still raised, one elbow higher than the other.

I sit next to him, watching gravity inch his limbs closer to the earth. I wonder if he actually can hear us, if he can think, and if he's panicked, realizing he's trapped inside of his own body. His eyes are wide, staring like there is a horrible creature on the ceiling.

"Galveston has a medical school," Vincent says. "Perhaps we can find a cure there. Or an asylum."

"He's not going to an asylum!" I snap. "If I have to work myself and buy a little cottage and care for him, I will."

"How would you both work and care for him?" Vincent asks gently. "Clara, I don't want to send him away, but this might be beyond us. We must let Grandfather know what's going on."

I raise my chin. "I will not abandon him."

"Haven't you given enough of your life to him?" Vincent snaps. "I love Father, Clara, as much as you do. But listen to yourself! You have one chance to break out from beneath him, and you're pledging to sacrifice the rest of your life caring for him? Are you going to marry Billy, too? I'm sure he's perfectly capable of navigating you through this with all his worldly experience."

"You were listening?" I ask. "I saw you peek in, but you had no right to linger and spy!"

Vincent looks away, grinding his jaw.

Angry words swell in my throat, but I swallow them and dig Father's watch from his pocket. It's nearly 9:00. I wind it, listening to the tick with my eyes closed as I have done so many times before. It's nearly two hours before Father wakes with a shudder that runs through his body. His left arm still hasn't reached the floor, but now it circles once, then goes to his temple as he blinks. I watch his eyebrows twitch, as confusion sweeps through his irises. I usually let him wake slowly, but Vincent surges forward onto his knees.

"Father?"

Father trembles as he shifts his face toward us. "Wha...what..."

"You froze," Vincent says.

I realize Father may not remember it, but this is the first time he can't deny it after spending one moment standing at the window talking to Mr. Meyers and the next waking on the floor with only his children nearby. Even Father can't pretend or believe that nothing at all happened.

Father pushes himself to a sit, then sways, setting his head into his hands.

"Are you dizzy?" Vincent asks. "What do you remember?"

"Don't overwhelm him," I warn. "He always wakes up confused."

"I don't..." Father trails off, like talking is too much of an effort. Then he jolts. "Wasn't Mr. Meyers here?"

"Yes, he was, but he's gone now," Vincent says. "We sent him home when you stopped responding."

Father goes rigid again, then collapses as he slowly lets out his breath. "Oh, god."

I reach to touch his arm. "James thinks this is something that can be cured," I say. "Perhaps not here, but we will find someone who knows why it's happening."

"It's always happened," Father whispers. "I suppose. They told me...even in school. But I didn't know..."

His voice leaks into a breath.

"Well, then it isn't anything that we can't handle," I say quickly. "Let's just sleep for tonight. Tomorrow we'll find some way."

Father's eyes are already glazing over, but perhaps I can coax him into bed before it happens again. Tomorrow, we'll ask James to the house and see if he knows anyone who can see Father.

"She's right, Father," Vincent says. "Everything will wait until tomorrow. And we're not going to leave you. Whatever happens to us, we're going to face it together."

Father rubs his head again, letting out another sharp breath, but he nods and pushes himself to his feet. "It will be all right. Good night."

Vincent and I glance at each other before we leave, honoring the dismissal. I worry about leaving Father alone, but for now it feels like our only choice. Vincent walks ahead up the stairs, but I touch his elbow when we reach the top silently begging for his thoughts. He stills, gripping the railing, but he doesn't turn toward me.

"I'm going to write Anne," he says. "I've got a bit put aside in savings. Not enough to save the company, but perhaps enough to rent a place to live. We'll work from there."

I swallow, realizing except for reading and writing, I have no skills. Even without Andrew's arrival, my life is changing forever. It's never going to be Father and me in this big house. I should be excited, but I'm terrified.

I manage to keep tears at bay until I shut my door safely behind me. I've spent nearly every day of the last eleven years within these walls, and I cannot imagine life outside of them. I don't want to leave my home by the sea. Will I still be able to see Scarlet?

I wind the music box over and over again, watching the spinner whirl until it blurs into a translucent circle. The dots pull up each lever until it snaps back in place with a tiny ping.

Scarlet either doesn't hear or she doesn't answer, but I continue playing the song anyway, listening to the wind rustle through the trees outside my window. I cock my head, hearing a violin from somewhere far away. It must be from the hotel. I scoot closer to the door, wishing it was Andrew's, and again wondering what had happened if I had joined him in the hallway that night. The song slows, echoing each note coming from the music box. I sit up. That's Andrew's song.

I grab the winder, halting the music box and the violin fades with it. When I release it, the music floats around the room and within a moment, the violin fades back in. I clutch the music box, closing my eyes and concentrating on the violin. Andrew is the only one that knows the song, but there's more.

The tone. The vibration of the strings. Perhaps this connection that spans distances is not Andrew's music box, but the song itself. I can't pinpoint the direction. The music floats around me, coming from one wall, then the other. The tunes collide, joining on one note, then dragging as the music box keeps its steady rhythm and the violin slows and wavers. Something is wrong.

"Andrew?" I whisper to the music box, since it's the only explanation that I can hear him at all.

The music goes loud, then soft, sounding like the time Scarlet and Keith were fighting over the volume of the radio in the car. The music box slows, syncing again and the violin grows louder just before the tinkling stops. I wind it again, waiting for the answer.

Andrew's violin fills the room, so loudly that I jump and expect Vincent to run inside. The tune has slowed even more, the vibrato lingering in a doleful and sloppy wail that doesn't sound like his playing at all. The next phrase speeds up, but the shake remains part of the song. Matching tunes but one wobbles like a top as the music box races steadily ahead. I hold the lever, sending the room into a frustratingly quiet wait, then play again, trying to sync the music.

"Andrew?" I call again, a little longer.

The violin answers in a trembling drawl, like the bow is jumping away from the strings as it passes. Then the room goes quiet, except for the steady solo of the music box, which plays on until its call dies mid-song.

21

SCARLET BELDON

Summer, 2012

MY ENTIRE LIFE FITS INTO A SUITCASE.

I sit on Clara's bed with my ankles crossed, hugging my knees and trying to decide if that knowledge is liberating or just depressing. I could grab that handle and end up anywhere — well, after I'm eighteen and have some say in the matter.

But sometimes I feel more like a dandelion seed being blown aimlessly. For all my speeches to Keith about how he has to take his life into his own hands and make it happen, sometimes I feel like life is going to whisk its carpet from beneath my feet no matter what I do. I told Clara that I'm leaving, and she said she had to go, too. I haven't wanted her time to pass, but I hope Andrew returns and they're together before I leave.

Dad's ready to go again. He didn't even last the freaking summer here, so I could be starting school anywhere this fall. I tell myself that it won't be that bad. Either the music box will keep us connected no matter where we are, or I'll never see her again after one of us steps out of the front door.

That's going to suck, but I have a feeling it's inevitable. When I hear the music box, I don't run like I used to, because it's getting too disappointing when it doesn't work. But I step over my suitcase to pick it up. I'm not expecting it to work, since it hasn't the last few times.

It jolts, and I squeal as Clara's fingers materialize. "Clara! Gah, I didn't know if I was going to see you again!"

There's so much to say, that I don't even know where to start. I haven't told her that Keith and I got scholarships to the same college so we might be going together. Vincent would be so proud. But I pull back, because Clara should be more excited than she looks.

"What day is it?" I ask.

She swallows before she says, "It's . . . that day."

"He'll be fine," I answer like a parrot.

Clara nods, but I'm not sure she believes me.

"All right," I say. "What's going on right now? What are your father's plans for the day?"

"I don't . . . We're staying home," Clara says. "Even if he had plans, I don't think they're happening. He went into the catatonic state last night while the Meyers were here. He knows now, and he didn't protest when Vincent and I talked about finding someone who can help him. He did know about it though," she adds like she just remembered. "He said it happened when he was young."

"I'm telling you," I say, "it can be a symptom of trauma. I'll bet there's a lot about your dad that he's not telling you."

"Well, I wish he would," Clara says. "It would make our lives a lot easier." She glances toward Edmund's bedroom, then whispers, "I haven't heard him at all this morning. Vincent said to let him sleep before he left for work. I don't want to wake him, but Father never sleeps this late."

"My dad always sleeps late when he doesn't have work," I reply quickly. "That's a good thing. The longer he sleeps, the less we'll have to watch him."

She takes a breath, then changes her mind, asking, "Do you think you'll be able to stay the entire day?"

"I hope so," I answer. "But if not, it'll be okay. You're strong enough on your own. You can take care of your boys."

She laughs, then bites her lip. "You're taking the music box with you when you go, aren't you? Perhaps we can still travel and—oh, and my ring. I don't want it to stay in the attic."

"Your ring?" I ask.

"The pearl ring. In the envelope." She pulls on a chain, fishing the ring from her bodice. "It was from Andrew."

I wonder how it got into the envelope, ending up with Vincent leaving it for Clara, but I sit up with a grin. "Was it now?"

Clara bites her lip and ducks her head, then laughs.

"See? You're already changing things." I spread my hands like we can all just peek in the future and fix a bad choice. "Everything is going to be fine."

"Father doesn't know yet," Clara says. "He thinks I'm going to woo Billy, but perhaps Billy won't pursue anything once he finds out our situation. So after Father is safe, we'll just have to stall another week. They're coming straight back to Galveston as soon as the *Titanic* docks, but they're taking the train instead of another liner so —"

I see her mouth move, but I have no idea what she's saying because my mind has snagged. "Whoa, whoa, wait!" I hold up my hands like she's a runaway horse. "Who's on the *Titanic?*"

"Grandfather and Andrew," Clara says. "I told you they were coming home early. They'll be docking in two days and—"

"Crap! Crap, crap!" I surge to my feet, pacing toward the door, yanking on my hair. "Clara, you have to get him off! Has it left yet?"

Clara's eyebrows tuck. "Yes, it left days ago."

I'm panicking. I, Scarlet Beldon, am panicking because I can travel through time, but I can't turn it backwards. And I'm suddenly realizing that Vincent and Anne never actually said the funeral was for Mr. Castle. "You have to get a hold of him," I say. "Call him. Send a telegram. They can do telegrams, right?"

I need to calm down. Clara's staring at me and panic creeps across her stunned expression. "Why?"

"It's going to hit an iceberg," I say. "You've got to send a note now and tell them to slow that thing down or a lot of people are going to die."

Clara stares at me. "How do you know?"

"Because the *Titanic* is like the biggest disaster in the history of ships!" I snap. "What's the fastest way you can get word to Andrew? A telegram?"

"I don't know if ships can get telegrams," Clara says.

"They can." I rub my temples and try to think. "It can because I saw it in the movie."

"What?" Clara asks, but I grab her hand, dragging her into the hallway. "Where in town has a telegraph machine?"

"I don't know," Clara sputters. "The newspaper office, perhaps, but it can't be the *Titanic*. This is the first time it's ever sailed, and Grandfather said it was designed not to—"

"It only sailed once, and nobody's ever going to build another with that name," I say.

I don't have time to argue. She has to believe me, and she does, because she only stares for a split second before she dashes down the stairs. She yanks on the front door so hard, it looks painful when it doesn't budge.

"It's locked," Clara cries.

I reach for the bolt that isn't there, realizing the only lock needs a skeleton key. "Where's the key?"

"Father has it," Clara answers.

We glance at each other, then turn to pound back up the stairs to Edmund's room, bursting in without so much as a warning.

I run toward the dresser, but Clara halts, staring toward the bed. "He's gone. Scarlet, he's gone!"

I spin, feeling my mind go three different directions. Right now, Edmund's safety is the last thing on my mind, but he does have the key to let us out of the house. "Maybe he went to the bathroom," I say.

Clara glances toward me, then the open door across the hallway. "No, he didn't."

"So he locked us in??" I demand.

"Father doesn't normally lock the doors," Clara says. "Perhaps Vincent did, so Father couldn't leave."

"I don't care who did it! Find them and get the key!" I wail.

We search every room, but the house is empty. Even the servants are gone.

"The spare is gone, too!" Clara calls, searching through the drawer for the key. "Vincent must have taken it. But when did Father leave and why didn't he tell me?"

"Why wouldn't he tell you he was leaving?" I ask. "That makes no sense. Why would he lock you in?"

"Because I'm alone?" Clara asks. "Hannah and Simon are usually here, but Father let them go yesterday. Never mind. We can climb through the milk window."

Her shoes make more noise on the stairs than my sneakers, but she takes them faster than seems possible. We rush to the kitchen, swinging out the miniature window frame. Clara hunches as she climbs through, bunching her skirt in one hand and jumping to the ground like a robber.

I follow, twisting my foot as I land. "How far is the newspaper office?"

"Only a few blocks. Vincent should be there."

For once, I'm relieved that no one can see me because I'd be turning every head. Clara is already attracting enough attention, the Castle girl on the loose, running down the road like a dragon is after her.

My legs burn by the end of the block, and I feel the bits of shell digging into my sneakers, but I flail on, putting one foot in front of the other, driven by a word I never thought would concern me.

Titanic. *Titanic.*

Out of all the freaking ships in all of freaking history, why does Mr. Mordaunt have to pick that one? Can we even change it? What would happen if we manage to warn them, to change the future and past of so many people? Would we wake up and find everything instantly different? People born, whose grandfather previously didn't even exist? Would people remember the change, or would the *Titanic* fade into the pages of history as the forgotten predecessor of cruise lines?

The newspaper office is a tiny, brick building with two windows in front. Clara bursts through the door like a gunslinger.

"Is Vincent here?" she asks.

A young man with greasy hair slicked to one side looks up from a drawer he's rummaging through. "He left."

Clara sets her hands on the desk. "I need to send a telegram. It's very important."

One side of his mouth perks as he continues to arrange bits of iron blocks with letters on them. "It would have to be for me to send it. Rodge is the wireless operator. He's out."

"But..." Clara falters. "Couldn't you do it? Surely you know how."

"It'll cost you."

His eyes are twinkling, but Clara pales anyway.

"He's flirting with you," I say. "Just play along with it."

"I can pay you later," Clara says, because Clara doesn't know how to flirt.

The man ambles over to the counter, digging a small pencil from his pocket. "Who are you sending this to?"

"Callaghan," Clara says. "Andrew Callaghan."

The man whistles. "That's a long name, Miss, for a favor."

Clara snaps the chain from her neck, sliding the pearl ring toward him. "Here. I've paid you. Now it's not a favor. I need to send a message to Mr. Callaghan, who is currently traveling on a liner called the *Titanic*. Can you get a message to a ship?"

The pencil stops as he glances up. "Mr. Callaghan the one who gave you that ring?"

"Yes, if you must know," Clara answers. "Now listen. I've just received word that there's ice and—"

"I can't send anything to the *Titanic*, Miss," the man says.

"But it's going to sink!" Clara says.

"It already sank. Early this morning. Already got news from New York, but not many details yet." The man slides the ring back toward her. "Your brother knows. That's why he went home."

Clara sags against the counter and the man hurries around the counter. "Now, Miss Castle. It's a bad business, I know, but listen here. Word has it that another ship picked up some of the passengers. Perhaps your Mr. Callaghan is on there."

Clara turns frantic eyes to me, but for the first time I have nothing to say. The man looks out the window, wiping his mouth like he's hoping he can hand Clara off to someone else.

Clara drops her eyes to the edge of the counter. "I think you're wrong," she says. "But thank you."

She turns for the door, calmer than I expect. The man swallows, crumples the paper, and tosses it into the corner as Clara steps onto the porch.

She forgets to let me out, but I slide through just before it squishes me. "Clara..." I have no idea what I'm going to say, but I jog to catch up with her.

"You can look it up, can't you?" Clara asks. "On your laptop?"

"Yeah, but..." I push my tongue against a bottom tooth, realizing just because I can travel through one point in history, doesn't mean I can change any of it. "I don't think I have to. That ship just picked up the people in the lifeboats. Everybody in the water froze."

"Andrew doesn't swim," Clara says. "He would have drowned. But perhaps he got in one of the lifeboats."

I turn my head away, biting my tongue, but it doesn't help because I can see the bay, sparkling like hundreds of evil fairies are creating a path to seduce unwary swimmers. Clara will discover the truth soon enough.

I wipe away tears, scolding myself not to cry. It's her fiancé, not mine. She needs that bit of hope while she gets used to the idea that Andrew is dead.

Andrew's dead. I've been worrying about Mr. Castle, and even wondering if anything bad happened to Clara. But I never ever considered that Andrew's letters stopped because he died.

"I heard him last night," Clara says, nodding like she's trying to convince herself. "I heard his violin playing the song with the music box, and I thought it sounded so...so..." she trails off before finishing quietly, "scared."

I walk with my mouth clamped shut. Maybe they changed their mind and didn't get on. Or crawled onto a door or something. Clara's story can't end like this.

"Scarlet, my grandfather is dead," Clara whispers.

So is her fiancé, but if she's too shocked to talk about it, I'm not going to remind her. I grit my teeth, feeling helpless as she rambles on in disjointed thoughts that make me worry she'll go into shock.

"This changes...everything," Clara continues.

"How so?" I ask.

"I don't even know yet."

I imagine poor Andrew freezing to death like Jack from the movie, hands clutched to his violin, probably thinking about Clara. If you can think about anything in freezing water. Great. Now *I'm* thinking about it.

"It's over," I say to both myself and Clara. The same thing I tell myself every time Dad leaves another woman behind. "Whatever happened, we can't change it. But he's not scared or hurting anymore." I know it's a crappy consolation but, honestly, there is never any good thing to say when someone dies.

"No. Just me," Clara replies.

"Clara." I grab her hand. "Stay with me in my world. Maybe that's why we couldn't find information. Maybe you came forward in time."

Even as I talk, I see her shaking her head.

"But you could!" I insist. "We could find a way. You could go to school and study music. Girls have so much more now than they did back in your day. You can do anything you want."

"I want to marry Andrew," Clara says.

"But you can't." I brush over it. I don't want to pretend nothing happened, and it's going to be a long time before Clara is okay again. But our time together is running out. If she comes forward, she's going to have to do it soon. If I get sucked back now, I don't know if I'll ever see her again. "Do something else. Come now and—"

Clara shakes her head and whispers, "I can't live in your world, Scarlet. Even being there a little makes me sick. It makes me feel old. I cannot live ahead of my time."

My shoulders slump. "Clara."

"I will be fine," Clara says, though her voice shakes more with each sentence. "We don't know that he's dead. And I have Vincent. And Anne. And Father..." She jolts, lifting panicked eyes toward me. "Father! Where's Father?"

"We'll find him," I say, though I'm realizing how many promises I'm making lately that I really have no control over.

Clara spins. "The lumberyard. He must be there or the bank or..."

"Lumberyard," I say quickly. Out of the two, it seems the most likely place to hit his head.

"I can't lose him, Scarlet," Clara says. "I can't lose him, too."

"Don't panic," I say, but Clara's already taken off like a bolting horse. The lumberyard isn't far, and I smell fresh wood even before we arrive. We both see Edmund standing with his back to us, silhouetted against the sky on top of a stack.

"Fath—"

I grab Clara's mouth, hissing into her ear. "Shh! Don't startle him."

But, alerted to his daughter's voice, Edmund's head whips around, scanning the crowd below. He sees Clara and frowns, but he looks sane as he swings over the edge, climbing down the ladder without so much as tearing his coat.

"Clara! What are...why are you here?" He reaches to pull her against him, though his voice wavers between bewilderment and anger.

Every tear that Clara has held back breaks through. "Andrew's dead."

Edmund stiffens as every face within hearing range turns toward us. His eyebrows draw inward, and he actually looks a bit stricken.

"What?" he asks. "What do you mean? Isn't he with your grandfather?"

"The ship sank," Clara chokes. "It hit..."

"Shh." Edmund cuts her off, as alarm fills his eyes. "You misunderstood, surely."

"No," Clara says, but he puts a finger against her lips.

He's feeding her lines, but his reaction jolts Clara into a confused pause as she, like I, tries to understand the situation.

"Let's go home," Edmund croons softly. It's bizarre seeing how easily he swings the pendulum, and suddenly Clara looks like the mentally unstable one as Edmund turns to the foreman. "George, I'm taking her home. If Mr. Meadows stops by for the payment, direct him to my address."

"Yes, sir," the man sputters.

Edmund wraps an arm around Clara's shoulder and nudges her back to the house. She complies quietly, while I follow, glancing around for anything that might fly out of the blue and cause them injury.

"Now tell me what's happened," Edmund says. He tightens his arm around Clara's shoulder, but it looks more like a hug than an imprisonment.

But Clara shakes her head. Edmund frowns as her eyes soften, roving to and from nothing. "Where did you hear that the ship sank?"

"From the newspaper," Clara whispers.

Edmund stops. His breath goes in and stays in until I wonder if he's going to freeze in the middle of the street.

Clara tugs on his hand. "Please, let's just go home before something happens to you, too."

Edmund stands like an anchor, catching her hand as she steps toward the house. "Darling, nothing is going to happen to me."

"Get him into the house," I say, partly to distract Clara from Andrew and partly because the roars of cars and clatter of wagons and clanging of hammers are driving me crazy trying to figure out which device is going to hurt Edmund.

Clara lifts her face toward her father, taking a breath and then pausing like the perfect way to coax the man back inside has occurred.

"Father," she whispers. "If Grandfather is dead, and..." She swallows Andrew's name. "That leaves us. Vincent and I. Doesn't it?"

The world around me fades as her meaning falls. Vincent and Clara are the only grandchildren — the only ones who will inherit Mr. Mordaunt's wealth.

Edmund nods, whispering, "Yes," though his eyes are crumpling like he's already anticipating ways that Mr. Mordaunt will intentionally jab him in that will.

"Then we're saved," Clara whispers. "Vincent already has a house. He's not..."

Penniless.

Her eyes dart back to me. Things have changed, some better and some far, far worse. We changed Vincent's future. So far we've saved Edmund's life. Clara doesn't have to marry Billy anymore. They may not even lose their house. But Andrew is dead. It doesn't mean that we changed his story as well — but what if we did?

I close my eyes as Edmund looks toward the footsteps behind me. Vincent trudges from the direction of town with slumped shoulders and hands hiding in his pocket.

"Vincent," Edmund says, but his son waves him off.

"I know," Vincent says.

He digs a hand out of his pocket, pinching something between his fingers. The pearl peeks out from the band that catches the sun.

"You left it," Vincent says.

Clara eyes it dully. "I meant to."

And then she begins to cry.

22

CLARA CASTLE
Spring, 1912

WITH MY EYES CLOSED, I CAN SEE THE MEMORY ALMOST AS WELL AS I COULD at the dance the night it happened. The dancers have departed, couples and families loading into wagons and automobiles, rumbling across the boards away from the pavilion. I sit at the edge, waiting for Vincent and Anne to stretch out their walk until the last possible moment. A man is packing the crystal cups into crates, which are hauled away by people I have never seen before.

The musicians break up, some snagging the last of the punch, others hurrying into the darkness, and still others playing bits of songs on their own. Andrew is among them, leaning forward to catch something the cellist says.

He grins, shaking his head as he answers, but he doesn't seem truly annoyed and the smile turns up a bit more as he spies me. He glances around, perhaps looking for Billy or Vincent, then approaches with his head cocked.

"Vincent and Anne went for a walk," I explain. I glance toward the shore, but it's impossible to tell which couple is them. "He said he wanted to wait for you anyway."

Andrew laughs. "How gallant."

"He can be quite gallant!" I play along, wishing Scarlet could see how well I'm doing, even while I'm glad that she's not watching. "When it's in his best interest."

"Can't we all?" Andrew asks. He sits beside me, leaving a bit of space between us. "Did you have a good time tonight?"

I laugh, feeling the evening wash over me once again. "Yes, I did. Well, most of it."

I don't have to tell him which parts put a damper on the evening. I drop my head back, watching the spray of stars from the window. "I'm a little sad that it's over."

"Me too," he says. "I would have liked to have danced with you."

My heart squeezes, interfering with its own beat. It was easier when I told myself that Andrew was working, and even if he wasn't, he didn't dance. Wouldn't dance, wouldn't even ask. I watched him play, swept into that place where music is the only thing that matters and the world around him is simply something he watches with a vague interest if he notices it at all. But now, knowing that he would have danced with me if he could, I feel the disappointment settle in deeper.

"Me too," I admit.

Someone begins to stack the chairs, clattering and punctuating the lost moment. Andrew sets the violin onto the bench beside him and stands, holding out his hand. "Will you dance with me now?"

Now? I glance to the men carrying a table past us, imagining their irritation. But every second is one less that we have before this chance is gone forever. And I've never actually touched Andrew for more than a few seconds, never danced with him or held his hand. I take it now, feeling warmth pass from him to me and back again.

"No music?" I ask, mostly to distract him from the heat I can feel rising in my face.

Andrew grins. "I hear it's overrated."

His hand twists in mine until his fingers close around my palm so lightly that I can feel the brush of its slight tremble. His other hand touches my waist, a light pressure that I can scarcely feel beneath my corset. He's taller than me, but he doesn't dwarf me like most of the other men.

I can't look away. I can't see the workers or Vincent or the starlight or anything besides his face, his eyes that hold me, yet quiver a bit. I feel his fingers tighten, tremble.

"I don't dance much," he whispers. "Not like those other boys."

"Neither do I," I say, though at this point, even if he stepped on my feet, I would adore him. I shrug. "I hear good dancers are overrated."

I feel his breath as he chuckles. He sways without stepping, first to the right, then the left and once we've gotten the feel of the silent rhythm, he steps toward me, guiding me back and around. It's a waltz, but it isn't. Our stance is wrong. We're not turning as much as we should.

But it doesn't matter, because we're stepping together, first one foot, then the next, and I have what I've wanted all night. It doesn't matter that James can't cure Father or that Billy thinks Andrew ought to fade into the corner and just provide the music.

Around us, glasses are stacked in unceremonious clinks, instructions are passed from mouth to mouth, and furniture protests in short screeches. But the mellow tone of a bow drawn across strings recaptures the fading feelings as though they were left behind by the couples like dust laying on the floor, waiting for music to stir them up again.

Andrew and I glance toward the lone cellist who has retaken his seat, swaying gently with the instrument. His eyes are on us, and he winks. I should be mortified, but I'm enveloped with gratitude that sweeps around us, blowing away time itself and granting us this moment.

Perhaps it knew that the water that lapped gently in the moonlight that night would grow still as glass, reflecting each light of Andrew's ship as it slipped beneath the surface. Perhaps it foresaw that the violin that Andrew abandoned on the bench, would play its last song within a year before its strings were frozen and its music silenced forever. Perhaps time is a conscious thing that goes out of its way to give us one memory that embodies all of the best of life, so that we have something to cling to later, when we discover that it is just as helpless as we are to halt the inevitable.

I trace the pearl on the ring, wishing I had kissed Andrew before he left. I don't suppose I'll ever know what kissing is like, for, like Scarlet, I have decided that I will never marry for convenience. And, like Father, I cannot imagine falling in love a second time.

I did not marry Andrew, did not kiss him, but that doesn't make the love less real than Father and Mother's or Hannah and Simon's, or even Anne and Vincent's. Death can end experiences, but it cannot shatter memories. Andrew might even be alive. He could have survived. The paper could be wrong.

I eye the newspaper with it's screaming headlines and long list of notable names, including Grandfather's. Andrew isn't mentioned. He's lost somewhere among the other 1,500 people who aren't rich enough for reporters to care about. His family may not even realize he's gone, since Grandfather booked him under Mordaunt and not Callaghan, which must be why Scarlet's searches never found him before.

How has my future turned so hopeful and so bleak at the same time? If Grandfather is truly dead, then money will no longer demand my choices. I could buy my own house if I want to. I can bring in the most expensive specialist to help Father. I could pay off all of his debts, recover the lumberyard back from the bank, and relieve every bit of stress that has ever driven Father into his study. I will be wealthy with no need to marry at all.

But I want to do more than that. I want to live. Live for Andrew and Vincent. Live for Scarlet in the future. She's going to go to college, and she's already promised to send detailed notes of her lessons and perhaps even books if she can manage. I'll never earn a degree, but I want to learn everything that she does.

Likewise, knowing that my time will leap far ahead of her days, I will keep a journal and write what I learn about life, about growing up. About the mistakes that I make that she can avoid. And the wonderful things I discover that she can't learn from a textbook.

If I can find a way to be content without Andrew. If I can ride out the storms I know will happen: the Great War and the Depression, and perhaps even the second war if I live that long. If I can learn to be happy through the turbulent years ahead of me, then surely I can teach her how to face her own uncertain future, no matter what it holds.

Then I will return to this house and leave the journal in the chest with the music box. She will find it. If not she, then someone else. Someone will remember that I lived. Someone will feel as though I am their friend, though I may never meet them.

I flip open the lid, wondering how in the world I could send the journal where Scarlet can find it from wherever I go next. Perhaps it will not need to be in the house. She leaves it in the chest. I find it in the box. Perhaps it could work opposite.

There is a letter inside the chest, still in a sealed envelope with my name on it, but no return address. But it doesn't look like Scarlet's handwriting. It looks like Andrew's.

I can't breathe. I sit, hand pressed against a stilled and aching heart. The postmark date is ahead of time by nearly a week. Scarlet must have found the letter in her time and slipped it into mine. Which means, I was to receive this letter a week from today.

I read the words again — the letters are too sloppy to be Andrew's careful scroll — for even after learning to read and write, he has corrected many of the blunders that made his first letters so endearing.

And once I open this, the truth will be known that it is not Andrew. But I force my fingers under the seal, willing it to start out, *Dear Clara. I am safe.*

If Scarlet was here, I'd hand the letter to her and let her open it. But I am alone, and I flip the envelope. It is probably something to do with the move to Galveston. Perhaps an employer. Perhaps—

I spy a picture of a red flag with a white star on the heading, and my eyes fall on the date.

April 12, 1912

Dear Clara,
We have left Queenstown, and my next stop will be New York.

The rest of the words blur, and I'm pressing my hand against my mouth because if I cry the way I want to, I'll alarm everyone downstairs. This is Andrew's last letter. I'll never receive another.

He really was on that ship and he really isn't coming. My fingers crumple the envelope, pushing a second paper free. A second letter, stuffed in separately, written with the same hurried scrawl that smeared the envelope. I wince as I unfold it, for Andrew never does anything sloppily.

> *Clara,*
> *They are loading the last of the lifeboats, but I don't think*
> *there will be enough, unless another ship comes along before we*
> *go under. I must send this along with someone else to post. I never*
> *wrote to my family. I thought I could tell them. Please, copy my*
> *letters and send them home. Tell them I love them. Forgive me,*
> *Clara. For not coming. I love you. I love you.*
> > *Andrew.*

I read it, then read it again.

I love you. The words I never heard him say.

But at the bottom, even smaller — even more difficult to decipher is one last sentence.

> *Please, don't stay locked up.*

The pressure in my chest swells. Andrew was stranded on a ship he knew would sink and he was worried his family won't know what happened, and I'd stay shut up in a house with someone who locks me into pantries.

The screen door slams, followed by the front door, and I hear the key click. We've had quite a few people stop by to ask after Grandfather, but I can't imagine why Father is locking the door in the middle of the day. I wipe away tears, stuffing Andrew's letters into my pocket as I hurry down the stairs.

Father grabs my shoulders, steering me toward the study. "Clara. Clara, come. We must leave." He digs into his pocket for the key to the secretarial, stabbing it shakily three times before he manages to get the key inside the lock.

"What?" I ask. "Why?"

"They want the money, and I don't have it," he says.

"But they'll get it, surely they know that," I sputter. "Father, even if Grandfather left you out of the will, Vincent and I will have enough to pay off the lumberyard."

Father hunches at the desk, rubbing an eye. "They don't care about the debt, Clara! They want me gone. They're going to arrest me before I have the chance to sell the house, because they don't want me here."

The gleam of terror in his eyes transfers to me. "Arrest you?" I ask. Can they do that? I glance back toward the door for Vincent, wondering if Father's mind has finally broken beneath the stress or if he truly can be arrested and held. "But we have the money," I try again. "Everyone knows now that—"

"It will be months, perhaps years, before that paperwork is done, if your grandfather hasn't decided to spite us all and leave the inheritance to someone else." Father grips his head, doubling over like his skull is breaking. "Clara, if they put me in, if they find out, they'll never let me out."

An engine stalls in front of the house, then shuts off. I step toward the window to see who has come, but Father grabs my arm. "No, don't! We must go."

"Go? Go where?" I ask, but Father is already dragging me toward the kitchen. I tug against his hand, but his grip is as strong as if it's frozen. "Father, my letters! I can't leave without my letters!"

And I need the music box. I need to travel to Scarlet's time, to put my own on hold until I can figure out what has happened to drive Father half-mad with fear.

"You don't need them!" Father snaps.

"It's probably Vincent outside!" I protest, though if Vincent has the car, there is no reason why Father would be dragging me through the kitchen toward the garage.

"Vincent!" Father's fingers clench my arm until it hurts, and he shakes me. "Vincent is no longer part of this family!" He spins back, hissing in my face and spraying bits of spit. "He's been with your grandfather this whole time, trying to destroy us!"

I search his eyes, expecting them to glaze, but I see only rage covering a bright glint of pain. I'm not sure what Vincent said; if he told Father he didn't think the mill was worth saving, or that the townspeople no longer trusted him, or even that he thought he needed to live at an asylum, but whatever it is pushed Father's illness into deeper depths.

"What happened?" I whisper.

Someone bangs on the door behind us, sending us both into a panic. I jolt away from Father, racing toward the dining room and snatching the music box, but I only get one turn in before Father grabs my elbow, dragging me down the back steps.

Grandfather's car reflects the sunlight off the golden chrome like a siren offering the sweet song of wealth that can buy anything except more time on earth. Father shoves me into the seat, and I grab the music box before it tumbles to the floor. I manage to wind it a second time, but the song is covered by the engine's roar.

Father swings into the driver's seat. He throws the car into reverse, backing out of the carriage house so quickly, that I grab the edge of the seat. The wheels crunch on the shell, covering Vincent's shouts that ring from the front yard. "Father, stop!"

I hear other voices calling, but as I turn to look back, Father takes a sharp turn to the right, throwing me off balance. I feel the tiny vibration as the music box plays like a tiny soldier marching steadily as the battle rages around him.

"Father, slow down, please!" With one hand clutching to the seat and the other protecting the music box, winding it again is risky, but I twist the key again, calling, "Scarlet! Scarlet, help me!"

April 16, 1912. We have changed our story, but it's still the day my father dies.

"Father, stop the car!" I say. "Please, please stop!"

Something screams like a thousand voices at once, covering the rumble of the motor. From the corner of my eye, I see black smoke trailing the sky behind the train engine that rumbles down the tracks ahead of us.

Another wail behind us yowls like a cat, and I spin in the seat. The police car is hardly marked, but the hand-cranked siren battles with the blast of the train. Good heavens. The police really are after my father.

I spin ahead, switching my plea to spur him on. "Go. Go."

But I see the train thundering toward us, barging toward the crossing. Father speeds up the car and I scream, "Father, you can't beat it!"

"It will trap us if we don't pass!" Father says. "There's room, Clara! There's room!"

There isn't room. I've never driven a car, but for once I'm positive I know how things work in the outside world. I reach for the steering wheel, yanking on it until the car jolts, sending my music box tumbling to the floor.

Father straightens the wheel, knocking my arm away. "Clara, don't! You'll kill us!"

"Please, please stop the car!"

Father blurs, and I backhand the tears away as I snatch the music box. A large crack spiders across the top as I twist the lever, screaming, "Scarlet!"

I glance back at Father, but his eyes have lost their focus, fixed across the field instead of on the train. I reach for his hands, trying to pry them from the steering wheel.

"Andrew!" I'm not sure why I'm crying for the last person on earth who can help me, but there's no time to think about it. *Stop the car. Stop the car.* The wheels jolt, pitching the car to the right as we hit the tracks at an angle. The train blares its horn. Metal screeches against metal as the train wheels lock onto the track, sparking as they slide toward us. The train looms large, casting a shadow over Father's face as he blinks, then swings his head toward the side.

"Get out!" I scream, but there's no time to save Father.

I shove my door open. The music box flashes in the sunlight as it falls, shattering against steel and wood. I jump, but the train smashes into the car, scooping me back into the cab as metal crunches.

Father cries out, and I feel his arm wrap around me, offering an illusion of safety that lasts for only a second. The seat rises to my left. The ground shatters the window beneath me.

We're knocked apart by the ceiling. Something slices my arm, then batters my head. I tumble against something soft, then something hard, then Father, then the steering wheel, every impact snapping, stabbing, sending pain shooting into a different part of my body. The car lurches, then stalls with a series of shrinking rocks, coming to a halt with the steering wheel inches from my head.

I lay still, afraid that any movement will snap something else in my body. It hurts so badly that I can't scream, can't even manage to pull in more than a sip of air. I'm trapped beneath Father with my back pressed into his chest. His arm drapes across my shoulder, dangling a limp hand just in front of my face. As close as he is, I cannot feel his breath. I cannot sense his heartbeat. I can, however, hear the ticking of his pocket watch. It dangles above my head, swinging from the steering wheel.

The second hand vibrates behind the shattered glass in brave attempts to move forward, despite its loosened screws. I close my eyes, listening to the tiny ticks.

Once.

Twice.

Then they stop forever.

23

SCARLET BELDON

Summer, 2012

"WHAT IS WITH THE COUNTRY MUSIC!" I SNAP MY SEAT BUCKLE INTO place and turn twisted eyebrows onto Keith. "Why does everyone around here listen to that?"

"Cuz it's good," Keith answers.

"You're driving a car!" I say. "You can't listen to country music unless you drive a truck."

"Can't afford a truck. They have terrible gas mileage."

"I can deal with the clunker." I spread my fingers to ward off the speaker. "But the music has to go."

Keith rolls his head toward me, then punches the scan button on the radio. It flips through a few fuzzy stations before landing on a new sound.

"Happy?" he asks.

"Yes. Thank you."

I settle against the seat, making a show of breathing a sigh of relief before I realize that the melody is played by an accordion. The lyrics start, sounding like an opera singer, and I wince as Spanish words that mean nothing to me float through the cab.

I blink twice, trying to think of how to get out of this one and watching the grin creep up the side of Keith's mouth. I punch the search, waiting while it flips through the numbers and lands on another station where a guitar starts another country tune. I punch it again and it scoots along, then blares, "*Siempre te amaré.*"

Keith's shoulders shake, and I collapse in defeat. "Fine. You win."

Keith chuckles and punches the preset, bringing back the original song. I fold my arms and pretend to be pissed. "Your radio's broken."

"Well, what kind of music do you listen to, girl?" he asks, like he's suspecting something illegal.

I go through the list of my favorite singers, probably the only area in my life where I actually match the tastes of most other teenage girls. You know, the songs everyone listens to, but won't admit liking. "I said you win." I hedge.

He laughs. "Before you leave, I want to take you back to the bookstore for coffee."

"That sounds too much like a goodbye outing," I say.

"What's wrong with that?" Keith asks.

"I suck at good byes!" I wail. "I'm no good at goodbyes. Besides, we're going to go to the same college. So we're not going to say bye. We're just going to say . . . see ya . . . in like . . . a year."

"Okay," Keith says. "But I still want to have coffee with you."

I look out of the window, forcing down the swell of frustration. I don't want to leave. It's the point blank truth and no matter how I dress it up or ignore it, I'm furious at being uprooted again and having no say about it. But I'm not ready to deal with all the emotions I just managed to get rid of, so I counter it with teasing.

"Well, you have my number. It's not like we have to resort to snail mail. I don't know what more you could want."

"I can think of a few things," Keith says, perking in the seat.

I slap his leg. "Shut up! Gah, you're as bad as your grandpa!"

Keith just laughs, then swerves, launching the car into a jolt. "Whoa, sorry. Pothole."

"That's not going to work, sweetie." I throw back, then pull the strap at my shoulder. "Seat belt."

"Well, it was worth a shot."

I roll my eyes, laughing, realizing Keith and I are going to have a lifetime of jokes nobody else understands.

But the laughter doesn't last, because I remember all over that Andrew is dead, and I'm about to move away from Clara's house. I nibble my lip, glancing down at the music box. "Do you think it will work?"

Keith shrugs. "I don't know. One test isn't going to be enough if it doesn't, because it hasn't always worked at your house. We'll just have to keep trying."

"If it only works at the house," I say, "you're going to have to have to keep it. You're going to have to keep in contact with Clara and tell me everything that's going on."

Honestly, the music box probably should go to Keith, since he's actually part of the Castle family. But I'm not ready to give it up unless I find that's the only way to stay connected to Clara. Keith has more of a chance to sneak to her house or even to the yard and try to contact her.

"I wish she would just come forward," I say.

"Would you?" Keith asks. "I don't think I would. Even if things were bad here, it would be hard never seeing anyone again and learning to live in a place more advanced than you know. At least now she knows a little of what will happen in her lifetime and how to navigate it. And her father is alive."

He says it like it might cheer me up, but I flinch. "Whoopee."

Keith sighs as he pulls into the parking lot of the bay. Our plan is to start out where Clara has been and though the pavilion is gone, the pier seems as good a place as any. Keith puts the car in gear but lets the engine run, wasting his precious gas. "Scarlet, I don't think it's your fault that Andrew died on the *Titanic*."

"Yeah, but I didn't fix it." I rub my eye. "And I could have. I just didn't know in time."

"You can't fix everybody's lives," Keith says. "Sometimes you have to do what you can with yours. Okay? Nobody can bring back their best friend's boyfriend. Nobody. You just have to be there for her."

I take a breath, then unbuckle. The music box sparkles in the sun as I climb out of the car and we walk down the pier as close to where the pavilion was as we can get. I wish I could rewind time and tell Andrew not to get on that ship. But this is as good as I can do, trying to keep in contact with Clara even after I move.

We agreed to try, but even now, I have no idea how much time has passed in Clara's world. She may even know for sure that Andrew is dead, may have seen his name listed in the papers. Or at least known that the Carpathia docked and no telegraph came from either him or her grandfather.

I swallow and twist the key again, winding it all the way. We stand there as it plays softly, its sound covered by the waves and footsteps of the fisherman that passes, peering toward us with perked eyebrows.

Keith waves. "Hi."

"Come on, Clara," I whisper.

I close my eyes, trying to send enough thoughts with the music that she'll hear and answer. But it keeps playing. I wind it again.

"Maybe they got the bodies," I say. "Maybe she's at the funeral. Or just . . . can't answer."

Or maybe she's trying to answer, but can't get the music to match on her side. I close my eyes again, listening for the echoing song, but there's nothing.

This has to work. If Dad sells the house, Keith is going to have a hard time sneaking close enough to travel without trespassing on someone's property. And I'm not ready to say bye to Clara. After leaving everybody behind all the time, I was looking forward to having a friend where distance didn't matter. The music ends, and I wind it again, shaking my head.

"We can try again," Keith says. "We can't just assume that because it didn't work this time, it won't ever work anywhere else."

I want to believe it. So we try it at the end of coffee in the bookstore where we met. We try it at the building where the newspaper office once stood. The lumberyard is long gone, but we stand on the porch of the grill. And then, to top it all off, Keith has to go to work, and I'm left standing in the front yard of Clara's house with a music box that isn't being answered.

I can't think of the house as home anymore, not with the smiling man in the suit and the couple who walks around the bottom story, oohhing and ahhing and talking about how much work it needs but it has, oh, so much potential. Dad's there too, smiling and talking it up like it's the Taj Mahal. Vincent might have left some things for Clara in the attic, but those things are coming with me now.

The potential owner sees me and offers a smile, catching me as I try to escape up the stairs. "What do you think about living here?" she asks. "How is it for teens? We have a daughter about your age."

"It's terrible," I say. "It's hot. Like really hot and you're pouring down sweat all the time. And it eats Internet signals for breakfast. Your cell phone probably won't work in here."

"Really?" she asks, already digging through her purse. "Does it work in the yard?"

"Yeah." I sneak a peek to the hallway where Dad is sending me a not-so-subtle glare. "I mean maybe your server is better than mine, but..."

"No, you're right." She holds it up. "No bars."

I grimace, sucking between my teeth. "It's bad. I don't really get why anyone would want this house."

"Oh, we've always liked it," the lady says. "I used to drive by and just imagine it was mine. I've always felt drawn to it."

I flinch, but Dad ends the conversation. "Mrs. Meyers, Scarlet just doesn't want to move. She loves this house."

Mrs. Meyers.

I open my mouth to inform her that she most definitely cannot have this home, but Dad's swept her into the kitchen, so I go upstairs, mentally begging Clara to take me back to when the house is fresh and cleaned by a servant who doesn't believe in coffee. I don't care if everyone is in mourning. The whole world feels pretty bleak at this moment.

I sit on Clara's bed, winding it again and again and again until the voices fade downstairs. I stayed for as long as I could on D-Day. We got Edmund back to the house, and Vincent was just coming when everything started fading around me. I got sucked back into my own life, which, quite honestly, is the last place I want to be right now.

"Scar." Dad barges into my room. "What was that downstairs? We're not staying here, and you need to get that into your head. Even if I can't sell the house, we're still moving."

"And then I'm turning eighteen, and you can give it to me," I reply.

His hands flail. "What are you going to do with it?"

"Stay put, for once." My voice shakes more than I mean it to. I glare through the pane of the music box. Where the heck is Clara?

Dad blows a long breath and sits on the vanity stool. "We're going to find somewhere, Scarlet. Somewhere that has a good school and lots of places for you to make friends. But this town isn't it."

I keep my eyes on the gears turning in the box, then wind it again so I have something to do.

"What is your fascination with that music box?" Dad asks.

I shrug. "I like the song."

"If you're going to play the same song over and over, can you be a normal teenager and start a band?"

"Can you be a normal father and not take me away from it?" I return.

Dad sighs. "When you're married, you'll understand."

"No, Dad. I don't think I will. I mean, sometimes things don't work out, I get that. But with you..." I finally look at him. "Things never work out because you run every time something gets hard."

"I don't run, Scarlet," Dad says. "I just don't see the point in staying in something that makes me miserable."

We both clamp our jaws and let the music play. This time when it runs out, I don't wind it again.

Dad folds his arms, then looks away. "Do you want to go live with Sherri?"

Sherri?

The world pauses around me. I can't live with Sherri. They're struggling with money already. I don't even know if that's legal, since she's my step-mother. But images flash into my mind, filling what was an otherwise uncertain future. I could work and help them make the payments — like Andrew did for his own family.

I peek up asking slowly, "Is that an option?"

"It could be," Dad says.

I'd have Kate back. And they want to stay in New York. And Sherri's a little flighty for jobs, but she's a great mom. She actually asks you how your day went, and if there are any guys you like, and if you're struggling with homework. With her support and Kate's humor and my drive, we would actually make a pretty good team.

"Maybe," I say, because there are still a lot of factors to think about. "Maybe you should give this house to her."

Dad laughs and stands. "Good try."

After he leaves, I stare at my phone instead of the music box, then take it downstairs to the yard to try and find the illusive signal. Sherri's still at work, but Kate is probably off. I wonder why I didn't look harder for a job here this summer and try to put money aside or send it to them. I take a breath and punch in the number that connects directly to Kate's phone.

"Hello?" Kate's voice comes across the line.

"Kate, it's me," I say, though I'm sure she already knows from the ID.

"Hi! How's your crazy beach life?"

"Crazy," I reply. "And coming to an end, apparently. Dad's got the house up for sale."

"Psssht." I nearly hear her roll her eyes. "Of course he does."

"I was wondering — and I need you to be truthful — how you feel about me coming to live with you and Mom?"

The silence kills me for three seconds before she asks, "Really?"

"Yeah. I was thinking, I could get a job, and we could all help out. With one more person, you could probably even afford a better place to live. But only if you think that would help. I don't want to make things harder than—"

"Yes!" she screams. "We'll have to share a bedroom, but I don't have much stuff and I can clean out half. And then you can meet my new friends and go to our old school and I want to meet your Keith. Maybe he can come up sometime."

I laugh. "Whoa, slow down! I don't know if it will happen yet. I'm just seeing if it's even an option."

"It's definitely an option," she says. "It's a good option. You should take it."

I laugh, and — like it's somehow giving approval — I hear the tinkling of the music box floating through the window. It's not nice to cut off her chatter, but I shout over her, "Kate! Kate, I have to go! I'll call you back later."

I hang up and slide the phone in my pocket, jogging inside. I'm halfway up the stairs when I hear Clara's voice, very faintly, though her tone sounds like she's shouting.

"Father! Father, stop!"

I catch my own shout, before it leaves my mouth and send the energy into my feet, pounding up the stairs.

"Scarlet?" Clara cries, but her voice comes from the music box like she's trapped inside. *"Scarlet, help me!"*

I snatch up the music box, trying to hear the tinkling of the song while I'm winding my own.

"Hold on. Hold on," I chant. "Clara?"

I release the lever to hear my song. It's there, and I halt it, listening for her tune until I can match them. But she's screaming so loudly that I can hardly hear the song from her end.

"Father, stop the car! Please, please stop!"

My hands shake so hard that it's hard to hang on to the lever, but I release it when I think the notes are close to the same phrase. Another scream jolts through me, filling me with a terror I can't place until I realize... it's a train. Oh god, it's a train.

"Father... beat..."

Clara's voice is static like a TV flipping channels in a warehouse full of screeches and clattering. I scream, bringing one hand to my hair before I snap it back to the box. "Work, work, work, work!"

I can't hear the music on Clara's end. I stop the lever, then start it, then stop it, as panic overrides any ability to think clearly. Clara's voice grows more shrill.

"Clara!" I yell. "Clara!"

"Scarlet! Andrew!"

She may as well be at the end of a telephone. A blare covers her voice, then the most horrific crash I've ever heard.

The music box jumps from my hand as though hit by an invisible force. I lurch for it, brushing the clear glass as it tumbles toward the floor. It shatters. It practically explodes. Tiny shards of glass scatter as the gears slide across the floor and disappear beneath the vanity.

All sounds stop.

The screams.

The metal.

The music.

I stand with both arms raised, squeaks hovering in my mouth, trapped by lungs that are as frozen as every other part of me. The house is silent and still. The only signs of life come from the twitter of a bird and the sunbeams that dance across jagged glass.

24

SCARLET BELDON
Summer, 2012

"DO YOU THINK HE KNEW?" KEITH ASKS.

I'm not sure if he's whispering because of the subject matter, or because we're in the back room of the library and he's scared to be loud. He's sitting at the table with a tiny screwdriver, trying to fix the gears of the music box with parts from one we found at a resale shop. I can't tell if he wants to hear the music again, or if it was the only promise that would make me stop bawling into his shoulder.

I'm in front of a machine that feels like a relic from the dinosaur days, peering at a screen showing the tiny print of old newspapers that was saved onto microfiche files. The newspaper Vincent worked for reported everything: who was visiting friends out of town, who fell off a tractor and broke his leg, and who hosted a party and everyone that attended. It's no wonder Edmund was private about their family.

But a fatal accident involving a car, a train, and a paranoid, bankrupt business owner with a daughter kept away from social events? There is no way even Vincent, on his quest to destroy family records, could keep that story from these pages. And even the tiny print on a machine in the back room of the library won't keep me from finding it.

"Know what?" I ask, spinning the knob and watching a page whoosh by on the screen.

"About the traveling," he says. "What if Clara did say something to Vincent about it, but he never figured out how she managed it?"

My head hurts, perhaps from crying, perhaps from squinting, and I turn in my seat, almost grateful for the distraction. "Why do you think she'd tell him?"

He shrugs. "I don't know. But what if he was looking for a passage, and he told his granddaughter about it? If he knew that Clara time-traveled, she obviously did it from the house."

"And when you started looking like him, she thought that he actually managed to find it?" I ask.

Keith nods. "Yeah."

Well, there's a time loop I don't want to think about. I shrug. "Makes sense."

I turn the knob again and my persistence is rewarded by a large headline about the *Titanic*. Beside it is the story I'm looking for, but it lacks the flair that described what was served at Mrs. Jones' party and how anybody who's anybody was there.

"Train collides with car," I read, as Keith sets down the screwdriver. "Tourists were shocked on Tuesday when their train collided with Mr. Robert Mordaunt's famed Lozier Automobile, which has brought delight to many residents of our town. Rumored to be a victim of the *Titanic* disaster, Mordaunt's vehicle was left in the care of Mr. Edmund Castle, who was driving with his daughter aboard. The collision flipped the vehicle, instantly killing Mr. Castle. His daughter was pulled from the wreckage, perishing only moments after the collision. No injuries were reported from the passengers aboard the train, who join the residents of our town in mourning the loss of Mr. Edmund and Clara Castle. The funeral was held at the Presbyterian church on April 19th."

"Sounds like they were more upset over the loss of the car," Keith says.

"Vincent wrote it," I reply. "I guess he was trying to direct attention away from his father's actions."

For once, I wish the nosy newspaper would have reported the juicy details, like why Edmund was driving around with Clara in the first place, why he refused to stop the car, and what possessed him to drive it in front of a freaking train.

But Clara is gone. Her life is over, no longer running parallel to mine. Instead, her death is reported right next to reports about Andrew's ship, and Keith and I are left with a newspaper clipping on tiny film and a broken music box.

Keith studies the springs and stems of the music box movement, finally admitting what I've suspected all along. "I don't know if I can fix it or not."

I blink back tears. "We can find someone who can."

He growls. "It's just this one piece."

I stare at the article. "She's dead, Keith."

Keith hesitates before saying, "I know."

"I guess I was just hoping she survived somehow," I say. "Even if I can't see her, I want her to be alive somewhere."

He pauses again before peering like he expects I might slap him. "I found her grave."

I flinch, then reach to push the button, watching the film wind itself back onto the reel. "Really?"

He nods. "It's actually pretty close to where my parents are buried. We can go — if you want."

I chew on the inside of my cheek.

I've seen Clara's name on letters a hundred times, but I'm not ready to think of it etched in stone.

I blink. "The box."

"What?" Keith asks.

"Clara's box. The one she kept the letters in. Once we get the part that plays fixed, we can put it into that."

"The part that plays is called a 'movement,'" Keith says, with a grin. Then he continues twisting a tiny screw until he takes a breath and winds it. The fanfly begins to spin, turning the gears, and the cylinder plinks the tune from the comb.

I stand. "Oh, my gosh. You fixed it."

Without the original box, I have no idea if it would work even if Clara was alive, but the song tinkles back to life, and I cover my mouth to stifle a laugh.

Keith spreads his arms. "I'm amazing."

I snatch the whole thing from him before his cockiness breaks it again. But I set it on the table and throw my arms around him. "You're the best. Come on. Let's get it back into a box."

We tiptoe past the rows of computers and the librarian's station, then walk home with me cradling the music movement like it's a baby chick.

"It might still work," Keith says. "Didn't you say you saw Clara before she traveled when you were playing the piano?"

"Yes…" I answer slowly. "But she didn't see me."

"Because she didn't line up the music with you. But what if it's actually the music, not the box that syncs up the time passage?"

I'm getting the sneaking suspicion that time travel is becoming an obsession with Keith, but every time he tries to explain any of his thoughts on it, I just get confused. "How so?" I ask tentatively.

"Like frequencies," he says. "Frequencies carry radio waves. What if it has to do with the frequencies of this particular song, lining up with when it was played in the past?"

The fly is brushing my palm like a tiny butterfly as it spins. I scrunch my nose, trying to process Keith's logic. "Then why wouldn't Andrew have traveled when he wrote the song?"

"Because it wasn't the right frequency," Keith answers like it's obvious. "Think about it. You played that song from the music on the high keys of the piano, and you saw and heard Clara, but it was a momentary thing. Then, when you got the music box, you saw her more clearly, but it wasn't until she also had it that she actually could travel back and forth."

"Okay," I answer slowly, worried that if he goes on, I'm going to be lost again.

"Okay. So Andrew never played that song as high as the music box could, but Clara said he was playing it the night the ship sank and the violin connected with the music box, giving her a chance to hear him, but not travel."

"Because he was playing in a lower key?" I say slowly.

"Exactly," Keith answers. "So it's the song he wrote that's been connecting everybody, but the traveling wasn't triggered until it was played closer to the frequencies projected by the music box. And only one music box exists, so..."

"So that's why no one else has traveled," I answer slowly. "And we could only travel back to her time because Clara was playing the music box, so the frequencies already existed. But once she died, the music box shattered..."

"And the window is closed," Keith finishes.

"But why wasn't it shattered when I got it?" I ask.

Keith frowns. "I don't know."

"I do," I say softly, staring ahead so I don't have to look at the land where the lumberyard once stood. "She didn't have it with her the first time. We changed it."

"How do you know?" Keith asks.

"Why would she take a music box on a car trip, unless she was deliberately trying to make contact with me? She must have realized that was how her dad died. She was still trying to save him. She just didn't know it was when she died, too."

Keith blows a slow breath and falls to musing again as we turn into my yard. We hunt the garage for a drill and a bit. I ignore Dad as I take the stairs and rummage through the chest until I find the small cedar box. Cleaning it out, I set the ill-fated love letters aside and hand it to Keith, flinching as he turns it over to drill a hole.

"What if it doesn't work?" I ask.

"What do you mean?" Keith pauses with the bit poised.

"What if it won't do the time glitch?"

"Scarlet." Keith stares at me.

"Well?"

"Scarlet." The drill sags as he uses his free hand to run through his hair.

"I thought you just wanted it as a keepsake."

"I want to change things back. To travel time. To—"

"Scarlet. She's already dead," Keith whispers. "Even if it worked, you'd have nothing but an empty house to return to."

"I have to try," I whisper.

He's going to argue with me, but he changes his mind and closes his mouth, squeezing the trigger to the drill. I watch tiny shreds of wood dig from the hole, accessing a part of the wood that smells fresh and new. Keith's hands shake as he fastens the movement into the box. "Shall we see if it works?"

I nod, and he hands me the box.

I twist the key and the music tinkles the melody. The box feels different, the vibrations traveling through a thick wall of wood, resonating with a deeper tone than before. But, as Keith's fingers touch it, the room darkens around us.

It's not like traveling. It's like being surround by the screen of an old movie, maybe like what people talk about when they say their lives flash when they think they're dying. I have never once in my life considered that I might be witness to an antique car colliding with a train.

It's not pretty, even on the wall. The train pushes the car, caving the hood on the driver's side, until the wheels catch the rail and flings the car aside like it's a bug. It rolls, smashing one side, the top, and coming to rest on the opposite side. It happens so quickly, I can barely register it, and there's no playback. All I can think about is that Clara is in there.

And she's not dead. Yet.

The car is swarmed by men as the train slows, still carried along the tracks by the momentum. White faces peer from the windows as passengers stare at the collision. I can't decide if I want to watch or not as one of the men climbs on top of the wreckage. He peers inside, calling something to the others.

"Clara!"

I gasp the same time Keith does as Vincent swings out of the cab of another car. He rips across the yard toward the Lozier, plowing through the men who try to barricade him. He shoves three men aside and vaults onto the car, balancing on the side.

And then he's pulling Clara out, and I wish I could make my eyes close, but I can't. Clara is a bloody, mangled heap, and the men are right when they shout that she should not be moved. But I know she's going to die anyway, and I'm not even sure that she's aware of Vincent's pleas.

Why did I rewind this music box? I don't want to watch this. I wind it, just enough to hear one click.

The picture backs up, like the movie is reversing.

My mouth falls open, and I give it a good twist.

The frame freezes on the moment when the car is mid-flight in an upright position that a car should never be.

"Keith!"

I gasp and give it another whirl, laughing with something between desperation and delight. I'm turning back time — or at least the story that's playing on the wall.

"Scarlet, what…" Keith reaches for the box, and I turn my body to block him, almost giddy with delight. "It's going back! It's going back."

Another twist, and Clara is winding her own box in the passenger seat of the moving car. Then it skips like someone has spliced the film, and she's resting her chin on the table, eyes moving from the music box to the ring in her hand.

That's almost far enough. If I can line up the music with the box in her time, I can tell her not to get into the car with her father. But if I'm actually turning back time, I want to go even further. I give the music box two more turns, witnessing scenes I never saw.

Clara's family is in the dining room, during what looks like an argument between Vincent and Edmund. Then I see myself, giggling over Clara's engagement, right before I figure out that a wedding is not going to happen.

And I'm almost back far enough.

Almost back to the night the *Titanic* sank. I see Clara sitting on the floor by her window, highlighted by the moonlight. She looks so blissful. She's messing with the music box and then—

Clack!

"Scarlet, stop!" The music box is jerked from my hand, but not before the winder gives a decisive little click, refusing to budge one more inch.

"You over-wound it!" Keith shakes the box, and it lets out a few notes before the gears jam.

"No!" I launch desperately for the box, glancing at the frozen picture on the wall. "That's not far enough!"

But the picture fades and everything around me goes dark.

CLARA CASTLE
Spring, 1912

AIR FILLS MY LUNGS LIKE THE FIRST BREATH OF FRESH AIR WHEN I open the window in spring. My head hurts and the pain spreads through my body, concentrating in the pulsing throb of my arm.

The train.

I shove onto unsteady feet, turning to jump free, but I'm in my room. Moonlight spills across the floorboards, lighting the hem of my gown that hangs in a shredded loop where it's been ripped. It's dirty and bloody. I pull up my sleeve, breathing harder as I see dark blood running down my arm. But it dries, heals, and then fades. My dress shrinks into the beaded gown, evaporating the pocket that holds a folded paper. It drops to the floor, and I kneel to retrieve it.

> *April 12, 1912*
>
> *Dear Clara,*
> *We have left Queenstown and my next stop will be New York.*

Who found that letter when I died? Did they read it? I flip it, searching for the second, but the page is blank. Scarlet must have changed something. Andrew hasn't written the second letter yet. Andrew is alive.

I stumble to the trunk in the hallway, glancing toward the soft glow coming from beneath Vincent's door. I crack open the lid, easing it upright, and search for the music box. It's there. Clear and perfect glass encases the gears. I pull it out, retreating to my room, before I wind it.

My mouth is dry, forming words between short breaths. The music plays, and I worry Vincent will come to see why I'm playing a song in the middle of the night. Bits of memory piece together. The train. The *Titanic*.

Tears splash onto the glass, splaying tiny droplets in all directions.

"Scarlet, help me," I whisper.

I listen for her song, closing my eyes to block out the terror that crowds my mind but the faint music comes again from the box itself. Andrew's song resonates across the strings, filling the room as the notes collide, then stop abruptly.

"Andrew," I whisper, though I know I'm the only one who can hear it.

I glance at the second letter. He stopped midsong, perhaps not because he ran out of time, but because he thought to write to me and send it on a lifeboat. I let the music box play, pulling open a drawer to retrieve my writing box. Andrew will touch this piece of paper, provided nothing in his own story changes. I swallow, then dip my pen, touching the nib to the paper.

> *Andrew, darling, I can't explain what's going on, but I can see this paper. You must play the music higher, as high as you can, and at the speed of the music box. If we can match the notes, I think I can get you off the ship.*
>
> *Clara*

Poor dear, he's going to be so confused, but I cannot explain the music box on paper, even if he could spare the time to read it. But he may be desperate enough to try. If I remember dying, he must as well. Which means he probably woke up cold, wet, and disoriented. That's not going to make it easy for him to play a song or think clearly enough to write a letter.

I snatch the music box, twisting it once again. This time I control the winder, trying to slow the notes down to Andrew's pace, but I can't hear him anymore so I simply let it play, summoning whoever can answer.

It's Scarlet who answers first. I hear her song, and before I realize that she's traveled, she's shouting, "Clara!"

Her arms swallow me, and I see Keith behind her, grinning. Scarlet's crying.

"You were dead," she chokes in a voice so high, it doesn't sound like it belongs to her.

"I know. I remember," I say, but I'm too worried about Andrew's death to dwell on my own. "But look! He hasn't written the letter yet."

I see hope flicker across her face, then hesitation, because she realizes that he's alive on a ship that is still sinking.

"What time is it?" Keith asks.

"Late," I answer. "But I wrote him on the letter he wrote me, so he must see it. And he must know that something has changed because if I remember dying, he probably does as well.

Keith snags the paper, fishes a pen from his pocket, then clicks it and scrawls in letters so sloppy I wonder if Andrew can read them.

What time is it?

"Are you sure this is going to work?" he asks.

"It worked for Clara and me," Scarlet says, "when we used the same paper."

"So there you go," Keith says. "Clara, you can buy a journal, leave it somewhere where Scarlet can find it, and you guys can write to each other forever."

"Until her time skips ahead of mine," Scarlet says.

But Keith sits up with a shout. "Look!"

Andrew's script darkens the page like a ghost is writing it. I want to touch it, but I worry that would mess up his pen.

Clara?

I snag the pen from Keith's hand as Scarlet screams.

I'm here.

How?

Never mind that. What time is it?

There is a full moment before the ink starts again, and I wonder if he's trying to find a watch or if he's so stunned, he can't think clearly enough to reply.

1:45. The ship will sink soon.

"He knows," Keith says.

"How soon?" I ask.

"2:20," Keith says. "I looked it up last night."

I can't compute those numbers because they're too close together, but they freeze my entire body.

Scarlet snatches the pen, then scrawls.

Don't write. Go play as much like the music box as you can possibly get. Do not stop.

But more letters appear as Andrew wastes time, until I want to shove him away from the very conversation that I started. I watch, wincing as the sentence slowly forms.

Left hand is busted. I'll try.

"That's his string hand," I say. "That's why it's shaking."

Please, don't stop.

I'm not sure if he sees my plea or not, because he doesn't write back. When I hear the violin again, it's changed pitch on the highest notes of the strings. I clutch the glass. Without Andrew touching the music box, it may not work. But Andrew wrote the music. If anyone can recreate the frequencies of the box and travel, he can. But he's playing too slowly. Still with the unfamiliar shake, and this time it's worse because I realize it's pain, not fear, that mars his song. I hold the key to the music box, then release it when he's one note ahead in the song. The volume increases, sounding like he's in the room with me, and even the music chimes a bit stronger. But Andrew's song wobbles and the violin pauses.

"Don't stop," I whisper.

He picks up the song, synchronizing with the box's notes.

Scarlet claps. "He can hear it! He can hear it! Oh come on, baby, you can do it!"

He's touching his instrument and I've got the music box, so that's the best we can do to travel. I catch Keith's eye and his face looks as twisted as mine feels. Andrew's song changes, going even higher than I thought possible on a violin.

"There's no way he'll be able to recreate the frequencies of a music box," Keith says.

"Shut up," Scarlet retorts.

The music box begins to slow and I halt it, winding it as tightly as it will go. The violin stops, then chimes in when my song begins again.

"He can hear it!" Scarlet screams.

Downstairs the grandfather clock distorts our song. The melody I always loved hearing grates against my head and heart, ruining my orientation with the music box's song. The clock chimes once, then twice.

"We still have twenty minutes," Scarlet says.

"Twenty minutes until the ship goes under," Keith says. "It'll list too steeply to stand before that."

"He can hang on to something!" she snaps.

My ears roar like water is surrounding me, as I realize what Keith is implying. I lift my face from the box, whispering, "Not if he's playing."

I can't even tell him to stop trying and swim. The violin is our only chance. I close my eyes, feeling tears run down wet skin as I wind it again.

This time Andrew doesn't answer. Instead, we hear an ever increasing *ping, ping, ping,* each sounding higher than the last.

Scarlet's head snaps up. "He's tightening that top string."

We all wince as the string protests with higher ping until Scarlet grips the side of her face, "Stop, stop, stop! You're going to break it!"

"He can't hear you," I say.

Andrew's song starts mid-measure, so high that it's painful to listen to, though still below the music box's cheerful chime.

"Anybody play the violin?" Keith asks. "If he can't match us, maybe we could match him."

Scarlet shook her head. "Not unless a piano would work."

"Shh!" I hiss, because I hear a chorus of other stringed instruments, playing an entirely different song. The floor dips beneath me, and I glimpse a white railing on one side, a white building on the other, and the silhouettes of people.

"What?" Scarlet asks.

I glance toward her, toward the bed and vanity. "I just saw it."

"Saw what?"

"The ship."

"The melody just went to lower notes," Keith says. "You're getting closer to matching."

We stare at each other as Andrew's song strengthens and lessens, sometimes skipping a note altogether.

When the music box loops and the melody drops, I see it again. The rail. The moonlight and brilliant stars. I turn my head, spying Andrew, but then he's gone again and I'm stuck in my room.

"It's working!" I shout, then hunch my shoulders because I hear Vincent's chair scoot back.

"No, it's not!" Scarlet grabs my arms like my father's trying to drag me into the car again. "It's backwards! He's drawing you there! You have to get him to stop playing and play first!"

"What?" I ask, but then I'm on the ship again and cold blasts my body. I'm still kneeling, and I lift my face, glimpsing blue eyes. "An—"

"—drew." I finish the word in my own bedroom, falling forward as the floor straightens beneath me. Clutching the music box, I twist my body away from Scarlet as she lurches for it.

"No, don't stop it!" I scream. "I'll get him!"

"You shouldn't be traveling there!" Scarlet clings to me.

"There isn't time to switch!" I say as it loops to the beginning of the song. "The deck's already tilted. If we lose him, we may not get him back. Besides, if I go, he can touch the box."

Keith kneels next to me, reaching gently for the box. "Okay. We'll play it here."

"No! What if she gets stuck?" Scarlet wails.

"I have to try," I say.

"Try what?"

Vincent's voice makes us all jump. A candle illuminates half of his face, highlighting his frown.

Of course, he can't see anything. Just his little sister kneeling by her window talking to a music box.

"Can you hear it?" I breathe as Andrew's violin floats back through the room.

"Hear what?" Vincent asks.

And then the ship is back, and I twist and lurch for Andrew. I catch his trousers and he kneels, grabbing my arm. "Clara."

And then I'm back in my room.

"No!" I scream.

Vincent jolts in the door. "Clara, what?"

"Leave me alone!" I shout at him.

"Clara, what?" Scarlet asks.

"Please distract him!" I cry.

And then Andrew's song picks up the melody, and the floor sways beneath me again. I tumble forward, remembering the car and the music box smashing against the tracks. I cradle it as my shoulders and knees hit the floor.

"Clara!" Andrew grabs my shoulder. "What? How, no. No, no, no."

I unfold myself, thrusting the box toward him, grateful that the gears keep playing no matter what's going on around them. "Take it!"

The floorboards beneath us shudder as the ship tilts beneath my boots, nudging me closer to him. Andrew loses his balance, falling against the hand that holds the neck of the violin. His bow slides past us, and he lurches to grab it.

The floor shifts abruptly, and Scarlet catches me. I see Vincent take two steps into the room before his great-grandson picks up my writing desk and hurls it at the wall. It shatters, spewing pens and ink, and Vincent whirls toward the fluttering papers.

Three notes of the violin and the cold blasts me again. Andrew drops the bow, grabbing me as I slide down the deck. He's sitting, using the traction of his clothing to keep us from sliding. The bow slips past me down the deck.

"Hold it!" I shout, shoving the box at him.

The ship cracks, splintering wood and steel that cover the chorus of screams. Andrew releases the violin, grabbing a rail. He watches it slide down the deck, smashing against the railing, before it tumbles into the dark water. His hand wraps around mine. It's bloody. His smallest finger is missing and his ring finger is crooked. The blood slips between our hands, but he cries out and pulls me toward him, hooking his free arm around my chest to pull me against him. I reach for the rail, hoping the music box won't wind down.

The floor beneath us lifts like someone is raising a wall. I hear the echo of Scarlet's music box, but it's not matched up.

"Hold on. Hold on!" Andrew says.

The distant song stops, then starts again, closer to the tune that plays between us. Once the music box hits the water, the gears will stop.

"Let go, Andrew!" I choke. "We have to both touch it."

Andrew's eyes widen like I've lost my mind. A man tumbles past us, his body rolling toward the railing separating the upper and lower deck.

I release my own grip, reaching for his hand. "Let go!"

"We'll fall!" he shouts.

I feel myself slipping from his arm and launch for the railing again. We're out of time. The stars are disappearing as the deck rises. It's going to be a straight drop onto the railing of the promenade if he doesn't let us slide soon.

"It can get us off!" I shout. "We're going to die anyway!"

Andrew's chest heaves, but I can't see his face anymore because he's pulled me too close. He takes three breaths, moans once, and then we're sliding. The wood heats beneath me, ripping against my legs. All I can see is the music box and Andrew's hand grabbing it.

Pain crashes into my knee, arm, and shoulder, shooting up one side as I slam against the floor. Warm, sticky air replaces the cold that rushes in and out of my lungs. I feel Andrew's breath before we roll away from each other.

I see my bedroom ceiling, my curtains fluttering. My leg is burning, but I sit up.

Andrew's laying on the floor, cradling his bloody hand and choking on his own breath.

I grab his shoulder. "It's all right. We're back at the house. We're safe. We're off."

Andrew rolls toward me, sitting up, casting eyes around the room, then back to my face before he wraps his arms around me. We hold each other until his heaving breaths calm and my heart rate returns to normal.

"Clara, Clara," he gasps.

I pull away from him, searching for his face, but I only glimpse it before he kisses me. I don't care who's watching. I don't care how improper it is. I press closer, wrapping my arms around his neck and kiss him back.

"How did . . ." he whispers.

I shake away his question. "Never mind that. That story is far too long for here."

And the room is far too quiet. I pull back, glancing around. Andrew's letter lays on the floor. My writing box is near the window. But Scarlet and Keith—even Vincent—are gone.

26

SCARLET BELDON
Summer, 2012

May 3, 1912

Dear Scarlet,
  *I've been all over the house, and I cannot find the music box.
We now have enough money to keep the house, but we've decided
to relocate somewhere fresh. Father's debt is paid off, but we
decided to sell the lumber yard. We're hoping to find somewhere
where he can rest and heal. I must soon make the choice of
whether I will travel by automobile, ship, or train, and I don't
relish the thought of any of them.*

Bits of Clara's last letter float through my mind as I tuck a bundle of letters beneath my books in my carry-on bag. The airport can lose my clothes, but I'm not giving them the chance to misdirect anything of Clara's. I can't find the music box either, but I suspect it's underwater.

  *We've arranged to rent the house, under conditions that the
furniture and the trunk are not to be removed. I've locked the
chest. The key is in Vincent's writing box in the attic if no one
has used it before your time. I don't know if you will still find the
things as you did at first, but it's the best I can do.*

I contemplate taking the family portrait with me, but we decided Keith should keep it since it's his family. All I have left of Clara is a selfie I snapped one day when we visited the bay. Since she was borrowing my clothes, I can show it to anyone I want and they will have no idea that girl was born 100 years before me. I haven't looked into the trunk yet, because I'm too afraid to see what has changed.

> *Tell Keith that we're on our way to Galveston for Vincent and Anne's wedding. Andrew and I will stay with them long enough to get Grandfather's will sorted out—his body was not recovered, so a memorial service is the best we can do. After that, Andrew is taking me to meet his family. His hand is mending, though it will never be whole. He's already talking about teaching himself to play with the other for songs he can't improvise with a missing finger. When we secure a house of our own, Father will come live with us. He won't speak often of treatment, but he does not protest it. I think he is as anxious as we are to understand his condition. For now, that is enough.*

I'm rather interested to understand Mr. Castle's mind myself. Keith teases me, but the more I think about college, the more I want to go into psychology. Keith still dreams of engineering, but he's unsure about the amount of math required. I also caught him on my laptop, researching time travel. Who knows? Perhaps he'll end up as an inventor instead.

> *Vincent knows now, about the time travel, and he's looked even harder for the box than I have. Perhaps someday he'll find it again or make a new one, and then what fun we'll have. But if not, dear Scarlet, I will not leave you to wonder whatever happened to the rest of my life. I'm going to keep a journal and when it is filled, I will return it to the trunk. I wish that I could know your story, but at least you can know mine. If I can write about my life, what I've learned, perhaps it will help you with yours.*

I zip my suitcase and slip the pearl ring onto my finger. One of these days, I'll compile the things into a shadow box, but right now I keep them as close to me as possible. I don't need the key to open the trunk and, for all I know, it's exactly the way that it was when I last saw it. But if it's not … Clara is years ahead of me.

That journal could be a detailed account of her next year, or an overview highlighting every event of her long and full life. Forget her wedding, it could have children and grandchildren. And I'm just not sure I can handle that. But I must. I have to let Clara's future become my past. Otherwise, I'll be standing forever, holding a key next to a music box and keeping both of our lives in limbo.

I take a breath and kneel down, opening the lid one last time. The newspapers, the lavender, the hand mirror. Little has changed, except I spy a blue, embossed book nestled inside the quilt. I pick it up and peek inside to the first page.

Dear Scarlet,

I close it. I'll read it a little at a time like they're letters to me. Perhaps I'll even answer some and keep them with hers. I'll have lots to tell her. Finding my first job. Life with Sherri and Kate. Graduation and college. If only I could get the letters to go back.

"Scarlet!" Dad calls up the stairs. "Are you ready?"

I stand, glancing around the house. No. I'm not. But life doesn't wait until we're ready. It takes away things we love and thrusts us into changes we're unsure of. I can drag my feet again, but that won't keep me here. I'd rather walk into a new day and embrace whatever adventure it holds.

I glance down at Clara's journal like she lives inside of it and whisper, "Ready?"

Keith's at the bottom of the stairs, spending his lunch break between jobs to see me off. He meets me at the foot to take my suitcase. I open my mouth to tell him I've got it, but Clara's voice floats in my head.

"Oh, let the boy take your luggage."

So I grin and follow him to the trunk of Dad's car, wondering whether Clara decided to travel by train or automobile.

"Thanks," I say.

Keith shuts the trunk and turns. "I'm going to miss you."

I raise my eyebrows and chin at him and he cuts himself off, then says with a sheepish grin. "I'll see you later?"

"Yeah," I whisper. I hug him, a little tighter than a normal goodbye. Then I shoo him off before I cry.

"Sure you don't want to come?" Dad asks when he joins us.

"He's got to save for college," I say.

Keith smiles and the last time I turn to see him, he's climbing into that banged-up car. I lift my face toward the windshield because I'm too proud to wipe away tears.

We drive past the graveyard on our way to the main road, and I watch the stones go by, wondering if Clara Castle is still etched into one of them. So many lives all reduced to a name and two dates. Everything they did between their birth and death is represented by a non-descriptive dash, and the only people that know what that dash represents are the people who knew them. Like Sherri, Kate, and Keith, whose dashes will weave with mine. The only person who can determine whether that dash was what it should have been is me.

I brush the cover of the book in my lap. Clara knew bits of her future; that the economy would crash, that the entire world would go to war. But her life was worth living anyway, and she walked into it with courage — and Andrew.

I would have liked to have changed history and been partially responsible for the *Titanic* safely reaching the New York harbor, but I helped rescue one person. In the end, I guess that's all anyone can do: make one friend, change one life.

And that's enough.

My phone buzzes in my pocket, and I fish it out, smiling at Kate's name.

Got your half of the room cleaned out. :) Can't wait to see you!!!!

I smile as I punch in the words.

Me too. As soon as I land, I vote we detour and find chocolate.

Yes!

Dad glances over. "You're going to come see me, right?"

"Yes, Dad," I answer, though I wonder if we'll both get so busy, we won't really try.

He nods and keeps driving.

When we part at the gate, I hug him a little tighter. Wanderlust aside, he's still my dad, and he looks a little sad to be left on his own. Maybe — just maybe — he'll realize that he's alone because he's the one who's always leaving and people won't wait forever.

Clara's ring goes through the tray at the airport, and Dad stays until I've put my shoes back on after getting through security. I stow the bag with her things above the seat and step back into a man.

He catches me, balancing a violin case in his free hand. "Sorry, sweetie!"

I hold my hands up with a sheepish grin. "My bad." I point to his case. "You play the violin?"

He nods with a grin. "In the New York Symphony. I came to Texas to visit some family."

"Really?" I smile and slide into my seat, thinking the summer before I wouldn't have talked to a stranger even if I had stepped on his toes. "I like violins."

And he's going to look good in the symphony. When the plane takes off, he puts in headphones, and I use Clara's journal to back a piece of paper as I begin a letter to her. Perhaps she'll never get it, but that never stopped her pen.

> *Dear Clara,*
> *Forget the train, boat, or automobile. I'm flying through the sky on an airplane. Your ring is with me, so whenever you see it, you*

can imagine all the adventures in store for it after it's accumulated yours. Oh, and tell Andrew I'm returning to NYC, so now I get to snoop into his old life like I did yours. Hope he's prepared.

Kate hits me with the force of a small truck when I step out of the terminal, squealing like a thirteen-year-old. I drop my carry-on bag and hold her so long it's almost awkward.

"I've missed you so much," she says.

"I have stories," I whisper in her ear, "that you are not going to believe."

She cocks her head with a grin as I pull back. Her eyes are sparkling with intrigue already, but I forget about the story, grabbing her face. "Kate! Your eyes look like..."

"Like who?" she asks.

Andrew's.

I glance around the airport, spying the man with the violin case disappearing into the crowd and realizing that Andrew had nine siblings running around New York and four generations later, there's going to be a lot of people in America carrying Callaghan traits.

"Weird," I say, and move to embrace Sherri. "Thank you for letting me come back."

"Sweetie, you are part of this family," Sherri says. She puts her hand on my face. "And you always, *always* will be."

Kate reaches for my luggage. "Gosh, Scarlet, what did you put in here?"

I laugh. "I'll show you when we get home."

She loops an arm across my shoulder as we leave the airport. A taxi drive and grocery shop later, I'm spooning chocolate ice cream into a glass and grinning as I remember that Clara always called it "iced cream."

Kate's only on her first scoop because she's too busy staring at me to eat it. "No way! Was it, like, haunted or what?"

"No. Someone was winding it," I say.

My phone buzzes again. Kate snatches it, grinning when she sees the screen. She holds it out. "It's your boyfriend."

"He's not my boyfriend," I say.

"Oh?" She glances at the picture. "Mind if I take him?"

"Don't you dare." I snatch the phone from her hand. "Hello?"

"Hi." Keith's voice is too carefully controlled to sound anything besides suspicious. "I've got a message for you."

"What?" I say.

And the stupid boy doesn't answer.

"What?" I ask again, pressing the speaker and turning wide excited eyes to Kate. "Don't tell me you're at the front door."

"Better," he says.

Then I hear a very soft tinkle of a music box.

THE STORY BEHIND
THE STORY

ONE NIGHT, ALMOST NINE YEARS AGO, MY FRIEND SHELBY SHEPHERD and I decided to create a movie together. We were teenagers, sharing a love of theater and music. The film would be shot in a family home that my grandparents owned. Interested in contrast, Shelby laid the foundation for Scarlet Beldon, and I created Clara Castle. We improvised scenes between the girls, a few of which conceptualized scenes that I included when I decided to write the story as a novel. Two rewrites later, the characters have taken on their own traits and the storyline expanded so much, it was difficult to decide what to include in this novel. So thanks, Shelby, for trusting me with your brainchild. I hope you like who she grew into. And I still hope that someday, there is a filmed version.

After I finished the drafted version of the novel, life changes set it on the back burner until I returned and revised large portions. I fell in love with Clara and Andrew's story and decided not to publish *Across the Distance*. My initial idea was to take the time-travel concept and create another novel with it, then write a historical fiction tale called *Distance Song* that explored Andrew's journey into Mr. Mordaunt's world and Clara's attempts to grow up, despite an overprotective father. The choice about which book to release delayed the project for years, while I worked on the historical story.

Across the Distance may never have been released at all, if it was not for the initial readers of the original proof and the short-lived kindle version, who loudly protested my change of direction. Thanks for fighting guys. I've combined parts of the historical into the original time-travel novel, and I love it, too. Clara and Andrew have a much more in-depth story which you may someday see as well.

But to all of those who continued to ask, "When are you going publish that time-travel one?" and especially to Dad who made it more personal,

"When are you publishing my book? That's your best book. Publish it."

Here your book. Thanks for your patience. Thanks for not giving up. I hope it was worth the wait.

Because it took nine years and four versions to develop, I had the chance to see parts of this tale acted out, first between Shelby and myself, and later when I roped my cousin Lauren, along with a few guys I had recently met, into helping me create footage for a book trailer. Philip, Thomas, and Nathan Brewer, along with Gerald Wall, are responsible for bringing portions of the original book to life, shooting bits of footage during a very cold November weekend, and helping me visualize what worked, as well as catching dialogue phrases that sounded terrible when spoken out loud. Also, to Jan Pierce who let us shoot a scene in the bookstore that served as the meeting place for Scarlet and Keith. Old Main Bookstore has served as a source of inspiration and coffee, along with letting me meet many of my friends.

Several people banded together to help me create the final form of this book. Jami dominated her own coffee shop to read through multiple copies of the finalized version. Shelby completed the circle from brainstorming the original idea to reading parts of the last proof. Valerie gave the manuscript a final polish. And Kyle Shepherd finished it off with his designing services for the cover and layout. You guys are great. To everyone who helped create this book and every reader who loves it, a big thank you.

With Love,
Lindsey

www.ingramcontent.com/pod-product-compliance
Lightning Source LLC
Chambersburg PA
CBHW050342030726
47503CB00008B/2570